Alpha Queen's Destined Hybrid

DESTINED SERIES
BOOK ONE

HIRAETH FAITH

To my family who never failed to support me, to my friends who motivated me to write, and to my younger self who had always doubted my writing capabilities yet somehow managed to look at things with wide-eyed wonder and unwavering determination. Finally, my dreams and imagination had found their right place, etched in these pages, my first book. I hope the right readers will find it.

- HIRAETH FAITH

Blood Moon

KAMILAH

There were times that I just wanted to disappear. To escape from everyone and escape this reality. Ah, how I wish that I could do that..

But I couldn't. Instead I am forced to face imbeciles.

"Watch where you're going, bitch!"

I cringed as I heard Jessica's high-pitched voice yell at me. I was just walking on my way to my house, but she took it as a chance to bully me. She flipped her ash-gray hair with blonde highlights that cascaded down her back, batting her eyelashes at me with her ponytail, as always.

She knew she could get away with that, just because she was the daughter of the past beta of the past alpha, Beta Drake… much higher status than a lowly omega like me.

I gulped, forcing my mouth to bear it for now. Never in my life did I expect to live worse than I had imagined. I mean, I had always been treated like shit, but most of the time it was bearable. I couldn't even count the times I was pushed to my limit, but I had managed to live because of the very thing that kept me living.

Darian Barnes, the son of the Alpha of our Shadow Pack. My heart fluttered at the thought of him and Jessica noticed my expression so she chuckled. "No way, are you thinking of your knight in shining armor right now?" she taunted. "Darian! Come save me! I'm scared!"

She said it in a tiny voice, as if mocking me. My eyes instantly snapped at her, now irritated. Gritting my teeth, my hands instantly met her cheek and she released a gasp, not sure if I had hit her.

"Did you just-"

"Yes. I did. And I will do it again if you won't shut up. I'm tired of dealing with your bitchy ass."

Out of everything, I didn't want anyone to mock Darian. Mocking me like that was like mocking him.

She gasped, "Do you realize the situation you're in? I can tell this to my dad."

I snorted, "Go ahead. I don't care. Continue licking after your dad's shadow."

Her dark brown eyes filled with rage and her hands were about to hit me when a hand stopped her.

"Quiet, Beta Drake's bitch."

I heard Darian's deep voice beside me. He was hovering tall over my 5'3" ass. His earthy scent lingered on me, tickling my nose. Darian is 6'1 in height, almost the same size as his dad now. His cerulean eyes seemed to drown my soul whenever we made eye contact. His shiny blond hair, that he kept in a neat style, and his exuding aura shone wherever he went, attracting and intimidating everyone around him. He was ready to take his role as the future alpha now. He looked drop-dead gorgeous and ravishing.

As much as I want to be with him, I am in a situation

right now. I glanced at him and he flashed me a concerned look. "Are you letting this bitch torment you for life, Kamilah?"

I shook my head, wanting to defend myself. "I did fight for myself, Darian…"

He glared at Jessica. "Are you going to slap my friend, beta's daughter?"

Jessica was breathing heavily. "She started it, Darian. And I have a name!"

Darian loomed over her, raising his eyebrows. "Are you talking back to your future alpha?"

"I-I," Jessica stuttered before glancing at me and snapping, "You ugly bitch! You won't get away with this!"

I smirked as she left us, and I could hear Darian's deep sexy laugh thundering from his chest.

Darian offered his hand for me to high-five before laughing out loud. "Did you see her reaction?"

I accepted his hand and we both burst into laughter. "She was completely mortified by you."

Darian looked at me. "It's the first time I saw you slapping her like that. How does it feel?"

I bit my lip. "Satisfying."

"Good. Now do that often, I want to see you defend yourself, Kamilah."

He ruffled my hair and I looked up at him. "Thanks for the backup, Darian."

He put his hands on my shoulders to comfort me. "No problem, you know I always got you. Go home. You have to prepare for tonight. I'm busy preparing so I'll see you later?"

He flashed me his boyish smile before leaving me.

I watched as he walked away from me. It was not just Jessica who would treat me like this. When I was still a pup, Darian saw me weak from being bullied, all bruised up from head to toe. I thought he would also join in bullying me but instead, he yelled at them and frightened them off with a protective stance.

He helped me up when I was at my worst, which let me be able to live comfortably for a while, but when everyone found that Darian and I became close, they tried to let me experience hell and did everything for me to get banished from the Shadow pack.

But unfortunately for them, I was tough. I held on. Held on every day… hoping for Darian to see me not just as more than friends…

All that mattered to me was Darian…

I smiled at the thought of him, realizing my infatuation for him was growing. I should know my place as an omega, but I couldn't deny his charms. I instantly went home and as I was about to enter my room, a yell from inside surprised me. I rolled my eyes as I saw who it was. Valentina. The only female I managed to befriend in this pack. Her family just moved here as they had trouble from their past pack, and our alpha took them in. I guessed that was the bright side of our pack, we had a nice alpha.

"What took you so long?" she asked, then clicked her tongue, realizing the answer. "Let me guess, Jessica the bitch bullied you again?"

I shrugged.

She heaved a heavy sigh, as I propped against my table. "You should fight back!" she said in exasperation.

"I did. Darian came, and I won."

Her eyes lit up and she hugged me. A huge banquet would begin, celebrating our alpha stepping down and the new alpha, Darian, taking his place. Plus, the expected time of the Blood Moon was also tonight. Blood Moon enabled us to sense our mates nearby and it only happened once every year, and since I will be eighteen tonight…I had to take the chance. It's now or never. I prayed to the moon goddess to let me be Darian's mate, hoping that my suffering was just a test and Darian was my end game.

I grabbed the red lipstick from my table and put it on my dry lips, staring at my reflection in the mirror. I also grabbed a concealer to hide the bruises that were left from my training every day. Since I was one of the lowest ranks, my healing abilities were almost nonexistent and I was practically a human, so wounds would stay with me for months. Geez, being an omega I never had a break.

"It's finally tonight," Valentina said.

I pouted, realizing I was getting ready for nothing. "Well, I'm on a patrol."

Sadly, as an omega, I had a bad schedule. Everyone would be at the packhouse, where the ceremony would be held. They got to enjoy everything, except me. Great.

"Good luck, my friend. I'll make sure to bring some food to you," Valentina offered nicely, breaking me away from my thoughts.

I grinned at her. "Don't you know that you are the best and great friend out there?"

"I know," she replied cheekily. Locking my room, we went outside and parted ways midway as she was going in the direction of the packhouse while I was off to my night shift on patrol.

I was wearing the best outfit I could find, a pair of black leather jeans and a black top with a red flannel over it. My hazel brown hair, and ocean blue eyes that shift to red whenever I transform, are as glowing as ever. I wore my black, heeled boots and wore the necklace I had been wearing since I was a child.

I was not even sure why but I felt safe whenever I wore it.

I felt like the necklace had some magical powers as it gave off a warmth that kept me calm and I felt I was somehow connected to my parents.

I mean, since I was just an orphan as a baby, I couldn't even remember if I had any parents left alive. I'd like to think they were killed in the war and hadn't abandoned me.

"Hey, you're late!" said our delta as he saw me going to the tree, my resting place every time I was on guard duty. I flinched, expecting him to hit me but he didn't. Instead, he just shrugged it off and left the area. It was kind of unusual but also I won't complain. Another night, another fight for my survival.

I got on my favorite tree branch, which overlooked the whole packhouse and I was able to see a glimpse of the bright lights and loud music stretched from afar. I wished I could go there and witness the happy moment…

"Hey, have you heard that someone who came to the famous necromancer is now dead?" I heard one of the she-wolves say from below. I didn't know their names since I was not always exposed to all the members of our pack. And even if I was exposed to them, I might just be an unimportant member to them.

"Yikes, that necromancer gives me chills. You know he could give you everything you want, but fail to give his conditions and there is a price to pay," responded her friend.

"Hmm, about that necromancer, that rumor has been going on for decades now. I'm quite intrigued…"

"Oh, you know what, let's stop talking about that necromancer, but instead I want to talk about Alpha Magnus. I'm excited to see him if given the chance!"

"Gosh! That man is drop-dead gorgeous. Such a shame that he is not invited here…"

"Be careful what you wish for, you know how his and our alpha's current state is..."

My ears perked up at that. Alpha Magnus? I'd never seen that man, so all I knew was that he had a large scar on his left cheek, was charming and drop dead handsome with a sexy and muscular body, according to the she-wolves. He happened to be flush with the women as he was a womanizer who had different women every day.

The two gossiping she-wolves then walked to the pack-house and my eyes followed them. Despite my weak abilities, my eyes were still able to see clearly in the night, which I was thankful for. Well, I would have been driven away in this pack if it wasn't for my white wolf. As the elders said, a white wolf was a blessed wolf that the moon goddess gave. I didn't even believe that crap since I didn't hold any special abilities, except being a big white furry animal when I transformed.

The cold wind brushed past me and I shivered slightly. I was a damn wolf but I couldn't even give off natural heat. I sighed. Suddenly, a branch of a twig snapped and I immediately turned in that direction. No one.

I blinked, not trusting my eyes. Hmm, it might be a rat or some night owl but then I heard some weird sloppy noises, sucking and then spitting some saliva behind the tree, twenty feet away.

I frowned, knowing everyone must have left for the celebration.

"Who is there?"

Catching my breath, I feigned courage and spoke up, grabbing the branch of the tree tightly for support. Silence fell instantly, and then a woman came out from the tree, looking at me with an irritated look, huffing before walking away.

Okay? I know damn well everyone is irritated with me but I kind of do not know the girl.

Just then, the bushes opened and a tall figure revealed himself, his black suit and red necktie were messy as his buttons were popped open. I sniffed the air and a trace of blood was on his chin.

I froze, realizing I also did not recognize the man before me. With the woman coming out from where he is standing, his lips all swollen and his suit in a mess, it's so obvious what they were doing there. Goodness, I was alone here, why did they have to do their lovey-dovey thing there? I cringed in disgust.

He looked up at me and formed a smile, acting as if nothing happened. "Oh, did the party already start without me?" his deep husky voice asked.

He was just questioning but I felt every part of my body churning, my wolf inside cowering in fear at the intimidating aura that exuded from his body. I could sense his pheromones lurking, and it was affecting me strangely.

"Uhm…yes?" I responded unsurely. He nodded, buttoned his shirt, then grabbed his coat he had hung from a nearby branch. I quickly took a careful look, my heart pounding, not knowing what to do. He was clearly not from our pack. What was he doing here?

Judging from the scar on his face, and his tall stature and deadly charms, I could quickly deduce he was Alpha Magnus, the man that the two she-wolves just talked about. He was the strongest alpha and had the strongest pack in the country, but I knew damn well he was not invited.

Out of all, our alpha might have been kind, but he was competitive as hell and hated Alpha Magnus to the core. He treated him as his rival and he made everyone train…So this was it. Alpha Magnus was deadly. He might be mischievous and playful to the she-wolves, but one wrong move and you'd end up dead. I noticed he was alone here. Did he…plan to attack us when all our warriors were at the celebration?

I wanted to press the bell that we were under attack, that someone trespassed on us, but the gorgeous man below me just flashed me a smirk.

"Normal werewolves have a very calm flow of blood, just like humans…" He sniffed me, and I flinched, feeling a bit embarrassed.

"You have a unique flow of flood. I could just hear it gushing like a waterfall… so tempting," he said, again closing his eyes as if savoring it. Now that he was close, I could see the golden specs in his iris that were now turning a red color, and what I noticed was that his skin was too pale for a werewolf. He groaned, shaking his head to concentrate.

Was he saying I was different or unique? I couldn't make sense of it.

"What is your name, beautiful?" he asked softly. I couldn't hear him clearly as my head was filled with racy thoughts about the way the piercings on his tongue rolled as he talked to me. I blinked, feeling myself giving in but I shook my head to resist. I wanted to leave right then and there. Before I had the time to react, he quickly went up to the tree and was in front of me. He stood by the branch, looking at me with a heavy look.

"Care to tell me your name, baby?" His voice was rather sexy and raspy in my ear, and I felt tempted to push my lips to his but I held my breath. Why would he ask for my name? A useless omega from his enemy's pack? I decided not to tell him just for my own safety.

He sniffed the air. "Your heart is racing, sweetheart." He then looked at my knee. "And you're bleeding."

I glanced at my foot to see blood dripping from my ankle.

In an instant, he scooped me up and I flinched when I felt a cold slippery liquid slide on my ankle. It just occurred to me that he was licking my wound. I gasped, feeling the warmth from his body and his saliva tingling my skin. I looked at my wound to see it healing quickly, the blood had disappeared.

Hmm, he was not an alpha for nothing. I couldn't help but feel envious for that super-fast healing they had... if only I was born with it too...

He licked his lips, eyeing me with a smirk and putting me down. "Careful, princess."

I gulped. Then I remembered my duty to my pack. I'd be in trouble if this continued on. Suddenly, I grabbed the rope from the bell and yelled loudly, "We are under attack! Everyone! We are under attack!"

He quickly covered my mouth to silence me, and I knew right then and there that this night was my last one. Goodbye, Darian. Goodbye, Valentina. I expected his hand to aim at my thin neck but I only felt his strong hands gently being removed from my mouth.

"You seem to misunderstand me. I am invited here."

I looked at him suspiciously. He may be drop-dead gorgeous but I wouldn't be deceived. Plus, he was dangerous.

He sighed. "Your alpha is stepping down from his throne, I have to be there. We are old friends after all."

Old Friends? I didn't know if he was sarcastic or bluffing with me, but I cleared my throat.

'He's invited. Let him in.'

I heard a familiar deep commanding voice in my head. Oh, It was Darian's father, Alpha Rufus, our alpha. He might have sensed Alpha Magnus's scent, so he informed me. Oh... so the ceremony still hadn't taken place? I felt a bit happy knowing I might be able to not miss the chance of his night.

But I felt a bit embarrassed, knowing I made a mistake in

front of Alpha Magnus but scared for my life, knowing I would be dead soon. I cleared my throat, trying to hide the shame I was feeling.

"Alpha Magnus. We could have escorted you," I said with respect, bowing a bit.

"There's no need. My beta came already before me, I wanted to come along and explore the Shadow Pack." His eyes darted to me. "You have more beauties here, I should have lived here," he added. I almost choked on my own spit but tried to hide it.

"Oh by the way, why are you here? Aren't you joining the party?" he asked. I bit my lip, wanting him to leave now so I could guard him in peace. That was a false alarm.

"I'm on duty, Alpha Magnus," I replied. He looked at me pityingly.

"That's a bummer. Tell your alpha not to worry. It's a party, everyone should be included, and you are alone guarding here. It must have been so hard for you."

I felt a bit surprised. I expected him to be an uptight, commanding alpha but he seemed so chill. His aura was not as intimidating as our alpha's, but with the way he calmly leaned back, as if nothing could even faze him, he sure was strong as hell. Was he controlling it? His aura?

Just then, when he was about to jump out of the tree, the tree branch snapped and I yelled in horror, seeing the ground closer as I was falling headfirst. I felt a sharp pain in my back and I cursed under my breath. I didn't have time to brace for the impact!

I could feel my shoulder dislocated now, my right hand strained. I glared at Alpha Magnus, knowing the tree broke because of his heavy weight. He was 6'3", almost the same height as our alpha, of course he'd be heavy. I kind of somehow expected him to help me from the landing but he didn't care.

"You didn't jump on time," he stated, looking surprised. "The omegas in my pack can even lift a whole tree."

I winced in pain. "I apologize, my abilities are too weak."

"Not surprising," he commented, looking at my weak body, and I took it as an insult. So he might not be the intimidating type of alpha, but he could be so degrading with his words.

"It was your fault though," I spoke up. Well, I wasn't scared of him.

"Feisty," he commented again. "I see that I'm responsible for this so I'll take you to your pack doctor," he said, offering to carry me.

I shook my head, grabbing my arm and yelped a bit. "I'll walk. I experience pain every day anyway, this is no big deal."

It was a big deal. I just lied to keep my face and dignity. No way in hell would I surrender and be treated so pitifully. But with one sweep of motion, I felt him scooping me up in the bridal style. I held my breath, stunned at this. This was my first time being carried like this, other than Darian. I could smell the earth's scent with a hint of lavender.

I wanted to complain but I shut my mouth as I saw his jaw clenching, his eyes deep in thought. He was very fast in running, much faster than Darian, and in no time was at the packhouse. He let me down gently and looked around.

Some wolves surrounded us, completely shocked how Alpha Magnus was in our pack, but mostly they stared at my poor state, while also giving confused looks and whispering to each other. Great. Another reason for them to bully me.

"I'm not late, am I?" Alpha Magnus asked as our alpha came to greet him. I watched the two of them, kind of strange for two alphas to be on good terms, much more so those two who had been on bad terms… I didn't recall them being this civil to each other.

"Kamilah!" I heard someone yelling, and it was Darian.

I broke into a grin. "Have I missed the good part?"

He shook his head. "No, the moon is just appearing."

The ceremony then started as everyone settled in. We watched as Darian took his oath. I couldn't help but glance at Alpha Magnus, who was watching everything with no emotion.

When it was complete, I could hear Darian's mind-link to me and he grinned in my direction. I blushed a bit but was happy for him. He had finally achieved his dream. He was finally our new alpha. The red color of the moon somehow escaped through the window, letting us know that it was time. Time for mates.

I glanced at Darian nervously and closed my eyes, praying once more for him to be mine. And when I opened my eyes, he was gone. He was walking in Valentina's direction, his eyes completely mesmerized. Valentina gulped and grinned as Darian took her hands. She looked in my direction and smirked. I halted, feeling everything pausing before me and nothing else was there except Darian and Valentina, my friends. I looked at the blood moon again and cursed it.

Darian was not my mate.

I felt my heart dropping, my stomach churning, and my chest tightening. I felt suffocated from the pain of knowing.

I knew it would end like this anyway. Love had always been cruel to the weak. I hated being born weak. An omega who had no rights and is treated like trash. An omega who had to keep quiet and obey because it would be a shame to do otherwise.

Why do I have to be so weak? Why do I have to be an

orphan poor girl, who had no one by her side other than some friends who pitied me?

My inner wolf instantly took over as I couldn't handle all the overwhelming emotions right now. There was only one place I could think of right now, my inner wolf wanting to rampage.

And I let her.

I couldn't clearly remember what happened, but a glimpse of it told me I was in a cave.

There was an old man sitting by a chair in front of me. His growing beard that reached his knee was in view and his eyes were almost hidden from the black cap that he was wearing. He had candles everywhere, books scattered to the sides, and some rats were even walking around.

I blinked. I didn't recognize him, but I knew him. If I was not mistaken, he was the necromancer who could do almost anything.

"Please make me stronger," I said without thinking.

The necromancer looked at me. "Who are you?"

"Kamilah. An omega of the Shadow Pack of Alpha Rufus."

He nodded. "Kamilah, do you wish to be stronger?"

"Yes."

He looked at me straight in the eye. "My dear, don't you know who I am? Every wish has a consequence. It will be hard for you. You will be a threat to the world, and the world will be your enemy. You won't have a mate until you meet with the child of prophecy, the hybrid. He was born from a vampire and werewolf. A sign of the greatest tragedy to ever come."

Hybrid? What was this old man saying? "I don't care. Just do anything to give me power."

He fixed his composure and looked at me. He opened his

eyes to see clearly and was muttering a few words. Pain suddenly flashed everywhere and I couldn't remember everything.

His eyes suddenly flashed fear. "Your future looks dark. You'll become a leader, a frightening one."

"What?"

I wanted to ask more, but the necromancer suddenly lost consciousness and fell to the floor.

I was left with silence in the cave, now a bit woken up. I returned to my human form, now fully naked. I looked for anything that would cover me and found a big leaf. What I asked will come haunting me one day, but I didn't even care.

Bloodlust Pack

KAMILAH

I immediately went back to the packhouse, fully drenched in sweat and a mind full of murderous thoughts. I could feel the newfound power surging within me, and it gave me confidence.

Looking around, I found Valentina huddled with Darian in the corner, laughing with each other.

"Kamilah? Where did you run off to? I was looking for you," Darian said, then looked at the only thing that was covering my private parts, which was the leaf I picked up earlier.

I ignored his question and glared at Valentina, "You bitch!" I yelled, gaining the attention of everyone in the room, including the alphas.

"The moon goddess chose me as his mate. Sorry about that, Kamilah," said Valentina.

This sly fox…she even pretended to be my friend!

"You're just an omega," she continued. "Did you think you'd have a chance with the alpha?" she sneered, grabbing

Darian's hands and I growled at the sight. Darian was just letting her, looking at me blankly as if he was under some spell.

'Stop it, Kamilah. This is my day', I heard Darian's mind-link.

I glared at him. So he was on her side. I growled and felt my inner wolf taking over. I felt the pain searing into my every fiber until I shifted in front of them.

Some left the banquet, some stayed to watch.

While I was too small compared to the other she-wolves in my human form, my wolf was a bit bigger than other omega's, which was a bit of an advantage. I instantly came for Valentina but Darian blocked me. "Stop Kamilah!"

I stared at the man before me. I was out of control and I couldn't even stop my wolf. Not that I wanted to.

"The moon goddess picked her, Kamilah," Darian spoke again.

"But what about me? Darian, you may act naive but you know that I… love you!" I cried out in anger.

He scoffed, "Love? I merely pity you because you're weak. I never loved you. Why are you such a weak omega?"

"We may have been friends but… don't you dare hurt my mate." When I still stood up in an offensive stance, he sighed. "I don't want to hurt you on this special night, Kamilah. But you give me no choice."

He came to me in a flash and grabbed my fur, slicing my cheek along the way. I whimpered as his sharp claws made contact, hissing at the pain. My blood dripped, but I felt nothing except numbness. All I could think of was disbelief and denial, hoping this was all a dream that the man who promised to protect me is not hurting me right now.

"Kamilah, now that you have done it, I don't have any more reason to keep you here in my pack. I banish you and you shall not take a step further or we will have to kill you." That was Darian, banishing me from his pack.

My wolf fought back and pushed him but he's strong, as he's now a full alpha, not budging from his place. I managed to get to Valentina who was snickering at the scene and I grabbed her throat, my body releasing a white light that blinded everyone.

Rufus, Darian's father, and the past alpha came at me. "I knew this would happen."

He attempted to stand and stop me but he struggled with my power. I could see Jessica, my bully watching with a wide grin, clearly enjoying this.

I released all the overwhelming energy in my body, which made everyone faint right there.

Then a hand grabbed my shoulders, stopping me from releasing further.

"So everyone here just hates you? Poor thing," Alpha Magnus's deep voice said from behind me, holding my hand, but I stopped when his hands collided with mine and I felt sparks.

He flinched, seemingly feeling it too. His eyes flashed red and he seemed angry and confused. His eyebrows furrowed at me. He looked at the Blood Moon, that was fully showing up in the sky, before turning back to me.

I felt an electric touch the moment our hands collided again and darkness took me in.

I woke up ticklish, feeling someone was licking my wound.

I opened my eyes to see a strange man licking a wound on my right. I winced.

"You're awake," he said, still licking, almost drinking my blood. I realized he was Alpha Magnus. But why was I here? The place was... different from my room.

"You have been sleeping for the whole day."

I touched my forehead, wondering what happened. "Where am I?"

"You're in my pack," he simply announced.

"What?" His pack… the Bloodlust Pack?

He sighed. "I know things might have shocked you but… Your alpha banished you. They believe you died that night, and I took you here in my pack."

I nodded, now remembering what happened. Darian and Valentina were mates, and I attacked them and that was all I could remember. I can't believe I am in the Bloodlust pack. I felt a sharp pang of a headache and I held my breath.

"What happened after that?"

Alpha Magnus was still licking my right side, and I felt ticklish now. "Uhm…why are you still licking me?"

"You have a wound. It needs to heal. And you have such unique blood," he pointed out, as if it was the most obvious thing in the world, now standing up and licking his lips, while wiping his chin.

I checked for any more injuries and found my shoulders were sore but they were slowly healing on their own. I blinked, now remembering I had gained power because of my rash decisions.

'You're alright. I'll always be here."

I blinked, now hearing my own wolf clearly. Last time when I was a weak omega, her voice was faint and I could only feel her when she was too hurt or scared.

I felt a bit relieved knowing I had someone inside me that I could rely upon. And she just became so strong.

So this is what it feels like to have power…

What will happen now? I didn't plan for any of this to happen to me.

Then I realized I didn't have any clothes on except the thin layer of a blanket. I blushed, glancing at Alpha Magnus who was deep in thought, gazing at me quietly as if analyzing me.

A delicate metal dangled from his hands. The design was intricate, and I just realized that it was mine. The one I had always been wearing since I was a child. The only thing that had kept me sane throughout all these years.

"This fell when you fainted at your past pack. I figured this is important to you." Alpha Magnus handed the necklace to me, and I glanced at it for a minute. Looking at it now, I suddenly don't feel any emotions attached to it other than the feeling of emptiness.

"Well, that's not important to me anymore. You can discard that."

Besides, I do not want to keep seeing something that will remind me of the Shadow pack. I have to move on. Alpha Magnus understood what I meant and he set the necklace aside.

Now that I could see him clearly, I noticed he was shirt-less, revealing his hard-toned body with six-pack abs. He stood by the wall, leaning his back against it and looked at me with a serious expression that I couldn't read.

I couldn't help but think how I would ogle at the sight if I was the me of the past, but now it was different. Since that night, I knew all too well that there was no past Kamilah anymore.

Only the new and stronger Kamilah.

My focus returned to his words earlier. About my blood. "Uhm…what did you meant when you said that I have unique blood?"

He shook his head. "Oh, it's nothing…"

Hmm… he was acting a bit weird…

"You still haven't told me your name, feisty one," he muttered.

I blinked, he saved me back there, helped me, and took me in, yet he still didn't know my name.

"Kamilah. Kamilah Ziraili," I replied.

He nodded his head, mouthing my name in a low husky voice as if saying my name was a strange thing. "Kamilah…"

"Are you not scared of me?" he asked all of a sudden.

I stared at him, raising my eyebrows.

I shook my head in answer. "Why would I be?"

He responded with a smirk and said nothing.

I forced myself to stand up but he stopped me. "Where are you going?"

His question struck me. Shit. I forgot that I have no place now. I am banished from the Shadow Pack. Till now, it still hadn't occurred to me.

"I'll be leaving now, I seem to have overstayed. Thank you for helping me, Alpha Magnus."

I attempted to take a step but my knees failed me. Alpha Magnus was quick to catch me before I could fall to the ground, "Careful there, you are in my pack so this is the safest place for you right now. Soon, word will come out about how you asked the necromancer for power that will disrupt the balance," he tried to explain. "We wouldn't want some elders and Lycan kings coming for you, right?"

I pursed my lips, processing what he said. Right, he had some points. They would all come for me. But what bothered me was how he learned that I went to the necromancer for help… was it that obvious? I couldn't even deny it as it was the truth.

With a final glance, he went to the door and stopped. "Stay here and wait for my beta, Dimitri. He will help you."

"Wait!" I yelled, stopping him in his tracks. "Why are you helping me, Alpha Magnus?"

He shook his head, "I just see myself in you. The past me. Scared and… unique."

The magnificent and perfect alpha, Alpha Magnus is right here saying he was scared?

I shook my head in defense. "I'm not scared."

In an instant, he approached me and placed his hand on my shoulder. "Then why is your heart pounding, sweetheart?"

I released a gasp, my heartbeat just quickening up at how close we were right now. He seemed to get the reaction that he wanted from me, so he turned away and left through the door, leaving me alone.

It didn't take long for another werewolf to knock on the door and let himself in.

"Hello, I am Dimitri, Alpha Magnus's beta," he introduced himself. He had a bulky body with tattoos all over his arms, making him look so unapproachable. He was wearing a plain black shirt with denim jeans that seemed to be made for his body. He looked proper and uptight.

I nodded in silence, not in the mood to talk more as I was still confused. He laid down a white T-shirt and black pants with slippers on the bedside table.

"You can change into these. And you should also eat dinner." He then got a tray with some food, motioning for me to eat it.

When I was still not moving, he sighed. "I'll leave you alone for now, but I'll be back to get you checked out by our pack doctor."

"Wait, I have a question! How about my past pack?"

"They treated you like shit, and you're still looking for

them?" he asked. "They already banished you, so why return?"

His words struck me. I watched him leave the room after asking me those words. When I made sure he had left, I struggled to reach for the food and spoon-fed myself.

I could feel myself getting stronger and my vision was now clearer. As I finished eating, I dressed in the clothes that Dimitri left and saw a mirror at the side.

I glanced at my reflection, seeing that my normal ocean-blue eyes were different. My right eye had turned red and I had a scar from my forehead across my cheek. I could remember the way it burned that night when Darian sliced my face, but now it was fully healed.

It looked ugly, and I didn't even want to stare at it any longer.

I didn't know that I stayed the whole night in the room, despite being monitored by Beta Dimitri.

I didn't even have the will to stand up. I had power now, but what was the use if Darian just betrayed me?

"You know, we're not confining you in your room. You are welcome to come out," Beta Dimitri said from the door after giving me breakfast the next day.

"I know. I just want to stay here," I replied.

I could hear him sighing, "You need to mingle with the pack. You're now a part of us, Kamilah."

I bit my lip, forcing out the words. "But I don't know anyone here."

There was a pause and a voice of sadness. "Do not worry, I'll be your guide for the day. Come on, I'll show you around."

Still skeptical, I sighed and finally opened the door. Guess there was no use keeping myself locked inside. Besides, I was curious too since this will be my… new home now.

Dimitri was shocked a bit but then immediately smiled, bowing a bit before offering me his hand. "Then shall we go, Miss Kamilah?"

I accepted his hand reluctantly, and as soon as our hands met, he gently motioned for me to follow him as he carefully started to walk. "Expect to get some stares on your way as you're our new member here… but I hope you won't mind that?"

I shrugged at his question. "Depends on their stares."

He chuckled a bit. "You're quite funny, eh? But just stay close to me for now to avoid some inconveniences."

I looked around... so this was the famous Bloodlust Pack. I heard rumors of how gory, bad, and vicious they were to their enemies since their alpha himself was merciless. I expected to even get eaten alive…

But looking at them all, walking around and minding their own business like normal creatures, gave me a bit of comfort. "I hope you'll adjust well. We don't bite here, although there are some mischievous ones who'll poke around for fun. You'll meet some good ones, I promise."

I didn't know if Dimitri was even giving me some reassurance with those words, so I just nodded. Hopefully, things would be good.

Some even paused to look our way just to greet Dimitri and gave me a curious gaze. Dimitri just gave them a friendly smile. Seems that everyone here loves the beta as they approach him without even an ounce of fear. It was not that they didn't respect him enough, but they had enough balance of respect, admiration, and camaraderie. But I didn't blame them though, even I, a newbie here, instantly felt comfortable around him… He's pretty chill for a beta, unlike my past pack.

As much as their alpha was intimidating, their beta here

was so friendly to everyone. My first impression of him was very much opposite now that I finally got to know him.

"You're too approachable for a beta," I commented without much thought, and he gave me a look.

"Nice observation there, honey. And I'll take that as a compliment," he replied. "I guess it's just my charm doing the talking? Well, don't tell this to our alpha, but I just want them to be reassured that I'll always be here as their brother. I'm second in command, but I don't want to scare them off as much as our alpha does. I need to be the one who balances things here." Saying that, he ruffled my hair. "But don't worry, you can also act friendly around me. I don't mind."

I smiled, offering a polite smile at him before going back to observing everything as everyone seemed to be working too much. "What are they doing? Why is everyone busy?"

"There will be an event later," Dimitri casually answered.

I raised my eyebrows. "For what?" I asked nervously.

"Oh… he didn't tell you? Well, it's part of our pack rules to welcome new members. Alpha Magnus will be holding a welcoming feast for you," he simply replied and I blinked. Alpha Magnus would do that?

For…me? The thought itself gave me excitement, uncertainty, and fear. I didn't even know what to feel. Why was he being extra kind to me?

<h1 align="center">Pack Initiation</h1>

KAMILAH

"Oh, seems that Alpha Magnus wants to see you, I'll escort you to his office," Dimitri suddenly informed me.

Just then, I could sense someone staring at me. I glanced up and saw a woman from afar. "And who is that?"

Dimitri looked at the woman and rolled his eyes, heaving a tired sigh as if he was done dealing with the specific woman. He smiled sheepishly, holding my arms. "I advise you not to deal with her."

He was about to grab my hand when a voice stopped him.

"Dimitri!" the woman called out and Dimitri muttered a curse.

"Here she comes," he whispered.

I blinked, feeling confused. Was there something wrong with the woman?

"Oh… look what we have here. This is the new one?" The tall blonde woman came, smiling at me, but I would have been stupid not to notice the look behind her eyes.

"Serena… good to see you," Dimitri replied.

"It's so nice of Alpha Magnus to host a party just for… this kind of being," she insulted me, and I raised my eyebrows at that.

"Excuse me?" I defended myself.

She smirked, already feeling how irritated I was.

Beta Dimitri grabbed my arm. "We have to go. Now excuse us, Serena—"

But Serena cut him off. "Oh, that fast? I want to hang out with the newbie."

Dimitri glanced at me. "I received orders from the alpha calling for her."

I stopped him, not backing down from just a mere fight with this random woman. "No, I'll go with you later, Dimitri."

Dimitri sighed at me and glared at Serena. "You know that bullying won't do any good, right? I'll report this to Alpha Magnus."

Serena scoffed. "What? Bullying? Me? Dimitri, I am not hitting her here."

I rolled my eyes, really, this situation was familiar.

It seemed that wherever I went, there would always be people like Jessica who were not afraid to trample on people just because they had power.

Serena instantly grabbed my arm and motioned for me to follow her. "Bye Dimitri! See you later. I'll take good care of her."

I shrugged her hand off. "Let me go, I can walk on my own."

She peered down at me. "Oops, I apologize. You're just so tiny that you might get lost in the crowd."

There was not much difference in our height, merely a few inches, but why was she so keen on harassing me?

She motioned for me to go into some dark alley outside and was about to hit me when a hand stopped her.

"Oh look, what we have here," said the man who grabbed her arm, peering over her.

The smile on Serena's face left as soon as she saw him. "Oh… Owen, what are you doing here?"

"Saw you directing this beautiful woman here. Didn't know if you would do some… immature tricks." The man named Owen was tall and had tanned skin. He had a bulky body, and his gray orbs and jet-black hair stood out.

He glanced at me, knowing I checked him out. "Don't you know the alpha's orders? Don't touch her."

Serena pursed her lips but slowly kept her distance from me. "Yeah, whatever."

"What is going on here?" A thundering voice said from behind us. We looked behind and saw it was Alpha Magnus.

Owen, standing beside me, tensed up, along with Serena. Alpha Magnus's eyes trailed on me and to Owen.

"Good day, Alpha. I was just making Serena go away," Owen spoke up.

Alpha Magnus stood firm, raising his eyebrows, and asked, "Dimitri, didn't I tell you to come and take Kamilah to me?"

Dimitri nodded, "Yes, Alpha. But Serena butted in."

"She did?" Alpha Magnus then walked toward her. "Are you defying my orders? Don't touch her."

Serena gulped. "I-I didn't, Magnus-I mean, alpha…"

"Scram off."

She gasped. "You! Just because she is here and you're not giving me attention anymore!"

Alpha Magnus glared at her, his eyes freezing her in place. "So you did that just to get my attention?"

He motioned for Dimitri. "Dimitri, teach her a lesson."

Dimitri nodded and grabbed Serena by the arm.

"Stop. I can go by myself." Serena threw one last glance at me.

"I can take things from here now," Alpha Magnus informed Dimitri.

Serena yelled as she was being escorted out by Dimitri. Dimitri cast a glance back. "See you later, Kamilah." Then winked at me, before leaving us alone.

Alpha Magnus turned to Owen. "You did a good job, Owen. You may now go."

Owen nodded and left us alone.

Alpha Magnus clicked his tongue at me. "And as for you, I need to teach you a lesson."

I gasped. "A lesson? Alpha Magnus, I was invited—"

"You should have rejected her offer. You should be careful since you're new and received special treatment. There is no guarantee that they won't nitpick at you."

I went silent as he guided me to a room that seemed to be his office. It looked rather… bland and typical for any alpha. Well, I only got to see Alpha Rufus's office so that was the only place I could compare this to. They had the same things… the table, the chair, the mini sofa to the right, and some lamps to brighten the room.

"This is my office. You should memorize where it is. Come here when you need me," he explained, and motioned for me to sit.

He stood beside his chair, his arms propped up on his table, making his muscles flex. "I believe that Dimitri has already briefed you about the party later. You need to prepare for tonight. Open that box."

I noticed that there was a box placed on the desk. I did as he told me and saw a dress inside. The elegant blue dress

embroidered with the beads that were patterned up beauti-
fully, shone against the light.

"Wear that for the party later," he said.

I blinked. "But what about the punishment you said…"

"I changed my mind. I'll let this pass since you're new
here. But the moment I hear about this again, I'll have to do
something. Just keep away from people like Serena,
understood?"

His cold voice shot at me, and I nodded.

"Make sure to be ready before seven." He then dismissed
me after that.

I then returned to my room. I realized that the room I was
currently staying in was at the same packhouse as the alpha.
Aside from me, Dimitri was the only one who lived here. The
others had their own houses from afar.

Since the party will start at seven and it was six in the
evening, I decided to get ready now. I took a quick bath from
the shower attached to my room and put on the dress. Just
then, I could hear a knock at the door. When I peeked, I saw a
beautiful woman standing outside.

I opened the door and she smiled at the sight of me. "Hi!
My name's Thora and Alpha Magnus asked me to help you
get ready." She motioned to the makeup bag that she was
carrying.

"Hi, I'm—"

"Yes, yes, I already know you're Kamilah. Now hurry up
and open the door, I can't wait to get started!" I opened the
door wider for her to enter.

Once inside, she took an overall glance at me from head
to toe, squinting her eyes and thinking before deciding. "I'll
have to use light makeup just to emphasize your features."

I blinked. "Is there something wrong, Thora?"

She shook her head, humming a happy tune. "No, just realized why the alpha chose you."

I tilted my head. "Excuse me? Can you repeat that again?"

She grinned, keeping it mysterious. "Oh… nothing. I'll start now."

She only did my makeup for about fifteen minutes. I made it in time and went outside to see Dimitri waiting for me.

"The alpha is waiting."

I nodded, taking his hand as he offered to escort me. As soon as I stepped into the hall, everyone stared at me. There were beautiful designs in the hall and the tables were full of meat. There were vases of roses in almost all the corners, giving off a wonderful scent across the hall.

I spotted the guy who saved me earlier, Owen, with Thora who did my makeup, and another woman beside them, smiling at me. I smiled back and continued walking as I saw Alpha Magnus sitting at the very front. An empty chair was sitting beside him and Dimitri made me sit there.

Alpha Magnus stared at me, his gaze glued to me and I bit my lip, feeling self-conscious but I held my head high. Dimitri came up on the stage and he signaled everyone to quiet down.

He held a microphone in his hand as he smiled at me. "Everyone, it is such a lovely night for all of us. Let us all welcome our newest member of the pack, Kamilah Ziraili."

Everyone clapped their hands and Alpha Magnus smiled at me. He whispered in my ear, "Welcome to the pack. You can say this is an initiation."

I smiled, my heart heavy. Not from sadness but from happiness. My past pack never treated me well. I was all alone there, and now that I was banished from there, Alpha

Magnus's pack was now welcoming me wholeheartedly and I felt like bursting into tears.

I took a deep breath, holding in my tears behind my smile.

"Are you alright?" asked Alpha Magnus and I nodded my head.

Dimitri then continued, "Everyone, we all know the tragedy that befell the Shadow Pack… and we have to follow our alpha's orders on not spreading any information to the enemy. Alpha Magnus, do you have anything to say to our new member?"

Alpha Magnus got on stage and everyone got quieter, giving respect to their alpha. "Everyone, we all know that this is our pack's traditions that have been passed down to us."

Alpha Magnus motioned for me to come up on stage and I blinked, not expecting this.

"You still haven't made your oath to me. Come on up," he ordered and I realized that that's why he couldn't mind-link with me. How could I have forgotten?

I stood up on stage and stood beside him, my heart beating so fast from the stares I received. If my past pack had fifty members, Alpha Magnus's pack was twice the size, and everyone was bigger and looked strong here.

Alpha Magnus removed the microphone so I was the only one who could hear him. Everyone was eagerly watching us on the stage and I could hear Alpha Magnus's breath, fanning against my nose as he stepped closer to me. I could feel the warmth of his body as we were now inches apart and I gulped.

He noticed it. "Don't be nervous. It will just take a minute.

Once I was calmed down he asked if I was ready and I nodded.

"Alright, grab my hand."

I did as he ordered and held his big hand. I could feel the veins and the callousness on his palms.

"From now on, do as I say, Kamilah. Look into my eyes."

I did as he told me, seeing his chocolate brown eyes melting my own as he concentrated.

"Follow after me. I, state your name, are now free from my past pack and are now in the Bloodlust Pack, under Alpha Magnus. I will do whatever my alpha asks me to, accept his orders, and let him mind-link."

I said the words he uttered and after we were finished, I could feel a sharp pain in my mind, a strong magnetic field on our hands that were still clasped together, and my inner wolf battling inside. I groaned in pain, falling to my knees. Alpha Magnus caught me before I could hit the floor and he grabbed my arm, whispering in my ear.

"Calm down. I didn't mean to harm you. You just need to go through this process quickly and it will leave soon."

"I-I know."

I took quick breaths, closing my eyes and trying to make the pain go away. After a minute, the pain stopped. Alpha Magnus released my hand, but not before I felt a sharp zap between us and instantly withdrew my hand.

Alpha Magnus seemed to feel it too and he supported me as we walked down the stage.

My mind was hazy and my throat felt dry. He made me sit back on my chair and Dimitri spoke again to catch everyone's attention. "Now Kamilah is officially part of us. Let us have our feast now!"

"Are you alright?" Alpha Magnus said beside me, still checking on me.

I nodded, grabbing a glass of water and drinking it to quench my dry throat. "I'm fine."

He smiled. "You handled that better than anyone. Others passed out and woke up after two days as the pain was unbearable."

My eyes widened. "Really?" It must be because of my new strength blessed by the necromancer…I had almost forgotten about that fact…I had to test out my abilities soon and check out how I could utilize the utmost of it.

My thoughts were interrupted when Alpha Magnus spoke up again, "Now that you are fully well and officially one of us, I'll have to train you tomorrow. Don't be late."

I nodded. "Alright, Alpha."

"You can go back to your room and rest. But it's better if you can mingle with the others. Make friends, Kamilah," he suggested and I nodded.

I know that Alpha Magnus had a reputation for being ruthless and merciless to everyone, but from my stay of a few days here, I personally would like to refute that. He's actually nice to his members.

I stood up and looked around, seeing them now eating, drinking, and dancing the night away. A woman then came upon us and I remembered it was Thora, the woman who helped me prepare earlier.

"Hi, Kamilah! I hope you still remember me from earlier," she said against the loud background music.

"Hi, Thora," I replied.

I couldn't hear the rest of her words and she motioned for us to go outside. I followed her and saw Owen and the other woman with him.

"Gosh, it was so loud inside. We need to have a breath of fresh air," Thora complained.

"Hi, Kamilah," Owen greeted us as we approached them. "If you don't remember, I'm the guy who saved you from Serena earlier."

"Yes, Owen, I remember you," I nodded and smiled at him.

"Hi, my name's Leia. Owen's mate," the woman introduced herself and I shook hands with them.

Thora then carried on the whole conversation and I started to get to know them.

"You did great earlier. Congrats," Owen said. "You felt that strong magnetic field, right? That is how strong our alpha is."

We talked for a while about the pack's rules here. All we needed to do here was to train every day, get assigned to our stations whenever we were on duty for patrol, maintain a respectful relationship with the others, and always protect the pack.

It wasn't that bad for me, since I thought I could handle those things. Also, I didn't have the proper time to think about my current state.

Being banished from the pack that I grew up with, it was a hard pill to swallow. I couldn't help but feel sad, confused, and overwhelmed. I suddenly wanted to take a breather from anyone. I excused myself from them and went to the bathroom. But what I saw made my jaw drop.

Serena was leaning on the wall, kissing a man.

No. Not some random man.

From the way, the man was standing and his build, it was too easy to guess that it was Alpha Magnus.

I felt like I shouldn't have seen that... nor should I feel this weird aching sensation inside my heart.

Rage filled inside me and I don't know why. I instantly walked back toward where Owen, Thora, and Leia were.

Thora noticed my discomfort and asked, "Are you alright?"

I looked in the direction of Serena and Alpha Magnus, still at a loss for words.

"Hello, Earth to Kamilah?"

Leia looked at me. "She must have seen it."

I raised my eyebrows. "Seen what?"

Owen took a sip of his drink and cleared his throat, "We all know it, Serena is the latest fling of Alpha Magnus. Well, Alpha Magnus didn't care at first, but her father is one of the warriors here so..."

I didn't know what to feel about the new information. I thought that Alpha Magnus wanted me to avoid Serena? Yet here he is, staying close to that woman. The rest of the night felt bitter for me. After chatting with Owen and the others, I just went back to my room. I took a shower before changing into the clothes that Dimitri had brought earlier.

I appreciated how nice and accommodating Alpha Magnus was. His pack was nice and welcoming, unlike my past pack. But strangely, something seemed lacking. Something felt off. I couldn't exactly pinpoint it, but there was a hollow feeling in my heart that told me I don't belong here.

I shrugged it off, thinking it might be just because I was still new and adjusting. I would get comfortable in this place soon. I was strong, I knew I could do it.

But left alone now, as I heard the distant music from the packhouse, it felt lonely. And I was left alone with the thoughts that I had been forgetting.

How was Darian doing?

I gulped, wanting to rip away the memories I had with him. Darian was my past now. I couldn't return to them now.

I was dead, hidden, and now in a safe place.

Why did I still think of that man?

And Alpha Magnus... Sure, I thought Alpha Magnus was

caring for me. He probably was just pitying me, that was why he took me in.

A short creaking sound was heard and I instantly sat upright.

Everyone was at the open field, partying so I was sure I was alone here. Was it Dimitri?

"Who's there?" I asked through the thundering silence, my heart thundering for some reason.

Just then, a tall figure appeared from the darkness and there was a knocking on the door.

"Kamilah? It's me."

A deep voice said. I hesitated for a bit, knowing it was Alpha Magnus. Mustering my courage, I opened it.

"Did you enjoy this night?" he asked.

I nodded. "I did. Thank you, Alpha."

His eyes darted to my eyes, down to my lips, and on to my collarbone. "I saw you talking to Owen…" He trailed off as if wanting to say more.

I saw you kissing Serena.

I wanted to say that, but I didn't. As much as Alpha Magnus was now evidently nice, I didn't want to risk my life for this mere matter.

It was his personal life after all. He is the Alpha, of course, he could do anything he wanted to.

"Yes, he's a nice guy. And Thora and Leia too," I replied instead.

He nodded. "That's good.

"I also came to say one thing."

"What is it?"

He blinked, deciding against it and turning around. "Go to the training grounds tomorrow. We'll train you, so wake up early."

Trainings

KAMILAH

"Wake her up."

"Kamilah, you must wake up now."

I blinked as the bright sunlight hit me. What time was it?

My body instantly alerted me that two tall men were standing by the door, watching me.

I realized it was Alpha Magnus and Dimitri.

"What-What's wrong?" I asked curiously, not remembering why they were there.

"The sun is high up now," Alpha Magnus remarked sarcastically, his tone so cold that it could slice a saucer.

I glanced at Dimitri beside him who was giving me some signals. I just raised my eyebrows, asking him to elaborate.

Dimitri sighed. "You have training today. Remember?"

I instantly stood up, now remembering it. "Oh, right!"

"Get dressed. We'll wait for you at the training grounds," Alpha Magnus said before leaving.

I furrowed my eyebrows in confusion, wasn't it just yesterday that he was "nice" to me?

Dimitri walked closer to me. "He hates tardiness. Please understand our alpha."

"Dimitri! Come!" Alpha Magnus's voice thundered from down the stairs.

Dimitri sent an apologetic smile at me, before following his alpha. "Yes, coming now!"

I quickly grabbed some clothes and found some nice black leggings and a sports bra. Thank goodness Dimitri had brought me a few more clothes that I could borrow.

I instantly showered to freshen up before getting dressed and running down the stairs…

I muttered a curse, realizing I didn't know where the training grounds were. Forget about it. I would just figure it out.

I left the house with an empty stomach and ran toward the forest. Just then, I saw Leia coming out of her house as I passed by her.

"Kamilah! Do you have training too?" she asked, gasping. Gasping, I didn't know we were even neighbors.

"Yeah, and I'm late! I don't know where it is!" I panicked.

"I'll guide you. Come!"

Leia led me to the location and we walked for a few more minutes. She guided me to the innermost part of the woods, wherein we could hear some loud yells of submission behind a tree. We continued until we could see an enclosed meadow, with trees surrounding us.

There were around fifty pack members squatting on the grass with Alpha Magnus standing tall in front, yelling orders to them.

Leia held my hand and motioned for me to come. "Damn, we're late."

I saw Owen and Thora by the side, looking at us in shock.

"You two are late. Give me twenty push-ups. Now."

Alpha Magnus's commanding voice sliced through the air, giving a hard stare to me.

I met his gaze as he raised his eyebrows. "Do you know the consequences of being late, Kamilah?"

"It's her first training here, Alpha. Go easy on her," said Dimitri, coming to my defense.

"Thirty push-ups. Now," Alpha Magnus said firmly, ignoring his beta's request.

I sighed, giving an apologetic look to Thora for being dragged into this.

I did as I was told and did the push-ups with Thora following me. I would have crashed doing 10 push-ups before but since I'm healed up and have the energy, I could bear it now.

"Continue your push-ups. We'll begin our sparring after this," Alpha Magnus said to the others, approaching our direction.

He crossed his arms as he watched us, making sure we were obeying his orders, his eyes lingering on me until we finished.

I could see Serena's mocking face, smiling evilly at me, her expression saying "Good luck, bitch".

I just rolled my eyes and focused on the task at hand, not in the mood to let Serena win this.

Making sure that we finished the punishment, Alpha Magnus then returned to the front. "Pair up everyone."

Instantly, Owen came to Leia beside me while Thora came and was about to ask me when Dimitri came up to us.

"Kamilah, the alpha says I'm to pair up with you."

I sighed, mouthing a sorry to Thora, who just shrugged.

Dimitri then stood in front of me, stretching his muscles

and smirked at me. "You can come at me anytime you're ready."

I stretched my hands before launching an attack at Dimitri, whispering to him, "Is he always like this to his new pack members?"

I know damn well that Alpha Magnus could hear me and I'm doing it purposely.

I could sense his head turning to us so I continued, "You need to tell your alpha that he should stop it."

Dimitri was quick enough to dodge my attacks and smirked, understanding what I was planning so he went along. "Pour all your anger at me. I know you're quite irritated now."

"I won't hold back." I launched another hard blow, this time much stronger. Dimitri purposely didn't dodge, accepting my full attack.

Dimitri budged a bit from his position, his face a bit shocked. "You really can punch."

I nodded. "Why? Don't I look like I can?"

He shook his head, chuckling a bit as blood came out from his lips. "Guess I don't need to be easy on you."

Dimitri then came to me with his punches and my body instantly reacted to dodge them. He looked at me with so much focus, carefully calculating all my attacks. Since he was much taller than me, he had the advantage of strength, and seeing him fight now really proved that he was a rightful beta for Alpha Magnus.

A claw managed to escape from his hands, wounding my arms and bruising my legs. I was sent to the ground, groveling on my knees.

Dimitri paused, carefully analyzing my earlier moves. "You have speed, Kamilah, but not enough. We need to train you more."

I instantly kicked between his legs and he yelped in pain. "You shouldn't let your guard down when you're with an enemy."

"That was a foul play!" he complained, now lying on the ground. I shrugged. "Everything's fair when you're in battle."

A bell suddenly rang, signaling the end of the match. I helped Dimitri up and he accepted my hand.

"You lost to me," I teased him and he limped a bit, clutching his groin. "That's because you cheated, Kamilah."

"Dimitri, you can report to me what happened later," Alpha Magnus said from behind us, startling me a bit.

Dimitri bowed a bit and left us.

I faced Alpha Magnus, as he was still watching me. "What?"

"Come to my study with me. I'd like to discuss something."

I followed behind him and he took a seat in his study. "You seem to be close to Dimitri," he stated and motioned for me to sit.

I did as he instructed. "Yes, your beta is nice." *Unlike you now...* I wanted to add it but decided against it.

"How about you? You're close to Serena?" my mouth blurted out without much thinking, and I honestly regretted it.

His eyes hardened, a golden hue circling his iris. He clenched his jaw. "That's another matter. You're changing the topic."

"Why? I was just curious," I muttered, "I mean why were you strict? Or are you like that to your new members?" I felt like he was just acting when he was nice and showing his true colors now that I am officially here. It's nice to speak out like that. Since I'm his new member, I guess I could say anything now.

"I did it with a reason. I want to toughen you up so that no one would come after you," he said.

"No one would dare to, Alpha, I assure you. As of now, I made friends with three of your pack members, four if you count Dimitri. And so far Serena, your woman, was the only one who dared to come after me," I spoke up.

He instantly stood up. "Don't tell me that she's my woman. She is not."

He's getting agitated for something so obvious. Why bother denying it? Did I say that wrong?

"I'm only strict with you so that they will not see you as a weakling, Kamilah. Tell me if Serena comes to you again. I am permitting you to fight back," he said and turned around. "Grab this box and head home now. You reek of sweat."

I saw the box on his table and grabbed it. Noticing there was food inside, I blinked. Alpha Magnus was strange. He would treat me kindly at first, then continue to treat me harshly saying it was to protect me, and now he's giving me food.

"Make sure you go to training tomorrow. You have to work harder than the others as you're new here," he said. "Just because I was easy on you doesn't mean I have to be easy on you always."

I blinked. One minute he was kind, the next moment he would say some harsh words to me...

I just shrugged it aside and left his study. I hoped tomorrow wouldn't be like this.

Encounter

KAMILAH

The next training day came. Alpha Magnus was true to his words of "treating me harshly" as he decided to stop my training with Dimitri.

"Step aside, Dimitri. From now on, I'll be her training partner," he said after a while, and Dimitri glanced at me. He sighed, nodding to his alpha and leaving us.

I clicked my tongue. "Don't you have other tasks to do as an alpha? I mean, like monitor your other members?"

He's so keen on the idea of "protecting" me… as if something was going to attack me. As far as I knew, I was safe here. Why was he so riled up and always on alert? No one would even come after a nobody like me.

Well, Alpha Magnus was one of the terror alphas after all. Of course, this harsh training would be normal.

"You can launch at me," he said, giving me many openings.

I did as Dimitri had advised me. Since I was small

compared to most people here, he wanted me to take advantage of it and be much quicker.

I managed to land a blow and he shook his head. "Still not enough."

He grabbed my arm and hit it, making me yelp in pain. I gritted my teeth, now attacking his sides but couldn't land a blow.

To think I was confident at how I could manage a blow at him. I had become stronger, but it was nothing compared to his strength.

We continued on like that, with me panting and catching my breath, and him not even leaving sweat on his forehead.

The bell rang, signaling the end of our training.

"Not bad," Alpha Magnus commented as he gazed down at me.

I rolled my eyes. "You're not that bad either, but you'll have to improve," I said carelessly, silently agreeing that he was worthy of his reputation, but I wouldn't dare say that in front of him. It would only make his ego bigger, and I wouldn't have that power over me.

Suddenly, I was harshly thrown to the lockers behind me. A gasp escaped my lips as I looked up at Alpha Magnus, not expecting him to do this.

"Improve, you say?" His lips were formed into a sly smirk and he whispered in my ears. "I think it's you who should be working on yourself, dear."

I clenched my jaw and I smirked back at him. "Let's see. I know I'm small, but I'm a fast learner, and don't forget I gained this newfound power. Don't underestimate me, Alpha."

At that, he removed his hold on me and I brushed myself off, flipped my hair, and walked toward Owen, Thora, and

Leia who had wide grins plastered on their faces as they watched me walk over to them.

"Damn girl, I could feel the tension from up here," Leia commented, smirking and patting me on the back.

"You did a good job back there, Kamilah," Thora commented. "I mean, our Alpha is kind but we never could do that in front of him… you're really one of a kind."

"What did you do to the alpha?" asked Leia once Alpha Magnus left the area. "He seemed too… caught up in you…"

Owen patted my back. "I agree, you're pretty close to him, Kamilah."

Thora nudged me in the arm. "Did you already find your mate? Who knows, maybe the alpha is yours."

I scoffed, hating the idea of it. "No way, that would never… happen."

But then… we would never know…

I gulped at the possibility. If anything, I don't want to be associated with him. I think I could settle for someone like Dimitri… but the Alpha… that's absurd.

I suddenly decided I wanted to explore the pack. I mean, sure I walked in some areas, but a bit farther from the pack-house… I still hadn't.

"Want me to come with you?" offered Leia, noticing my trailing eyes looking at the trees. "I mean if you want to explore the place. I know you're always locked up in your room."

Owen looked at her with a terrified expression. "I want to come with you two! But damn, my mom's been asking me to help her with her garden."

Leia chuckled. "Then go to her, you know how she'll scold you. She can be terrifying."

Owen leaned into Leia and smashed his lips into hers.

I rolled my eyes, disgusted at how I was standing really close to them, having a close-up look at their make-out session.

Owen smirked as he broke the kiss. "Want to join in?"

As if my face couldn't turn bitter, I grimaced. "Ew, Owen!"

Leia chuckled. "Leave her alone, babe." She planted a small kiss on Owen's lips. "You can go to your mom now."

I looked at Thora. "What about you?"

She smiled bitterly, her face hating the idea. "The Alpha asked me to report."

Leia rolled her eyes at her. "Yeah, then it's a date between me and Kamilah! Come on, dear!"

She locked her arms on mine and guided me to the woods. Owen and Thora walked away and we continued into the deep forest for a few minutes. Leia was busy telling me stories of their childhood. About the past alpha, and how they lived in harmony.

"You know, Alpha Magnus is strict, but his father was much more intimidating. Whenever he was in the room, we would shut up. We never even had any parties, for all the time I can remember..."

Leia was much more fun to be with than I had imagined. I found out that her parents died in the past war. Alpha Magnus took her in, which explained why her house was near us.

I didn't know someone that happy was alone... "I guess that makes us pretty much the same. I'm an orphan. So since my last pack, I never had anyone, no parents, no siblings... just some friends and some bullies."

She gasped. "No way, you had another Serena there?"

I chuckled. "Yeah, I guess no matter what pack, there will always be a bitch."

She busted into fits of laughter as we continued on a trail.

"How was Alpha Magnus when you were kids?" I couldn't help but ask.

Leia pursed her lips, thinking about it for a minute. "Oh, he was too quiet and never played with us."

"Really?"

"Yeah, he was a weird pup, not even socializing with us. He only stayed inside their house, as if hating the heat of the sun. I think that must be why he had gone pale compared to the rest of us."

I nodded, feeling that was some strange information. I really thought he would be that outgoing extroverted kid…

"What about his parents?" I asked more. "Oh, sorry, just curious."

Leia just smiled. "Well, I only know his father, who was a famous dreaded alpha at that time. According to what I heard from the others, since I was just a kid at that time, the former alpha killed his mate and disappeared with some woman…No one knew who the woman was, then suddenly, his father, who was in tears, reappeared one day carrying Alpha Magnus as a 5-year-old. His father was shouting to kill Drucilla that time."

"Drucilla?" I blinked, knowing full well who he was. He was the elder for our region who maintained the balance and kept our existence away from humans…

Leia was silent, then her ears perked up. "Did you hear that?"

"Hear what?"

She grinned. "A rush of water! We are near the river that we would play in when we were kids!" she happily exclaimed, grabbing my hand and running to the sound.

Hidden in the bushes, she opened them to reveal a river. I gasped at how clean it was. The smell of an earthy scent, leaves and the fresh air made it look so relaxing.

Leia instantly removed her pants and T-shirt, only leaving her underwear, and jumped excitedly into the water.

When she reappeared, she motioned for me to follow. "What are you waiting for? Jump!"

I instantly removed my sweaty shorts and sports bra before diving into the water too. I released a sigh as I felt the calming water soothe my body.

"Ah! This is the best! I could swim here all day!" Leia exclaimed, fully enjoying the water.

We played in the water. Being with Leia made me forget about my past, about my past pack, about what happened to me even after a while.

I swam to the side and relaxed my head. I closed my eyes, feeling that it was not so bad after all here.

We stayed there for a few more minutes until Leia got out of the water.

"I'll get dressed now. You're going to stay here?"

"I'll stay for a few more minutes. Let me just enjoy it more."

She smiled. "It's really calming, right?" Standing up, she grabbed her clothes and dried herself off.

I closed my eyes still until a loud yell woke me up. A few birds hummed, giving me melody and some crickets were in harmony.

"Kamilah!"

It was Leia's voice, breaking my trance. Sensing danger, I instantly got out of the water and hurried to where I heard the voice.

It was broad daylight and panic flashed in me.

Was it the humans? Or other enemies? Wasn't this still Alpha Magnus's territory? Leia was really in danger, but I couldn't find her! I instantly transformed into my white wolf sniffed her smell, and was led to a tree.

A gasp let out from my mouth as I saw a head dangling from the branches.

It was… Leia.

She didn't even have the chance to shapeshift and was still in her human form. Meaning that the attacker was too quick. And strong.

I felt a loss of words, my vision blurry and my mind hazy. I gulped, trying to stand still.

No, no. No. This was not happening. We were just—we were just swimming by the river!

Who would dare to do this in broad daylight and worse, in Alpha Magnus's territory?

I racked my brains for any information. No, the attacker was still here, judging from the smell of Leia's blood.

I couldn't wipe out the fact that Leia was dead. She was attacked. Right there, near me. And I couldn't even do anything to help her. I howled to inform the other members.

I needed to find the attacker.

In a far corner, a tall figure hid behind the trees, watching Kamilah who was in despair.

He looked at the dead body hanging by the tree, the foul smell and the gushing of blood coming out disgusted him. But the incident ignited a fire in his mind, blazing his thoughts to never miss this chance to poke his nose into it.

He had seen who the attacker was. He didn't want to get involved, but knowing Kamilah was here, living like a ghost, excited him.

"I've been looking for you… who knew you were here," he thought to himself.

What would happen if the others knew this? For sure, there would be riots… but it would be fun to watch.

He smirked. "This is going to be interesting," muttering those words, he quickly ran away to another location.

The Alpha

ALPHA MAGNUS

I gulped down the glass of wine in my hands and winced in disgust at the taste. My mate's blood is much more appetizing than this.

Ever since I tasted her blood, she was always the one I had been craving. It was intoxicating to me. And it killed me that she was not aware that she was mine. And her smell, oh her so lovely scent… It was a mix of flowers and honey, and tasted so sweet.

I could just inhale it for the whole day and never get tired of it. I didn't normally sleep, but that scent alone would let me snore for the night.

That was how much power she had over me. So much power that it was scary how she could easily manipulate me in the future… if she wanted to.

Knowing this, I knew I was damned.

No, I had to be patient. I had to let time pass and let her discover it on her own. I knew she had been adjusting to her new pack—my pack—and things were still confusing for her.

But a woman was standing in front of me. I glared at her, not in the mood to get laid tonight. She had been staring at me earlier and grabbed this chance to flirt with me.

If I was my past self, I would have easily flipped her over and dragged her to the bathroom to drink her blood. But her blood tasted so disgusting now. No, everyone's blood tasted disgusting. Except for her. Kamilah. Damn, why did I always think of her?

Not to mention, my wolf was getting too picky. He hated the idea of being with another girl. Their once sweet smell to me smelt pungent and disgusting. I tried to get the least disgusting woman I could see but it was still not enough. I was not satisfied.

This was not what I came here for. I went to town tonight and grabbed a drink at a bar to let loose. I was aware that I was low on blood and would soon give away if I continued not to drink blood for one more month.

I could force myself to get with one woman, but the last thing I wanted was for my wolf to become triggered and go wild. What if I asked Kamilah for a taste? A sip of her blood again?

I shook my head. No. No, that shouldn't be. It felt pathetic for an Alpha to be like this. The mighty womanizer, Alpha Magnus, who always gets the girls who were drinking alone. How ironic. Damn it. I tried hard to get Kamilah out of my head but every day was hard if I couldn't see her.

Out of everything, I hated the customs and traditions. As much as possible, I did not want to be a puppet to my fate. But damn me for being born as the child of a prophecy. Damn me for being a hybrid.

Why did my alpha father and my vampire mother even have a child? They should have the decency to think of what their future would be. If they even considered my well-being, then I wouldn't have to drink the blood of girls every month just to live, while hiding my true identity from my pack.

For fuck's sake, I was tired of this.

I drowned in the glass of whiskey in my hand, while I mind-linked my beta, telling him to come immediately.

As always, Dimitri, my second in command, never failed as he appeared in front of me after five minutes. He knew I didn't like to be kept waiting.

"Magnus," he greeted, his tone condensing. I gave him permission to call me by my name whenever we were outside our pack, especially now we were in the human realm, but Dimitri the jerk always seemed to take this as a chance of belittling me.

Dimitri knows I wouldn't have the choice to command him too much as it would be a bit obvious from the human's point of view.

Well, we had to act normal outside our world. That was the law of the elders—the werewolves that were chosen to maintain balance in our world and keep our identity secret.

"Come join me in drinking, Dimitri." I motioned and he sat beside me, grabbing a drink for himself.

He didn't have to ask what happened as his lips turned into a smirk. "You're drowning yourself in whiskey, Magnus?"

"Shut up." He should be thankful he was my beta and my close friend for years. That was the only reason he was able to remark like this and stay alive. I would have already stripped his head off and hung it in my bedroom otherwise.

He seemed not to take my mood seriously as he continued, "You're too patient for a short-tempered alpha."

I raised my eyebrows at him. "Am I?"

He knows that Kamilah was my mate, and had been teasing me about it ever since. Except, he didn't know that I

was a hybrid. And I never planned on telling this to anyone…
even if Dimitri was my most trusted companion.

He nodded. "Aye, I have never seen you so passionate
about a girl. You've had all the girls and you never partied for
years until now."

I hadn't realized it myself…

Well, that was because even if I wanted to, I couldn't,
except now.

"I have my... special someone now, not like you, Dimitri,"
I reasoned out, leaving out the term mate so that the humans
who could hear us wouldn't get suspicious. Dimitri let out a
sigh of relief.

"Well, I'm thankful that I still don't have one. I'm still
having fun now."

"I'm older than you by two decades and don't forget, I am
your master," I said, using my alpha card on him.

He just laughed at my threats and downed the drink.
"Come on, let's go home. Your subordinates are waiting."

I shook my head. "One more drink."

We stayed there for a while, despite my not being able to
get drunk. I drank all kinds of beer available but still, they
couldn't get me drunk.

Dimitri then stopped me from drinking further and
escorted me back to our packhouse.

Our packhouse is situated far from the city and deep in
the woods, where we are free to train and hunt as we needed
without the humans noticing us. Just as my father had, I
trained hard to be the best alpha. So, when he died, I didn't
hesitate on taking the role.

I went straight to the shower to get myself cleaned up.
Stepping under the spray, I ran my fingers through my hair,
then grabbed the body wash and shampoo to thoroughly
wash up.

While lathering my body, I thought of Kamilah, reminiscing about her lovely scent on me, her beautiful hair framing her doll-like face and the way her eyes froze me every time she gazed at me.

I gulped, letting the water fall on my shoulders, to my biceps, and to my six-pack abs, to rinse off and imagined it was Kamilah touching me.

I could feel my member between my thighs hardening and I reached for it, wanting to stroke but then stopped.

'Alpha… something happened… I need your help.'

My eyes widened and I instantly went on alert. It's Kamilah. She's in danger.

I instantly moved out of my bathroom and grabbed a towel to dry myself.

'Stay where you are and don't move. I'm on my way.' Ordering that, I then mind-linked my warriors and got dressed. Outside, I located Kamilah's lovely scent and knowing her direction instantly, began to follow it.

Don't Blame me

KAMILAH

I gulped, to think she had just become my friend.

And she was Owen's mate. What would he do if he knew?

Alpha Magnus soon arrived in his black furry wolf form with ten backups, including Dimitri, trailing behind him. He approached the tree and sniffed.

'The attacker is nearby. Dimitri, trace him!'

Dimitri, in his sandy fur, quickly ran off, with five of the others with him.

Still in my white fur, I faced Alpha Magnus. *'Him? How'd you know?'*

He gritted his teeth. *'He must be the only one judging by the claw and the markings. From the looks of it, he did it very abruptly.'*

He then looked at my body checking for any signs of bruises, *'Are you hurt?'*

I shook my head. *'I'm alright.'*

'Good, report to me everything that happened and leave

no details,' he sharply ordered and I spilled every detail. How we got here and what we did. Alpha Magnus focused, his eyes menacing.

When I was finished, he clenched his jaw. *'Who would dare to kill my pack members, right in my territory?!'* he raged, howling before turning around. *'We must get back to our packhouse and settle things. Keep yourself to your room. Are we clear?'*

I shook my head. *'No, I need to go to Owen and tell him what happened to his mate.'*

He stopped me from moving. *'No, it would be best to stay still. Leia is Owen's mate. And you were with her when it happened. He might get blurred with rage and kill you.'*

I gasped. *'But-But I'll explain, Owen, is my friend—'*

'It's not about the matter of friendship, Kamilah. Just listen to me. It's really starting.'

I furrowed my eyebrows. *'What's starting?'*

With a final look, he pursed his lips. *'You'll know soon.'*

As soon as we got back to the packhouse, we shifted to our human form, then I went to my room and locked the door. I took a shower to wash away all my regret and unease.

If only I had gotten out of the water and protected Leia. If only I had made it in time.

Regret filled my mind and ate me alive.

What now? What will I do? I couldn't turn back time. A tear that I didn't know I was holding escaped from my eye and I let it fall—let myself be vulnerable.

She was so dear to me. That little trip we took to the river gave me a chance to get to know her better. Just when I finally got comfortable with someone, this happened. Whoever the killer was, he wouldn't get away with it.

I got out of the shower and dressed in my pants. I instantly climbed onto my bed when a piece of paper fell out of my blankets. I picked it up and I gasped as I read the words written in blood.

Missed me?

Judging from the smell, it was Leia's. I would have panicked, but now that I am a member of Alpha Magnus's pack, I know that he would help me. I instantly got out and went to Alpha Magnus's study where he was filling out some papers, pack warriors with him. He sniffed the air and looked up at me with wide eyes before making his pack warriors leave.

He stood up to grab my shoulders, then saw the paper I was holding. "What is that? Why do you have Leia's blood?"

"It's a note. I found it on my bed after I took a shower."

Alpha Magnus read it before grabbing it and putting it in a stash of plastic bags. He muttered a curse.

"It must be sent by my past pack," I spoke up and he looked at me. "I mean the only one who's brazen enough to bully me here is Serena, which I doubt. She's not that strong."

I started thinking. From my past pack, the only person in my mind who could do it was Darian and Valentina. Darian had the ability—he was strong enough to do this. But I knew he didn't have the intention to do so.

If it was Valentina, she might have the intention to ruin me. But she didn't have the power or ability to kill Leia, one of the strongest members of the Bloodlust Pack.

Alpha Magnus grabbed my hand, cutting off my thoughts. "Whatever you saw from the incident or on this paper, don't tell anyone. Understood?"

I nodded and he made me return to my room, reminding me not to leave until he told me so.

I waited for further information from Alpha Magnus… any instruction or command from him. However, I haven't heard anything from him for a while now, and I had fallen asleep for a few hours. A knock from outside the door woke me up.

"The Alpha wants you outside. Let's go to the funeral," Dimitri's voice said and I stood up to open it.

He then guided me to the funeral where Alpha Magnus was standing at the front, looking at each of his pack members.

Candles were placed on each side as the pack members surrounded Leia's grave, their expressions grim.

I joined in with them beside Dimitri as Alpha Magnus started his speech.

"We have lost a member today. Leia will forever be remembered in our hearts. I am taking this as a chance to warn everyone. Do not do something suspicious, I am watching you all. Not until the killer is caught. I've raised the security patrols in the area and no one will be allowed to leave." His eyes trailed at each of us, making sure that we had received his warning.

My eyes incidentally met with Owen's blue ones and the sadness in his eyes turned into anger, he stormed to me. "You killer! You killed my mate!"

Thora was quick enough to stop him from fully attacking me.

Dimitri came to my side, defending me from him. "Owen, calm down. Do not blame her for this."

Owen laughed out of madness, completely not himself now. Gone was the cheeky and flirty Owen that I knew for just a day.

"Then who should I blame? Tell me, Dimitri. Who? The

real killer is not yet found. And at that time, Kamilah was the only one with her."

Serena came in. "Yes, it was only you, Kamilah. You should have protected her, but you just let your dear friend Leia be killed just like that. Isn't that suspicious enough?"

"This is no one's fault," Alpha Magnus interjected. "I will take full responsibility, so stop blaming anyone until we have found evidence."

Serena scoffed. "You keep on coddling her ass because she's new to our pack. From the rumors I heard from her past Shadow pack, she's the one who attempted to kill the mate of her crush... isn't that right, Kamilah?"

Everyone was quiet at that, watching Serena with wide eyes.

Dimitri rolled his eyes. "Shut up, Serena."

I pursed my lips, gulping down the lump in my throat as I remembered that scene again. Serena had somehow known that this was my weakness and she was using it as a chance to put me down. Dimitri wanted to stop me but he sighed and just let me speak.

I cleared my throat and spoke up. "Let me be clear, Serena, since you brought up my past," I started, breathing in. "I was blinded too much rage and jealousy that time that I attempted to kill my beloved's mate. But I didn't manage since they stopped me. So technically, I didn't kill anyone."

I approached her and whispered in her ear. "So watch what you say. I'm stronger than you, so don't keep pushing my limit or you'll surely be out of sight," I added with a smirk and she shuddered, trembling at my words.

That should be enough to scare her, right?

"Did you hear that, Alpha Magnus?" She clung to Alpha Magnus's arm and yelled, "She just openly announced she'll kill me!"

Alpha Magnus shook her hand away. "Behave yourself."

Serena sniffed a tear, pouting.

I looked at everyone, especially Owen who was still glaring at me.

I gulped, wanting to talk to him, but I could feel Alpha Magnus's hard gaze on me, stopping me from even moving toward him. It was best that I should listen to his advice and not get closer to Owen…

It was best to talk things out, but better to let the other person who was grieving have his own space.

I cleared my throat. "I admit it's my fault for not being able to protect Leia on time. I should have gotten there sooner. I was the only one there to help her, but I didn't. I admit to my mistakes. But you don't have the right to pinpoint that I'm the killer when she's dear to me too," I explained to everyone. "I swear the moment I find the attacker, I'll give his head to you personally, Owen."

My speech somehow made the situation worse, the air around us tasting bitter and mellow. The night ended as the ceremony for Leia's burial finished. Everyone went back to their houses and rooms, except Alpha Magnus who was approaching me.

He glared at me. "I told you to not say anything until we found the killer."

"Why? They deserve to know and it's time to not hide in your shadows. As you said, I have to show them what I'm capable of."

He shook his head. "You should be careful with your words, Kamilah. Words are bullets that need to be compromised."

After leaving those words, he walked away, leaving me dumbfounded. I was quiet as Dimitri escorted me back to my room.

I looked behind him, seeing Alpha Magnus shifting into his wolf and going to the woods. "Where is he running of to?"

"He will personally take charge of patrol duty tonight. I'll be with to him too, after I escort you back to your room."

My ears perked up. "I want to come too."

"No, it's dangerous. We never know when the next attack will be. So you should be careful. I think the attacker is going after you especially."

I sighed, finally giving in. We reached my room and Dimitri said his goodbyes. I watched in silence as Dimitri walked out and transformed into his sandy wolf.

I wasn't able to sleep that night, completely alert for anything. I was prepared to transform and fight back if the attacker would return for me.

When I woke up the next day, I went to eat breakfast and wanted to go to train myself. Alpha Magnus was nowhere, and it was only Dimitri who stayed to keep an eye on me.

"Where are you going?" he asked and I shrugged.

"To the training grounds."

"No, Alpha Magnus cancelled it for today. You can sleep all day."

I shook my head. "I couldn't sleep that much, anyway."

Dimitri was keen on not letting me leave alone so I stayed at my room for a few hours. I waited for Dimitri to leave and I instantly ran out of the house. I looked in the direction of Leia's house to my left, seeing it was lonely and quiet.

I passed by Owen who had just went inside Leia's house and he didn't even bother saying hi to me.

He must really hate me right now. I couldn't blame him for that. I gulped, walking to the training grounds.

I jogged around and did some curl-ups, push-ups, and some routines before punching the punching bag, imagining it was Leia's killer.

The training grounds were empty today, which was good. I could be left alone with my thoughts and focus. The only thing that bothered me was the strange gloomy feeling that lingered in the whole pack. It felt unusual than it usually was.

"You need some help?"

Asked a man from behind me. I glanced at him, noticing that I was not familiar with him. I hadn't seen him around so was obviously not part of the Bloodlust Pack. Also, he was too pale for a werewolf.

I'd never encountered a vampire myself, but judging from the smell, I instantly knew… he was one. I cursed under my breath, wondering how the hell one vampire managed to infiltrate the pack. Were the members assigned on patrol today not doing their job properly?

I growled, howling to signal the rest of the pack members, and instantly prepared myself to transform and bite his head off when he stopped me.

"Chill, babe. I'm here to make friends with you," he calmly said as I grabbed his throat.

"Who are you and tell me what is your purpose for trespassing into the Bloodlust Pack?"

He raised his hands up in surrender. "Whoa, relax babe. You're playing a dangerous game for someone targeted by a killer. My name's Gusev. And I am friends with Alpha Magnus." He then whispered, "Want to know a secret? I know who killed Leia."

Caught in the Act

KAMILAH

I raised my eyebrows, still not trusting this stupid vampire. "You are not going to fool me, bloodsucking mosquito."

He gasped. "Mosquito? How dare you call my elegant appearance a mosquito."

He was too carefree, which was absurd for someone who casually entered this pack as if it were their own. Also, he was a friend of Alpha Magnus. I don't believe him.

"Why? Isn't it real?" I retorted, and he just pouted.

He then took a step closer to me, "If I'm not mistaken, you are Kamilah?"

I blinked, he knew me? Part of my heart felt nervous about it, but I feigned courage.

"Yes. How'd you know?"

His smile turned a little devious. "I heard a lot about you. You're living like a ghost. You're dead but here you are... alive and kicking."

My nose caught a whiff of his pungent rotten smell, and I scrunched my nose in disgust. "You smell rotten."

This was the first time I had ever encountered a vampire in my life, and this smell was strange, putting me in a daze.

He held his chest as if offended. "You keep insulting me when I come in peace." He then cleared his throat. "I was there when it happened, you know."

I abruptly stopped. "What did you just say?"

"Someone was following you when that incident happened. Looks like it was sudden, but it was planned," he started to explain, his tone now so serious that I believed it.

Part of me told me that he was lying and just baiting me... while something inside wanted to know more. "Tell me more. don't leave out any details," I urged.

His eyes narrowed. "You're curious, hmm. So you really want to catch the killer?"

"Yes," I admitted, I didn't lie about that. I was desperate to know and it irked me so much... so much that I wanted to kill someone.

"Well, you should be careful who you trust... that's all I can warn you for now... Actually, I just want to enjoy your company at the moment."

I scoffed at him. "What? You know who the killer is, and you won't tell me about it? How can I be sure that you're telling the truth?"

"I am risking my life here, Kamilah. Who in their right mind would go to a powerful alpha's territory, and most of all, a vampire?"

I was silent. He had a point though. But he still didn't answer why he traveled all the way here just to drop this mystery for me to solve. He was making it hard for me to believe him.

"Trace back to what happened before Leia was killed. You'll find the truth."

I sighed. "If you have nothing anymore to say, then leave this territory."

He chuckled. "You mistake me, Kamilah. I kind of went there not just to approach you… I came here for your alpha," he suddenly said. "Tell your alpha I'm here with some valuable information. He would be pleased."

I mind-linked Alpha Magnus. *There's a vampire looking for you. He says he holds some valuable information for you.*

There was a pause before Alpha Magnus replied. *Let him in our territory.*

I sighed and motioned for the vampire to follow me. "Let's go."

"Awe, my best friend still remembers me! The last time I saw him he was just a shy little kid," he exclaimed happily and I glanced at him.

"I'm your responsibility now, I hope you take care of me."

"Oh, we both perfectly know that you have no need of care, you can handle yourself."

He just smiled and walked quietly behind me. It took us a few more minutes of silent walking before we neared the packhouse.

Suddenly, we were stopped by a shriek. "Ew, why are you letting a vampire enter here?"

I didn't have to turn around to know it was Serena who stopped as we passed by her.

"He's Alpha Magnus's old friend," I replied shortly, not in the mood to deal with her right now.

Just then, Gusev took a step closer to her, raising his eyebrows. "You've always been such a rude girl, ever since you were a child."

Serena gasped, offended by the vampire's comment, "Excuse me? Do I know you?"

"You were just a little kid the last time I came here so you might not remember," the vampire said. "But you need to show some good manners and have some respect, kid. Your high shrill voice irritates my lovely ears."

Serena was too stunned to think of a comeback and she stormed off, mouthing a curse.

As we walked to Alpha Magnus's study, I asked again the thing that bothered me. "Just tell me who the killer is."

"Awe, where's the fun in that? The humans are at war now because of their stupidity, fighting over land territory, while we supernatural choose to hide in the dark. I just came here to pass the time."

I gritted my teeth, he took that topic so lightly.

"How old are you anyway?" I changed the topic.

"Is this an investigation?" he responded. "You keep on asking me questions. You seem so interested in my life. You are starting to like me, aren't you?"

I ignored his teasing.

"Why are you befriending our kind? And our alpha? Isn't this an act of treachery for your own kind?" I kept throwing the questions at him from my mind. "Come on, answer."

"It seems I have to drop the mysterious act." He sighed. "Fine, I'll answer just to gain your trust. Honestly, I don't side with anyone. I could be at my own clan's side, but it doesn't mean I won't help the werewolves' side."

I blinked, somehow confused. "So, what side are you really on?"

"No one actually, it depends on my mood. I could side with both or either. But I am on my own side. I do whatever I want," he replied with a lopsided grin, his fangs showing.

I shook my head. "You're crazy. So there will be a time that you'll betray us."

"Depends on the trust you put in me." As he answered that, we finally reached Alpha Magnus's study.

I didn't have to knock as they probably heard our footsteps, well, my footsteps since the vampire moved like air and didn't even make a sound. Dimitri opened the door and motioned for Gusev to enter.

I was about to enter too when Dimitri blocked my way.

"What about me? I want to hear what they discuss."

Dimitri shook his head. "It's an important and private matter."

I sighed, not wanting to argue more, and left them.

I ended up waiting outside the door. I tried to put my ears on the wood but I couldn't even hear that they were talking. It felt like they were not even having a conversation.

After an hour, the door opened and I pretended to wipe some of the artifacts.

"You're still here? Did you wait for me?" Gusev asked, his hand was about to grab mine when a pair of strong arms stopped him.

"Stop teasing her. I also didn't permit you to touch her," Alpha Magnus ordered firmly, and Gusev's eyes sparked with interest.

He stared at me. "Oh… this is going to be much more interesting than I thought."

I looked at the vampire with a confused face. I wonder what I was going on in his mind to find this situation entertaining? It was not obvious that he was not taking us seriously.

"Dimitri, lead the vampire to his tower."

Dimitri nodded and Gusev commented, "My dear best friend, I really love how you prepared a special place for me. I always know I am welcome here."

Alpha Magnus casted a side glance at him, "You're not

special. I just made that tower in case this happens. I don't want my pack members to get bothered by you."

Gusev's mouth opened in shock and Dimitri couldn't stifle his laugh.

"How could you, my dear best friend!" Gusev cried out dramatically, as if he was betrayed and Alpha Magnus groaned in annoyance.

"As I said, stop calling me best friend. I don't want to get involved with a lowly creature."

Gusev gave up on arguing with Alpha Magnus as Dimitri guided him to where he would be staying.

"I know what you're thinking. Don't get involved with vampires," Alpha Magnus warned me as we were left alone now.

"I was just curious." I shrugged. "Oh… what did he tell you back there?"

"It's classified information," Alpha Magnus answered.

I pouted my lips. "Please? Alpha?"

"No," he firmly responded. "Stop poking your nose in other things and just focus on keeping yourself safe."

I sighed. "Fine, I'll rack all the information from Gusev myself next time."

"Don't even bother. Talking with him might only drain your energy alive."

"I have a question, is he your best friend? You two look close, and he's the only one other than Dimitri that can tease you like that," I suddenly brought up now that we were on the topic.

Alpha Magnus released a chuckle as if I'd told him the most hilarious thing in the world.

"Are you serious about asking me that, Kamilah? Isn't it obvious how I dread him? That damn vampire only spouts nonsense."

I thought he was mocking me, however, he did the opposite and was laughing now. It was the first time that I had seen him look happy like that. I was used to seeing him frown and glare all the time and it was refreshing to watch him in this state.

I think I should tell him more hilarious things from now on… I suddenly felt a bit closer to him, and it felt like something was filling the gap between us.

Mates

KAMILAH

Nighttime came, and the window opened.

I saw a figure coming in as the cold breeze harshly hit my skin.

I sniffed and I could smell the scent of someone familiar. I furrowed my eyebrows. "Thora? What are you doing?"

"That swim in the lake was really cute."

I blinked, as she spoke up. "What are you trying to say?"

She scoffed at me. "You're so naive that I have to really come to you." Her tone was irritated and bored. "You're too slow to figure things out. I'm so disappointed in you, Kamilah."

It took me a minute to realize it. I clicked my tongue. "It was you?" I almost couldn't believe it.

"Yes, Kamilah, how are you so slow? I am a spy of Drucilla." Thora was the killer. This has never occurred to my thoughts, not even once. I must say that she had surprised me.

I growled at her as she laughed at me. I stayed still, alert, on my toes. I kept note of her movements.

"I am one of Drucilla's subordinates. I also wanted Owen for me, but now that my cover is blown, see you!"

My canines dug deep into her neck, wanting to stop her and she groaned in pain. A smirk played on her lips as she pushed me, overpowering my strength and making me stumble on the ground, "You won't win against me."

She instantly ran away, leaving me alone. Still in shock, I sat on the ground, not knowing what to do. Thora had become a friend of mine here… and I didn't know betrayal again would find its way to me here.

I instantly felt a presence behind me, and I looked up to see Alpha Magnus was already there.

"It was Thora…." I muttered as I looked in the direction where Thora left. "She's part of Drucilla…"

He nodded, instantly getting my point. "I'll investigate this. We never knew she had someone assisting her in the pack."

I scoffed, tired of all of this. "Seems that your "safest place on Earth" is not working, Alpha Magnus. Some rats managed to slip in. How can you be so sure that this thing might not happen again?"

"Kamilah…" Alpha Magnus tried to reach out to me but I stayed still. Just then, his ears perked up and he sharply looked around, standing on alert.

"Stay still."

A branch of a tree snapped and I instantly felt sharp fangs clinging to my shoulder. I groaned in pain and Alpha Magnus pushed the intruder away from me.

"Looks like Thora's friends heard of this."

He clicked his tongue, fury lacing in his tone. Judging from the stinky foul smell, he was definitely a rogue...

I stared into the claw marks my attacker left. Five more rogues then appeared behind him, circling us.

"No, the scent is different. Drucilla never works with the rogues," Alpha Magnus muttered as he protectively grabbed my hand and pulled me to his side. "Stay behind me, Kamilah."

I shook my head. "No, I'll fight back."

Alpha Magnus was firm as he forced me to stay rooted in my spot. He launched at all five of the rogues. It was the first time I had seen Alpha Magnus fight seriously in front of me. He managed to save me last time from my old pack, but my memories from there seemed to be a bit hazy.

Magnus was quick, precise and there was surely killing intent. He transformed into his black, furry wolf and in one swift motion, four of the five rogue's heads were dropped on the ground.

The last rogue was shocked, and panic filled his face.

He tried to run away but Alpha Magnus was quick to get him. "Uh uh, I won't spare any of you. Tell me who sent you!"

Even though on the verge of death, the rogue smirked. "You have a lot of traitors within your pack."

Alpha Magnus gritted his teeth, tightening his hold on the rogue's neck. "You seem to underestimate my power, filth. Spill the truth or your guts are out."

"Just kill me, I'm dead anyway."

Alpha Magnus rolled his eyes and dragged the rogue by his head. He turned to me. "Come. I'll show that pup who he's messing with."

He continued to drag the rogue behind him and I followed as Alpha Magnus made his way back to the packhouse.

He continued on until he stopped at the familiar house, knocking on the door.

The door opened and a shocked Serena came into view.

"Alpha Magnus? What is—" She stopped as Alpha Magnus harshly dropped the rogue in front of her.

Serena gasped looking at the bloodied rogue.

Alpha Magnus leaned on the wall. "How many more of them are here?" His tone was calm, but his eyes were menacing and throwing daggers at her.

Serena blinked. "What? I don't understand—"

"Tell me. How many more did you hire," he stated again. "Don't make me repeat myself, Serena."

Some pack members noticed the commotion as we were still in Serena's doorway. They instantly watched the scene in curiosity, wondering what was happening.

I stayed quiet behind Alpha Magnus, just watching them. "I don't—"

"Feigning innocence, huh?" Alpha Magnus kicked the door, breaking the interior of the wood.

"Everyone! Watch this traitor lying at me, the alpha, straight in my face," he yelled for everyone, and I even saw Owen in the crowd.

Alpha Magnus grabbed the rogue's head and made him face Serena. "Rogue, tell me who sent you to attack us there?"

Serena's eyes widened further. "I don't know that filthy rogue—"

"It's her," the rogue admitted and the crowd gasped.

Serena's eyes widened in horror. "What? I don't even know you, filthy rogue!"

Alpha Magnus dropped the Rogue and grabbed Serena's throat to harshly push her to the wall. "Tell me the reason, Serena."

Serena struggled, keeping his hand away. The more she struggled, the more his hand tightened.

Even as a spectator, I got scared watching Alpha

Magnus's wrath. He clearly lives up to his name as an alpha and his reputation. Serena was so red that it looked like Alpha Magnus would instantly snap her neck, but a hand stopped Alpha Magnus.

"We'll pass judgment on how we'll kill this traitor, Alpha," Dimitri said calmly.

"Shut up!" He was too mad to even calm down, that Dimitri had to push him off to snap him out of it.

"Clear off your head from anger, Alpha. Let me handle this based on the justice system you made."

Alpha Magnus glared at Dimitri and took a deep breath before closing his eyes for a moment. His hand let go of Serena who choked as she panted for air.

"If I weren't there with Kamilah, you could have killed her, Serena. Did you not know that?" Alpha Magnus asked, now a bit calmer. "You dared to cross my limits… you know how I get angry at traitors like you, right?"

Serena was on the verge of tears as she threw a glare at me. "What? Do you think I'm happy too? We had a thing until she came here! All of your focus went on the stupid mate of yours so I had to—"

"Stop blabbering." He shut her off. "You know what I made you promise, Serena. You're spilling it out here."

She snorted. "What? Can't take that I spilled the truth? Why bother hiding the fact that she's your mate? I am here, Alpha Magnus. I can make you so much happier if you're with me."

"She's nuts."

"Desperate she-wolf."

"If only her father was not one of the pack warriors, I would have killed her already."

Those were the words from the crowd that I heard. Serena glared at them.

I tried to process what Serena said. Mate? I couldn't remember about that... I glanced at Alpha Magnus, who was clearly annoyed with her. If Dimitri hadn't come to stop him, he would have already killed Serena a while ago.

"Dimitri, tell me what do we do with traitors?" Alpha Magnus asked sarcastically.

"According to the justice system that you made, we'll cut the traitor's hand off, then banish them from the pack, or cut her head off," Dimitri instantly answered.

Alpha Magnus nodded. "That seems not the right punishment for Serena, don't you think, Kamilah?"

I blinked, all eyes on me. Serena was on the verge of throwing her hands and digging her fangs at me. I shrugged, somehow liking the idea that she was at my mercy.

"Give her a chance if she apologizes and bows to me. If not, just kill her," I answered with a teasing look at Serena.

"What? You are a newcomer, how dare you?!" Serena complained, yelling and fighting, but Alpha Magnus kept her still.

"You heard her, Serena," Alpha Magnus urged.

Biting her lips, Serena shook with anger as she didn't have a choice except to do as he said. Serena bowed to me. "I apologize, Kamilah."

Alpha Magnus turned to me. "Is that enough?"

I shrugged, wanting to see her suffer more but Alpha Magnus seemed to hear my thoughts as he nodded.

"I am not satisfied with that. I got a better idea." He then grabbed her and the rogue outside the house.

He asked Dimitri to grab two knives and Dimitri came back with them, throwing them at the two. "I am going to give you both a chance to live. Only if one of you kills the other."

Serena gasped and the rogue laughed.

"Alpha Magnus, are you out of your mind? How could you!"

Alpha Magnus ignored her pleas as he sat back beside me. "Remember, no shifting. Just the knives. You may start now."

We watched as the rogue didn't hesitate to attack Serena with the knife. Serena was quick enough to dodge him as she fought back. There was no denying that Serena was strong and quick when I saw her training, but the rogue was much stronger.

I glanced at Alpha Magnus, noticing how he was enjoying this. He was clearly just and fair in treating his subjects, intimidating and strict when handling them, but he was also controlling and demanding along with merciless when they dared to cross his limits.

He was not hailed as the strong and merciless Alpha for nothing.

The rogue was on the verge of killing Serena. Serena ran to us for help.

Alpha Magnus raised his eyebrows, went to the rogue to kill him and Serena sighed in relief.

He shook his head. "That's boring, Serena."

Serena's tears suddenly gushed down like a waterfall.

"Consider yourself lucky and thank Dimitri as I would have already killed you."

He then looked at everyone. "You see how I treat traitors. If any of you dare to do the same, then you are more than welcome to leave now," he threatened. "Now clear the area."

The other pack members left the scene as they removed the rogue. Dimitri then grabbed Serena's hand and took her away.

Serena looked behind her to tell him. "My father will know you killed me, Magnus." Serena just smirked devilishly before going to where Dimitri led her.

"Nice show!" An excited voice exclaimed from the crowd, and I saw Gusev, the vampire, commented as he walked over to us, as happy and carefree as always.

"I love how you demonstrate your love for your mate, Magnus. You're really my best friend!"

He tried to cling his arms to Alpha Magnus, but he pushed him away. "Shut up. I don't want to deal with you now."

Gusev pouted and scrunched his nose in disgust. "What a bummer. Everyone here smells filthy, except Kamilah. I want to spend some time with her."

Alpha Magnus just ignored him and started to walk, motioning for me to come with him. "Let's go."

Gusev's mouth opened, and he clutched his chest as if in pain. "I came here to have some fun, not to be ignored and locked up in the tower!"

"Read the room, Gusev," Alpha Magnus demanded and Gusev stopped, looking at the way Magnus's hand twitched and he sighed before leaving us alone.

Once we were alone, I looked at Alpha Magnus. "We need to talk." I wanted to know about the mate thing.

"We will. In my study." He made me follow him and led me to his study.

I didn't bother wasting a moment as I dropped the bomb, "Tell me what Serena said. About that mate thing."

He pointed at my bleeding hand, which was bitten earlier by the rogue. "Let me heal you first."

I shook my head. "I can heal on my own. Stop changing the topic."

He sighed, "I waited for you to remember it on your own."

I raised my eyebrows. "Remember what? What is it?"

"That Blood Moon night," he blurted out. "Try to remember what happened."

I closed my eyes, wanting to remember it but still couldn't. I groaned in frustration. "Tell me what it is?"

"You're my mate, Kamilah" he blurted out, which took me aback. But deep inside, my heart already knew it and was not even surprised by it.

He grabbed my arms and pinned me on the wall. "And now that you know, I want you to know that I want to keep you safe here. As long as you're with me. Forever."

I blinked.

The thought of forever had a strange ring to me. Especially now that I didn't believe in the concept of 'mates' ever since that night happened.

I struggled against him and pushed his hand away. "No."

His eyebrows instantly furrowed, as if never heard of the word. He must not have been used to being rejected and only experienced it now, "What do you mean, no?"

"I said no. I don't want to be your mate," I firmly said, keeping my ground.

I expected him to scold, or even attack me.

Instead of yelling at me, his voice softened. "You can't just say no. The Blood Moon already chose us." He cleared his throat. "Is it because of me?" he meekly asked.

"No—"

"Then why?" he asked.

I pursed my lips, averting my gaze to the ground. "It's complicated."

He grabbed my hand softly. "Explain it to me so I can understand."

"How could I when I don't even understand it? I hate the concept of mates. I hate it, Alpha. So much."

"You're not a child of prophecy," I said, remembering

what the necromancer told me. Unless the necromancer deceived me or Alpha Magnus lied to me, I didn't believe he was my mate. He was an alpha, not the hybrid that the necromancer mentioned to me. The hybrid that would bring tragedy to the realm.

"He said my mate will not be found until I find a child of prophecy—"

He paused as if knowing something. "So you know your mate is a child of prophecy?"

"Yes." I answered.

He smiled at me, a pained expression on his face, as if he knew something yet he chose to keep it.

The thought of being stuck in this pack, with ongoing fights, betrayals, and everything, as if I just went back to my past pack… This would be my new life from now on.

My breath hitched at the thought. I couldn't imagine myself staying here, being a subordinate to someone again, and acting like a puppet for them to control.

Just then, he instantly wrapped his hands only around my waist and directly looked at me. My eyes went wide as he trapped me between him and the wall behind me.

He gazed down at my lips as I licked them, then gulped down. He glanced up at my eyes and instantly smacked his lips on mine. I froze, not realizing what was happening.

He was… kissing me?

I couldn't even bring myself to smack him away and hated to admit that I actually enjoyed it.

Alpha Magnus was the first to break away as he looked into my eyes again, waiting for any reaction. I looked back at him, stunned. "You liked that?"

I gulped, not wanting to say yes.

A strangled noise came out of my lips and he smirked. "Then I hope you won't protest with what I'll do."

I could feel his cold hand grazing mine as he trailed his eyes on me, up and down. There was lust, eagerness, temptation, and hope, all bottled up in his eyes.

In an instant, he slammed his lips on mine again and said in between breaths, "If you don't like what I'm doing, then tell me to stop, baby doll."

I accepted his lips and I could feel him push the door of his study closed with his feet without breaking our kiss. He closed his eyes, savoring the pleasure. He sucked on my lower lip, nibbling on it and biting it slowly. He parted my mouth, his wet tongue asking for an entrance. He was teasing me and taking my breath away all at the same time.

I could barely breathe with how his tongue was claiming mine. My heart felt like it was about to be ripped out of my chest at any moment. My blood rushed to my cheeks and I could feel that I looked so ready right now.

Alpha Magnus's hands were cold and he was grabbing my hair, almost like he couldn't get enough of me, but at the same time handling me so delicately. As if he had waited for this all this time and now, he was enjoying every second of it.

He broke the kiss and watched as I panted. He leaned in and sniffed my neck, his lips sliding on my collarbone while his hands that were wrapped around my waist, played with my jeans. I could feel his hard-on through his denim jeans, that were grazing against my skin.

He looked red, fierce and hot, his veiny hands were eager.

"Your blood really tastes sweet. And goodness, your smell, ugh," he growled out.

He breathed deeply, looking at me with heavy emotion in his eyes.

Our kiss had been hot and passionate, and I couldn't help but admit it. And it felt like there was a magnetic field that drew me in closer to him, not letting me let go of his touch on me. It electrified me and thrilled me beyond the core.

I couldn't help but want more. More of Alpha Magnus.

Right here, right now.

We both knew that once we crossed the line, things wouldn't be back to the way it was.

My usual self would have said no to this. This was so not me. Not the Kamilah I mastered the image of.

I should be pushing him away but it was like I lost control of my body. I felt tongue-tied and lost in bliss.

The way Alpha Magnus looked at me and tempted me to initiate the move now, I could tell he wanted to ask for permission to continue, but he was afraid so he kept quiet.

I stared at his lips, then into his lustful brown eyes, and the golden hues that surrounded his pupils.

Leaning to him, I instantly slammed my lips on his and grabbed his hair. Then my hands made their way to his chest and touched his hard abs. I felt him shivering at my touch, but he smiled against our kiss and trailed soft kisses from my lips to my neck, and down to my collarbone.

Suddenly he paused, stopping his lips on me. "I… need to stop, before I lose control, Kamilah."

I blinked at him as if a zap had woken me up from my senses. I averted my gaze to the ground and bit my lip as I struggled to comprehend what just happened. That was intense. And I instantly felt the connection between us.

"You might hate me tomorrow if we continue doing this," he added, trying to reassure me.

He's right. As I could think now, I am hating him for this. For making me feel this way. For having to make my thoughts run in circles, bothering and buzzing around my mind.

Great. Not to mention, my heart was not slowing from beating so rapidly.

I breathed deeply, fixing my stubborn hair that was messed up because of his hands and my wrinkled shirt, trying to think against the awkward silence between us. "I respect you as my mate, and I want to continue so badly, but I don't want you to get caught up in the heat of the moment, to be forced because I wanted to continue. I want you to want me yourself, to seek me yourself."

By saying that, he didn't even let me respond. "We'll talk later." He walked away and left me alone in his study.

I stared blankly at the wall in front of me, letting everything run around in my thoughts and sink in. It was a bit hard to let everything in at once.

Trust

KAMILAH

I walked toward my room with my head empty and Alpha Magnus out of sight. I'm so confused right now, that I couldn't even think straight. Fear for the future, scared of what will happen. The uncertainty…

But among all of these, all I could think of was how he was really my mate…

The thought scared and intimidated me earlier, but now, I didn't know what to feel.

But I wanted to be the one in charge. I wanted to be the one leading. And since I am stronger now, I could make that happen. Should I give him a chance? I bit my lips, the kiss we had playing in my mind again and the blood rushed down my cheeks, making my breath hitch.

Alpha Magnus seemed decent to me…although, do I even have the right to be picky with my mate? Someone as strong as Alpha Magnus should have a stronger Luna too…not me who just gained strength just because of my deal from the necromancer.

Never in my life did I expect to be an alpha's mate… It should make me feel honored, so why was I not feeling that way?

Millions of questions lingered in my mind and it had been bothering me. I needed to talk to him now. Going back to his office, I bit my lip nervously and wanted to open the door when a hand stopped me.

"Oh, hello there."

Dimitri's goofy smile greeted me.

I smiled back, acknowledging his presence. "Dimitri."

He glanced at the door and at my hand. "What are you doing here? It's past curfew."

"Oh." I didn't know it was past curfew. It was past midnight, so everyone was asleep.

Dimitri stood by the door and blocked my way. "And? Do you want anything from the Alpha?"

"I want to talk to the alpha," I answered, wanting to clear my head out. "I have a few questions I'd like to ask him before giving him a chance."

Dimitri looked at my eyes as if attempting to read what I was thinking. "You can't do that tomorrow?"

"I'm afraid I might forget."

He nodded. "But the alpha is busy." He was still blocking the door. I wanted to take a peek at what he was doing inside but Dimitri was keen on not letting me.

He was acting suspiciously. What was the alpha doing inside that made him act weird like this? Were they hiding something?

"Is he… having a meeting?" I asked suspiciously, attempting to take a peek behind him.

"No-I mean yes!"

"Then let me in," I continued pestering him, not keen on

backing down. "He said I could come in anytime I want. We had not finished our conversation earlier."

He suddenly pointed at the window to our right and muttered, "Wow, the full moon is captivating tonight, don't you think?"

I looked at the moon and realized he was distracting me. I instantly pushed Dimitri off the door. This made him lose balance and enabled me to see something unexpected inside.

In front of the desk was Alpha Magnus, holding a woman in his arms as the woman was closing her eyes, savoring the moment. Alpha Magnus was kissing the woman on the neck, creating a bitemark and I could smell the woman's blood all over his desk. No, it was not just some woman. It was a human.

My mouth opened and I was rooted in my spot.
Wow.

Alpha Magnus didn't seem to notice my presence, too enchanted at the moment…

I couldn't help but just gasp at the sight. He was saying promising words to me, saying I was his mate, when he had someone else in his arms right now…

"Alpha Magnus?" I called out.

Alpha Magnus's head turned to me, his eyes blazing red, breathing hard. His pale skin bothered me, his fangs were showing and he looked like he could jump and kill me any time, so I instantly closed the door and ran. Dimitri saw me, calling my name but I didn't stop.

After that incident, I stayed in my room for the whole week and purposely avoided Alpha Magnus. I had done a lot of rethinking about my decisions in life.

It was a good thing Dimitri sent me food over so I wouldn't starve, but no matter what I thought I'd do, the image still remained in my mind. Dimitri wanted to talk about what happened, but I only knew that he'd just give excuses for his master.

If Alpha Magnus wanted to talk to me, then he should come to me. But seeing the image again made my stomach churn. I wanted to kill the woman in his arms right there and then.

Looking at the open window, I glanced outside and saw no one was there except a few guards that were assigned to patrol the area. Other than those patrol guards, there was no one. It seemed that everyone was still grieving the loss of Leia. It had been a week but they still held memories of her.

But this would be the perfect chance for me.

To leave.

I waited for another hour before I took my chance. Since I didn't have many things here as it was all given to me by Alpha Magnus, I decided not to bring anything with me. I opened the wooden window and jumped down. The height wasn't that high so I didn't get injured on the way.

Taking a glance to each side, I continued walking normally but was stopped by a patrol guard.

"Hey, you!" I halted as he yelled at me. "Stop right there!"

I muttered a curse and sighed, now facing the patrol. "Hey." I awkwardly waved.

His mouth formed an O as soon as he recognized me and cleared his throat. "Oh, Miss Kamilah, the new member. Alpha Magnus specifically instructed us to take care of you… Can I ask where you are going? You're heading toward the town and that's out of Alpha Magnus's territory. We are on high alert now, as you can see."

I chuckled, thinking of a way to get out of this. A little lie wouldn't hurt, right?

"The alpha asked me to go grab him some wine, you know him."

His head cocked to the side. "Oh? But we still have some supply… as far as I know."

I shrugged, trying to play it cool. "He probably got tired of the taste, and wanted a freshly made one. If you don't believe me then you can ask him yourself—"

He shook his head instantly. "No! It's fine, I believe you. You're close to the alpha."

With one last smile and him motioning me to proceed, I continued on my way. The guard even waved at me before minding his own business.

I sighed in relief as I felt free as I got closer to leaving the Bloodlust Pack's territory, then I heard a deep voice behind me.

'It seems you chose to leave my pack.'

I looked behind me and saw Alpha Magnus, running up to me in his wolf form. He had transformed into his black wolf, which was a lot bigger than me.

"I appreciate your help but… I don't want to stay in your pack, Alpha Magnus," I responded, my feet were shaking a bit but I stood my ground. I wanted the ground to eat me up right then and there.

His face darkened and something in his eyes flashed with red, now in a rage. *'You've been avoiding me, Kamilah,'* he demanded, his voice sounding hurt for some reason.

"No, we won't do this," I replied firmly. How dare he have the nerve to show his face to me, like it was no big deal? Like nothing happened? I didn't know if he was playing some game with me, pretending to forget about that night, or if he was just thick-headed.

'But you are my mate,' he said with so much weight, his

voice growing and his eyes glaring at me. *'You have to stay by my side, Kamilah.'*

I swallowed, now turning away from him. I didn't want any mate thing for me. I was fine alone. Yes, he could protect me, he was the famous Alpha Magnus for goodness' sake.

But that was not enough to confirm my doubts.

Doubts about his loyalty. Doubts he would find another woman. He was too overbearing for me. And I was too disobedient. We were not a good match. Maybe he should have been with Serena. I couldn't help but think that.

"Just let her go," growled another voice, and I looked behind me to see Owen fiercely glaring at Alpha Magnus.

I furrowed my eyebrows. "What are you doing here, Owen?"

He just gave a glance at me before throwing daggers at Alpha Magnus. "If you love her, let her leave, Alpha."

Alpha Magnus's eyes darkened. "This is not your business, Owen. You are defying me as your Alpha."

"As an alpha? I'm tired of that bullshit hierarchy. It's best that I go rogue," he said firmly, making me widen my eyes in shock. "It's your fault my mate died. What happens if you let Kamilah die here too?"

Owen dared to say that in front of his alpha? Did he have a death wish? What did he eat today to be this courageous?

Alpha Magnus's glare didn't even make him back down. He was surely certain of his decision.

'I won't let her die on my watch. Never,' Magnus replied, his eyes holding a heavy emotion as he stared at me. Each word he dropped was heavy to bear. I avoided his stare. *'Don't you trust me, Kamilah?'*

I knew we didn't end on a good note with his mate Leia getting killed, but I was just surprised at how brave he was for defending my wishes and standing up against the Alpha himself.

That really took a lot of bravery.

He leaned toward me and whispered, "Just go, I'll distract him—"

'You don't have to. I'll let her leave,' alpha interjected, now giving up. *'Then do what you want, Kamilah. I won't stop you from leaving my pack. But remember, they will be after you and you will be needing my help soon.'*

I knew that. They would be after me but I would be strong. If they killed me, then let them. I would come at them for messing with me. And with that, Magnus didn't even move an inch from where he stood as I started to run away. I continued running. I even looked back to see him just watching me from afar, silently.

I could feel long strides that followed me and I didn't have to look back to see Owen was following me.

"You run fast," he commented.

"Yeah…" I said, not sure what to reply. "Thank you for defending me back there… but why are you following me? Did he send you?" I asked.

He shook his head, now matching my pace. "I'm leaving the pack too."

It didn't shock me hearing his reply, but it was just that I couldn't fathom how Alpha Magnus, the strict and one of the most feared alphas, let him leave easily and unscratched.

I wanted to ask Owen why but I seemed to know the reason. Of course, it was because of Leia. After her death, he looked lifeless. I guess he was not blaming me now, instead blaming Alpha Magnus for what happened.

I felt pity for him but I just couldn't judge him. I didn't experience losing a mate like that.

But then, I had just left Alpha Magnus, who was claiming

to be my mate. I was not even sure if leaving him like this would cut our connection.

"So where are you going?" I suddenly brought up, curious about his plans.

"I don't know. For now, I'm just going to accompany you and decide there. What about you?"

I shrugged at his question. "I don't know either." We both suddenly burst into laughter, realizing the situation we were in. It was like we carried a gun without bullets on a battlefield because of how unprepared we were. For now, we needed to find a place to settle in for the night.

I suddenly stopped when my ears perked up at a strange smell. A loud howling suddenly sounded, setting me apart. My heart was drumming so loudly but all I had was one thing on my mind. We were not alone now. I met Owen's eyes who also noticed that presence.

No...We were being followed. Surrounded even.

"Get your fangs ready," Owen whispered to me, shifting into his wolf, and as soon as he said that, a big sandy wolf attacked him from the right. Owen had transformed swiftly and fought back, signaling me to run as he wanted to distract them but there were five more of them.

I sighed, Alpha Magnus was right. We only crossed a city away from him and I was being hunted by the enemies now. How cruel.

"You can stop having fun guys," Just then, the bushes opened and I heard a very familiar voice. "Missed me, Kamilah?"

Same blond hair in a neat style and cerulean eyes that captivated my soul, but what caught my attention was his very familiar earthy scent.

Darian. From the Shadow Pack. From my past pack.

And my ex-love.

The air suddenly left my lungs and I felt like I couldn't breathe. My walls seemed to crumble down, suffocating me. With each smell, memories suddenly flashed back into me, putting me in turmoil.

Owen beside me who was fighting suddenly stopped and went to my side to protect me. "Stay behind me."

I shook my head. "No, I can handle this."

"I guess they really were telling the truth," Darian said, approaching me. Each step he took stirred me up. As soon as he was in front of me, he grabbed my chin and made me look into his eyes. His eyes gazed at me as if he couldn't believe it. "You really are alive."

I gritted my teeth, glaring at him. "Yeah, so what?"

I couldn't believe how he looked exactly the same since I last saw him, but his aura exuded nothing but arrogance. Was this the downside of being an Alpha?

He was so much different now. I couldn't believe how I fell in love with this same creature.

I guess time really changed creatures. Not just for humans.

"Why are you here instead of being with your mate?" I asked, trying to change the topic.

He tilted his head to the side, his eyebrows raised. "My mate? Oh, right, your best friend. Well, keep this a secret, Valentina doesn't know I am meeting you now. She's not aware that you're even alive," he said. "I think she would be delighted if she saw you herself."

I scoffed, rolling my eyes as I feigned courage and stood my ground confidently. I pushed his hand away from my chin. "Yeah, and you won't get to return to her for attacking me like this."

He blew a whistle and clenched his chest, as if hurt from what I said. "Ouch, so you really can fight now, huh? I thought you couldn't survive without me. What did Alpha Magnus do to make you this sassy?"

I shrugged. "I don't know, but fun fact, he's much stronger than you."

The five of his men behind him who were watching us cheered for me. Owen beside me looked confused but still stood on alert.

He ignored that comment and caressed my cheek. "You've become so beautiful now. I missed you, did you miss me? Want to return back to my pack and become my concubine?"

Gritting my teeth, I spat on his face and pushed him harshly. "Damn you, you bastard!"

He was so much worse than Alpha Magnus. Why did I even fall in love with a bastard like that?

He heaved a deep breath and paused, wiping away my saliva and licking it.

He gave a smirk to me, completely unaffected and I almost gagged at what he did.

"I guess Alpha Magnus made you stronger but he stopped you from learning some manners," he continued, keeping his cool. "What did he do to seduce you easily? You easily get swayed by men. Careful, that man hides a dark secret."

Something about the way that Alpha Magnus's name left his mouth made me want to punch his face. "Leave his name out of it. What do you really want from me? Say it," I snarled.

He paused, then continued as he circled around me, pacing back and forth. "Since that Blood Moon night, the moment Alpha Magnus helped you and attempted to kill us, he broke our treaty. And about what I want? Well, it's simple. I want you back in my pack. I know you left him, so stop acting strong here. We're now his enemies, and I just want to get back to him."

I rolled my eyes. "Is that it? Really? Come on, I expected bigger than that petty reason—"

"He killed my dad, Kamilah. Tell me if that is petty enough. My dad, the one who took you in as an orphan," he said, looking at me deadpan.

It took me a moment to realize what he said. No... way...

Alpha Magnus... killed the last alpha of the Shadow Pack? Alpha Rufus?

But I did not remember anything that happened like that...

"Clueless eh? Guess that prick hid it from you, so let me tell it to you directly," he said. "That night, your power got so out of hand that my father had to stop you, but that damn Magnus stepped in and stopped you from releasing further. He announced you were dead and then raged in anger. I had to fight with him, but he ended up killing my father."

As he explained, a tear escaped his eyes and he tried to wipe it off. "It has been months now. You should have been the one who really died, Kamilah. Now that I know you're alive, I won't rest easy."

His saddened expression turned into a smirk and pointed at Owen beside me. "Now come with us or I'll kill this one here."

"Run, Kamilah!" Owen said, pushing me behind him and transformed into his sandy wolf again.

I couldn't help but think that despite being in danger himself and at risk of death, Owen still showed his loyalty to his alpha.

"Is someone endangering my Kamilah?" Just then, my ears perked up at the familiar voice.

I looked up at the tree and saw Gusev standing by the

branch. His black robe was present and his fangs were evident, eyes flaming red as he glared at Darian.

"Oh, I know you. You stalked Kamilah these past few days," he said as he jumped down, standing in front of me. "You don't have permission to stalk her. I am the only one allowed here!"

"Gusev!" I yelled with a sigh of relief. I knew I could take them in a fight, but I worried that Owen might be dead before I even got a chance. I could not even control my power properly.

Gusev sent me a small smile. "Hello there, my little juice box."

I did not even have to ask him how he found me. This vampire was so nosy and too stalkerish that he appeared like a mushroom, always everywhere.

Gusev stretched his hands and prepared himself to fight, "Leave now, I can easily handle them,"

We were about to turn our backs and leave when our paths were blocked.

"Na uh, you cannot leave. I heard you had trouble with Serena, the beta Drake's daughter?" Mocked Darian and I somehow recognized the smell of the three wolves blocking our escape route.

"Serena's family is here to welcome us, great," commented Owen. "That bitch really has backups."

I just raised my eyebrows at them. "What? What are you bastards here for?" I rolled my eyes, tired of all of this. Really, why couldn't they let me live in peace? Just existing here and enemies were coming one after another.

'You imprisoned my daughter, Kamilah,' said the one in front with the light brown fur. He seemed to be the leader of them, so I was guessing he was Beta Drake, the former Beta of the Bloodlust Pack.

"It was Alpha Magnus who punished her by imprisoning her, not me. Take it as a lesson for your daughter since you coddled her so much that she has no manners," I responded fiercely, transforming into my white-furred wolf.

'What did you say, bitch?'

I scoffed. *'I guess an apple doesn't fall far from the tree.'*

Beta Drake was about to launch on me when Owen went in front of me. *'Serena deserves it for bullying the Alpha's mate,'* he said. *'You know what happens if you continue that right? You dare touch her and you'll be triggering Alpha Magnus. We don't want your whole bloodline ending, do we?'*

At that, they all growled in anger, snarling at me but couldn't even do anything as they whimpered and ran away.

'Tsk, Cowards,' Owen commented. *'We better leave now.'*

I glanced at Gusev who was busy removing the heads of three out of the five men. I hate to admit it but although both werewolves and vampires were gifted with their own strengths, vampires had more advantage than us.

I gave a smirk to Darian before turning around and leaving with Owen.

Clueless

KAMILAH

We got into town first, where we were sure that we wouldn't get easily attacked. No sane werewolf would attack another werewolf right in front of the humans.

The elders would surely assassinate them once that happened. No one would dare to do that.

Thank goodness Owen had a stash of money in his pockets as he managed to get a room for both of us. His money was only good for one room, so we didn't have any choice but to share one. It was awkward and my first time sharing a room with another man but he assured me he wouldn't dare do anything. I also considered him as my older brother so I trusted him. If it weren't for him, I wouldn't have any place to stay tonight. I should be grateful he was nice enough to share his room with me.

He let me take the bed and he took the sofa. Tired of today's activities, we ate at a local cheap restaurant and he treated me to some ice cream.

"Honestly, thinking about it now, this day was hectic. I'll

definitely remember this," he brought up, removing the tension filling the air.

I chuckled, nodding along to what he said. "Yeah, me too. This was really crazy for me." Things had been too dramatic for me these days. I was surprised I even managed to stay alive.

"So, what now? What will be our next move?"

He shrugged. "Just stay away from enemies and hatch a decent plan first," he said, his ice cream melting.

We were too tired to even go around the town and risk having another batch of enemies after us, so we retired to bed early for the day. I took a bath first to calm myself down as I reeked of sweat and mud everywhere. Good thing there was a robe so I temporarily put it on, washed my clothes and hung them to dry.

I was completely naked under it, so I worried a bit about Owen seeing me, but then again, shifting into my wolf and having to be naked afterwards had made me more used to it, so it felt relatively normal.

"You can sleep first, I'll take charge of keeping watch for the night," Owen offered.

"Wake me up when you feel tired. We'll take turns in keeping watch," I responded, stretching my limbs and heaving a sigh of relief.

He nodded, his eyes looking at me as if he wanted to say more. "Kamilah?"

"Yeah?" I answered, yawning.

He chuckled and just shook his head. "Never mind, I'll tell you tomorrow. Rest up now."

"Alright. Goodnight, Owen." He just sent a small smile and laid on the sofa. I slumped into the bed, closed my eyes, and immediately drifted to sleep.

In the middle of the night, I heard another man's voice.

"Is she alright?"

"Yes."

"Good, take care of her for me."

I somehow opened my eyes, still half-asleep, and saw a familiar dark figure by the window. Owen was standing and talking to it.

"Owen? Who is it?" I called out, rubbing my eyes to get a clearer view.

"Nothing, go back to sleep, Kamilah," he replied.

It seemed that I was hallucinating as I saw Alpha Magnus's eyes staring back at me from the window. My heart leapt, waking me up. I blinked, then he was gone.

Weird.

I seem to be dreaming of him… I closed my eyes and settled on the bed again.

I woke up with a start, feeling like my head had been hit by a truck. Yesterday's moments suddenly came to me, and I facepalmed myself.

I looked over to my right where the sofa was and found it empty.

I creased my eyebrows, wondering where Owen was.

"Owen?" I called out, standing up onto my feet and looking for him. I looked out the window to see the sun had already risen up high…

I looked at the wall clock that was hanging on the wall. Tick. Tock.

The sound of its two hands racing together felt monotonous, saying it was 1:30 in the afternoon.

Why did he not wake me up to take a turn keeping watch?

No way, did enemies get in last night and take Owen?

Panic instantly filled me and I overthought many more scenarios.

A piece of paper fell from my pillow and judging from the scent of it, it was from Owen.

I picked it up and knew it was a letter with his writing messily scribbled on it.

"Thank you for everything, Kamilah. You're like my little sister, and I want to stay and protect you. But whenever I see you, I am reminded of Leia and the pain of losing her... I feel like I could go insane in a moment and will only end up hurting you. I feel suffocated if I see anyone and I'm reminded of... That is why I need to leave to forget all the things about Leia.

If you're wondering where, I'll drop a hint. It's somewhere in the west. I treasure the moments I had with you, Kamilah. I'm sorry, but stay strong.

I believe in you.

-Owen

I reread the letter over and over again, still feeling shocked. Damn. So that is why he was acting strangely last night.

I could remember now that he wanted to say something but ended up not continuing as we were both tired.

I bit my lip, feeling regret. He must be feeling all of this, silently enduring it all on his own. I appreciate that he took the time to write me a note and explain his situation, as best he could.

I guess things are not meant to stay long for me. He was one of the people I was close to, and he offered comfort protecting me against his own alpha, against the enemies yesterday…

It felt sad, but I can't control things. I don't have the power to make them stay against their will. And I respect Owen's decision.

But I'm penniless now, I think Owen only paid for one night's stay here… guess I'll stay outside the streets next.

There was a knock on the door and I sniffed the air, smelling that foul scent from a certain vampire.

"It's me, Kamilah," The vampire said from the other side of the door, in a singsong tone.

I sighed, placed Owen's letter in my pocket, and opened the door.

A beaming Gusev greeted me, his same old robe and wide grin, flashing his dazzling teeth at me.

He went inside the room without waiting for my invitation and looked around, pacing back and forth, like a supervisor checking up on his employee.

Shouldn't he be hiding as the sun is up now? People are everywhere, and how did he even get here, without people wondering about his appearance? "It's broad daylight and you walk around, showing people that you're a vampire."

He shrugged. "I guess I'm just that dazzling for them."

He made himself at home as he sat by the bed and looked at me. "I managed to get rid of the enemies last time. Don't you want to compliment and thank me?"

I sighed, he was the same as always.

"Thank you for helping me, Gusev," I said, a bit against my own will but still said it.

He smirked. "You're welcome, anytime, my juice box."

"What about Darian? Did you kill them all?" I couldn't help but ask and he shrugged.

"I regret to say this but no… I killed his subordinates, but he was tough to fight with, I managed to injure him enough to stop him from seeing you for a while."

I nodded. Of course, Darian is an alpha. No matter how I say that he's a bit weaker compared to Alpha Magnus, he is still powerful enough to not be killed that easily. He's a tough opponent. Next time, I will have to be stronger.

He then looked around. "You are alone? Where's that other wolf you're with?"

I pulled out the letter. "He left."

His mouth formed an O in shock. "He did? Wow… that's selfish of him, knowing you're in a tight spot now."

"He has his own reason, Gusev," I defended and he raised his hands up in surrender.

"Alright, if you say so, I didn't come here to argue with you."

Standing up, he inhaled my scent, closing his red eyes as he did so. "It's your smell. Enemies are coming after you because of your sweet scent." His expression was serious. "You need to hide it… and the way to do that is to be with me."

I raised my eyebrows. "Are you doing that because you just need a reason to stay with me?"

"Yes, I just couldn't leave you alone. Remember, they're after you."

"Then so be it. Let them come, Gusev. I want to face it head-on."

Gusev shook his head, "You're really stubborn, eh? I'm the one offering to help you here."

"I appreciate it, but leave. I didn't leave the pack just to be treated like a kid." I said firmly.

He sat on the floor stubbornly, and pouted. "I won't leave. I'll call my best friend Magnus if you won't let me tag along with you."

I sighed. "Don't you have something to do? Like, suck some human's blood?"

He shrugged. "I have been roaming around this world for centuries. I've seen enough, but I love your blood."

I massaged my temples, feeling like I was talking to some kid. "Why are you and your best friend both obsessed with my scent and my blood? Leave me alone."

At that, he instantly stood up and held my cheeks. "So Magnus had a taste of your blood already?" he asked with widened eyes and a pout. "How lucky, wish I could do that too."

I scrunched my nose in disgust. "No, thank you."

"So why did you leave him exactly? Like what is the reason?" He now started to butt in, minding my business and I glared at him.

"Scram off. Stop minding other peoples' business."

He chuckled. "Alright, I won't ask again, but with the way you react, it seems that it's a bit serious… I kind of get the gist of it."

He then grabbed a knife, quickly wounded me, and drank some of my blood.

I watched in horror at him doing that. "Consider that as payment for protecting you."

I instantly withdrew my hand from him. I don't understand how this vampire loved my blood. Shouldn't he be repelled as our clans were naturally enemies?

"You could have asked for permission properly," I snarled.

"Oh, I apologize, I was just tempted by your blood," he answered. "But fine, If you still won't let me stay with you, then I'll stalk you and will update your mate."

I gasped. "Why do you think it's fun to poke into other's business?"

He suddenly turned serious. "You're a mess. You don't have a direction now. Tell me, what's your plan? Where will you stay? Do you have money to hide within the humans? Everyone is after you, Kamilah."

I gritted my teeth, not because of how stupid I was but because of how right he was. He had hit a good point. He clearly affected my stubborn ass and huge ego.

"I'll apply to work, to be able to fend for myself. I can handle myself."

He looked at me straight in the eyes, sensing if I was true to my words. When he was sure I wouldn't back down and was talking seriously, he gave up.

"Alright. Fine. I'll let you on your own, for now."

As soon as Gusev left, I went to the nearby coffee shop and tried to apply for work.

I found out that humans need some papers and requirements in order to work. Trying to find a way, an old woman was just strolling along the streets just in time, and offered to make the paper thing called a birth certificate for me and she'd input a fake identity for me.

I applied to the town's famous coffee shop and was hired. Since I was adjusting, I made a few mistakes but I was a fast learner so it took me only three days to master everything. From making the drinks to washing dishes to cleaning the shop.

The owner even praised me for doing so well. I guessed

humans tended to live the same as us. Except for the part where we tended to live longer than 100 years. How could they enjoy life the most with their short amount of time in this world?

They were weak and fragile…but still woke up every day to live.

Humans

KAMILAH

Living with humans also made me aware of how similar they were to us. They had various emotions: fear, love, and compassion. There were also those who betrayed, lied, and killed, like some of our kind.

I guessed in every creature, there would always be good and bad. No one was perfect. No creature was better than the others.

A year had passed and I was so used to living like this, working my ass off to support myself and somehow, no enemy had attacked me, which was opposite to what they all warned me about.

Maybe it was really the best decision to live with the humans.

I was assigned to take out the trash when I heard a low howling from outside. It sounded kind. Checking it out, I saw a lone kid sitting by the wall beside the trash can, his stomach growling as he closed his eyes and stifled a tear.

I kneeled down, but made sure to keep a distance so he wouldn't get scared of me. "Hello there, kid."

The child looked up and I was shocked to see how silver his eyes were. His hair was blond and he looked like he was around seven years old. Smelling him, I instantly knew he was the same as me. He was a werewolf too. But abandoned?

"What are you doing here, child?

His stomach growled and he looked at the black garbage bag in my hand. "Please don't shoo me away. I just need food."

He then grabbed the garbage bag from me and opened it to look for something. He found the rotten sandwich that the owner asked me to throw away as it had already expired and would cause harm to the humans.

He munched on the sandwich and I stood there, watching him silently.

I couldn't help but feel pity and wanted to cry at his situation. With his dirty clothes, bare hoodie, pale skin and bare feet full of scrapes and bruises, I wanted to take him in right then and there and offer him food.

I thought of a plan not to scare him. "Want to eat more? Let me take you inside," I offered, giving a smile to him so he'd know he could trust me.

"No, thank you. I couldn't afford it."

"C'mon, I know you're hungry. It's my treat. I'll pay for you." I noticed he was too skinny for a little kid. At this age, he must be eating a lot to nourish his fangs and strong paws.

He looked at me hesitantly before dropping the rotten sandwich and standing up. I motioned for him to follow me inside.

Thank goodness the owner wasn't there, so I sneaked in a few snacks for him and prepared them on the table.

His eyes sparkled at the sight, licking his lips as he was

salivating over the steak I cooked and he dug in. He looked like he hadn't eaten for a year and I sighed.

"You can eat slowly, the food won't disappear. If you want more I could cook more," I offered.

His eyes widened, his cheeks blushing red. "Really? T-thank you, old lady."

I chuckled. "Old lady? You can call me Kamilah."

He nodded and continued eating. I left him on his own as a few customers came in to order.

After a while, I returned to his table and saw he finished the food.

"How can I pay you, Kamilah?" he asked. "I can work here. I can wash the dishes."

I shook my head. "No, working is for adults. You're still a pup," I said. "Can I ask though? Where are your parents?" I asked after a while.

He was silent, now avoiding my eyes as he fumbled with his hoodie. "I-I don't have any."

It stuck with me. So he was abandoned too. He suddenly reminded me of myself when I was back at the Shadow pack. As an orphan, it was hard to survive in this world. But I was a bit lucky as Alpha Rufus, the last alpha from Shadow pack, took me in.

"You could pay me back, kid," I told him and he seemed interested.

"How?"

"I'm building my own empire. Want to become my right-hand man?" I asked. I can't believe that I was asking a literal child about this…It was not part of my plan at all. Truthfully, I was saving enough money to be able to have my own building and hire my subordinates…

The little boy tilted his head, confused. "I don't know what that is, but I'll join."

I grinned, giving him a high-five that I learned from the humans that they do when they're happy. "Good! Now tell me, what's your name?"

"Almiro."

I nodded. "That's a good name."

That was the start of our friendship. I took Almiro to the cheap apartment I was staying at and officially made him my little minion. I bathed him, let him eat, and enjoyed his childhood.

He would help me, and I noticed he was very reliable and mature for his age.

I took him to town for sightseeing once when I suddenly felt goosebumps. I could feel someone was staring at me. I looked from the dark alley to see a familiar figure. Alpha Magnus.

My breath hitched, and I nearly stumbled. He was standing there, looking at me silently, wearing a dark hoodie and a hat. Now that I saw him clearly, I knew it was him.

A horde of humans walked past us, blocking my view of him. Once they passed, I saw that he was gone.

Almiro noticed my discomfort. "Are you alright?"

I shrugged it off and we continued walking.

"Stop right there, kid!" yelled a store employee as he chased a girl who was running to us. I instantly knew that the girl was also our kind.

"Please hide me," she pleaded, eyes watered up with tears as she clutched onto my leg for dear life. When the store employee finally caught up, I stood in front of her.

"What is it? Why are you running after a little girl?"

He gritted his teeth. "That girl stole an apple from me!" he raged and I could feel the little girl's hold on me tighten.

"How much is that apple?" I asked, grabbing my wallet.

The store employee said the price and accepted my money before walking away.

"He already left. You can show yourself now," I said and the little girl hiccupped.

"Thank you, lady," she said. She wanted to leave but Almiro stopped her.

"Kamilah is still talking to you, don't run away," he firmly said, and the girl stayed still.

"I was hungry and didn't have any money… so I stole it," she answered honestly.

I kneeled down and ruffled her fluffy hair. "Pup, you know that stealing is bad, right? But don't worry, I'll take you in," I said without even thinking about it clearly. Goodness, I needed to stop pitying little children and take them. I was not an orphanage or some foundation.

The little girl shuddered. "You're suspicious. Who knows what you're like? You could be acting nice just to earn my trust and sell my kidney on the black market."

I gasped, feeling humbled down.

This little girl was smart.

Almiro stepped in. "If she was that bad, then I would have already been sold to the black market."

I smiled at him for defending me smartly. The little girl scoffed and gulped.

"Is there… food? If I go with you, will I never get hungry?" she asked, making sure I was honest.

I chuckled. "No, I assure you that so much more will happen. You will never get hungry and will even get so full you'll get sick of food."

She blinked, tempted by the idea, and nodded. "I am Louisa."

"Nice to meet you, Louisa." I smiled at her.

Goodness, how did I plan to start my own pack with just 2 kids and 50 dollars in my pockets?

GUSEV

I was dead but I was still alive. I watched the humans start from scratch, building their communities, and their civilizations, fighting over land and territories, and ending up destroying their innovation. They were known as the smartest and most superior creatures of all, but watching them fail as a human amused me with how ironic the truth was. Up till now, they chose to be ignorant. Some believed about our existence though, and they were outcasted in the process. I pitied them. I guess it was best that our existence was kept hidden and only viewed as nothing but fiction.

I woke up with a monotonous routine. Different times, and different eras had gone by, but I never met someone who I could call my mate. I sometimes envied those lowly werewolves. They didn't have the curse of living eternally as they could survive up to 300 years, neither short nor long... each of them had their own destined soulmates.

What did it feel like to have someone that was fated with you? I could only imagine it.

But recently, life had been thrilling for me. I had never tasted blood so fine and so sweet in my entire life of roaming this world. My nose didn't fail to disappoint me. With what I smelled, it was even better when I tasted Kamilah's blood.

I never felt alive like this, even though I was already dead. As soon as she pushed me back in the hotel, I made my way into my dear best friend's packhouse, but not before slaying some more wolves that were after Kamilah. They really didn't give up, did they? I had expected that they would somehow stop pursuing her. I mean, I couldn't accept that other than me, everyone would get to taste her blood. No, just thinking of it made my stomach churn.

As I was on the road, I breathed the fresh air. I looked at the sun, enjoying it. Despite the human belief that we hate the sun, it was partly true. We hated it before, but the same with humans, we also adapted to it and learned to coexist.

And no, we didn't sleep in coffins. Humans really made us so disgusting. I preferred my soft mattress and comfy bed to lay on, thank you very much. Although we didn't sleep, it was good to pretend that we did.

And about blood, sure, we loved it. We fed on people and had to drink it to survive, even though it was against our will. Those in the higher-ups had invented a juice box for us to drink in case of emergency. We could also drink animal blood.

Our higher-ups also limited us in killing humans to only one per year, if ever we were sick of animals' blood. Hence for the whole year, we were always hungry. Personally, though, I didn't like killing innocent people so I preyed on rapists, serial killers, or some others of the worst people, as disgusting as it might sound.

Life had been cruel, but that was how we survived and existed to this day. The other vampires had given up that rule though, as they wreaked havoc around some areas, slaying children and women.

I found that unjust and would never do that to children and women, so much that I even killed my kind who do that and delivered them to the high-ups. The higher-ups even rewarded me for that, thank goodness.

It was a bit hotter now compared to before since the humans' activities were damaging the planet. I could slowly watch the world being destroyed and the sun getting hotter each day.

I wanted to intervene and just slay them all… I always wondered about that. They were the ones who labeled us as "monsters" when in fact it was them who were more dangerous to the world. The innovations kept on growing and damaging the environment.

I marched in front of Alpha Magnus's study but didn't find him there. I spotted Dimitri, his beta, leaving a pile of papers on his table.

"Where's your alpha?" I asked.

"He's resting for now," he answered, and I raised my eyebrows.

"Resting? That workaholic perfectionist never rests," I said. Hmm, I smelled something fishy in here. Alpha Magnus was acting weird. He must be so down about his mate, Kamilah, leaving him, right in front of his face.

I instantly dashed to his room and arrived in less than a minute.

"Hi, best friend!" I greeted cheerily, knocking on the door. When he didn't reply, like he always did, I opened his door and found him lying on his bed, facing the ceiling and looking like he'd been rethinking his life decisions over and over.

He didn't even stand up or reply haughtily at my arrival. And that's when I knew how serious this situation was.

The famous Alpha Magnus, heartbreaker of women, soul destroyer of men, and powerful in the whole area, was here on his bed, depressed.

I stood there for a minute, watching and waiting for him to budge. He looked lifeless and dead, far more lifeless than my pale skin was. But he didn't even move an inch so I cleared my throat. "I tasted her blood. She smelled amazing."

Quicker than the air, I felt his hands grabbing my neck, his dead eyes now blazing with so much hatred. "You do not deserve to breathe the same air as her. Back off, Gusev."

I chuckled. "So that's what it took for you to notice me. I was watching you there the whole time."

He loosened his grip on me, to calm down. I sat on his bed and patted the spot beside me. "I never comforted anyone before so seeing my best friend now depressed, I don't know what to do."

He sighed. "If you're here to mock me, just leave."

I clicked my tongue disappointedly. "Why does everyone want me to leave? I just wanted to comfort you."

"Your presence here is not helping. I need to think."

"Why sulk here when you could go to her and see her? Even from afar?" I casually suggested and he turned to me.

"I could… do that to her?"

I nodded. "Yeah, of course you could."

He shook his head. "No, you know Kamilah. She's not that simple."

I sighed. "Better to do that than sulk around and pity yourself. I don't know about you werewolf guys and your mate thingy, but if your bond is that strong, you need to stay close to her, right?"

What I said seemed to bring light to his face. I patted myself on the back for doing a great job.

"You haven't even imprinted on her. Why are you so laid back just because she's your mate? She might find another one," I said intentionally, just to trigger him.

"Shut up, Gusev."

I hummed a tune. "Let's see. I tasted her sweet blood. I can understand how attached you are to her. I mean, if I were you, I wouldn't want to lose her."

I could see the killing intent in his dark orbs and the gold rings turned red. Thank goodness I was quick on my feet and dodged his attack, as I didn't think I would have left his room alive. I instantly ran away, leaving him with his thoughts.

"I'll kill you, Gusev!" I heard him yelling so loud, growling and howling.

I sighed, so much for being the fairy godmother for those two. One day, he would understand that I was doing him a favor.

A Hundred Years Later

KAMILAH

In this dominating world, only the powerful would stay at the top, trampling on the weaklings. It was not about the law anymore but those who were in power were the law. It had always been that way. And no one dared to change it.

And I was one of the powerful. Right now. I couldn't care less either way. I had gotten what I wanted… to be strong and to build my own pack. I buried what happened in the past and lived in the present.

In my 150 years of existence, I watched as the world evolved and delved myself in the human's business too. I became the CEO of Dark Crest Company.

Well, Vampires, Wolves, witches, dragons, and other supernatural's that humans could name, were all mingling around. Well, we had remained mostly hidden in the humans' eyes, but in the past, we were tortured and killed by them, but not anymore. We freely and quietly roam around now.

"How are things going here?" I asked my right-hand woman, my beta, my second in command, Louisa as I paraded around the halls. Simultaneous greetings instantly filled the room and I didn't bother to glance at my subordinates.

"You have to attend the gathering later, Alpha Kamilah. The elders are hosting a party and invited all alphas," she answered, her sunglasses perched on her nose as she looked at me with a calm look, not even fearing me at all. I had to give it to her, working under me for 150 years might have taken a toll on her, but she never quit. I was aware of my sassiness and bad attitude. She was a beta for a reason after all. I could even remember how we got here. How small she was when I first took her in.

I looked at the green highlights that fell from her short curly hair, highlighting her hazel eyes that melted into the sunlight, her tanned skin glowing along the way. I raised my eyebrows, seemingly passing that thought in mind... "Oh, is that today? Cancel that then."

Louisa gasped at that. "But the elders—"

"Oh, I'm sure you know me by all the years you have served me, Louisa," I said, smirking at her, and that made Louisa sigh in silence. Of course, I was a busy woman. I had to manage my pack, secure our safety, and expand my territories. I didn't have time for mere boring meetings where all the elders talked about problems and stared at me with so much hatred.

I was the first female alpha who changed the world a few decades ago. I knew what I was capable of and they were aware of it, that was why they have been careful of me and held meetings in disguise to check if I would suddenly change the world and rampage again. Besides, it was no good going there anyway. They only invited me out of fear, but never intended to see me there.

Sighing, Louisa bowed her head at me. "As you wish, Alpha Kamilah."

"Good. You are now dismissed. Don't bother me again or I'll kill you," I threatened as Louisa just walked away without even flinching. That was also one thing I liked about her… she was immune to my harsh words.

I did my daily check of looking around the whole building I created in the past century. I had made this mansion when I left Alpha Magnus's pack last time. My pack, the Dark Crest, was situated in a nice and quiet nature with a hundred were-wolves. We had trouble finding the right place in the past. We travelled from the sands up in the east, to the cold winter air from the north, and to the hidden outskirts of the south.

We almost toured the whole world in a whole two years until we finally got tired and decided to rest here, in the middle of the east and west boundaries, between the Crimson Pack and the Bloodlust Pack.

"Good morning, Alpha Kamilah!"

"You look beautiful, my lady."

Several compliments came my way as I walked by my pack, and I just nodded at them, keeping some check in my head as I counted off my subordinates. Of course, my pack was filled with women. Well, except my male slaves and guards like Almiro if you count that.

"Have you heard of Alpha Magnus? I missed seeing him!" Giggled one of the omegas from the corner. "I heard that he's going to attend a party…. I wonder who the lucky woman is as his date."

My ears perked up, instantly turning to them as her friend responded.

"Shh, quiet, our alpha will hear us!"

I blinked, somehow getting interested in their conversation but also wanting to scold them for daring to talk about that alpha of the Bloodlust Pack right in my presence.

Well, Alpha Magnus never changed. He had always been popular around the ladies, with his amazing playboy skills and charms. I did everything I could to not get involved with that alpha again but I saw him once on a business trip and I swear I wanted nothing but to gouge his eyes out. Men like him were narcissistic and wanted nothing from women other than to play them. It was a good thing I chose to leave his pack decades ago.

"What are you two blabbering about? Get back to work," I ordered and the two she-wolves just returned to their seats. Deciding to not scold them further as I was in a bit of a happy mood, I walked to my office, my black heels clicking with each step. Once I reached the topmost level of the building, I sat down at my desk and looked at the pile of papers in front of me. I had always been into clubbing and parties the past few weeks but I had forgotten to work on this. I could just hear Louisa scolding me in my head but I ignored it.

The wind blew and a small note came out from the folders. Picking it up, I could smell the very scent of that man. Reading the note, I breathed in deeply.

"I want you to be my date. I'll be expecting you at the event ;)"
-Magnus

I scoffed, not believing the note. I could sense his trailing scent that was seemingly disappearing, meaning, it wasn't that long since he came here. How did he even manage to enter my office? No, how dare the nerve of that alpha, to invite me to be his date? He had always been watching my every move everywhere, what a creep!

I looked at the window and rolled my eyes.

"Almiro!" I called my loyal protector, the only man I trusted in this pack. He's little pup that I took care of along with Louisa. He was the only guard I placed outside my office to keep me protect me. If Alpha Magnus entered to leave this letter at my desk then he should have noticed Alpha Magnus's presence and report it to me. However, I never received any news from him. Silence…

He usually appeared instantly the moment I called, but now was a bit strange.

"Almiro!" I called out and heard Louisa reporting in my head that he came to the elders and alpha's gathering as a representative for me.

I gritted my teeth. I should go after him. I planned on not attending the elder's party but I guess I had no choice now. I gave orders to Louisa using my mind-link, and went to my room to put on my lovely red dress that hugged my curves, along with my red stilettos and red lipstick. I put a black suit over me and I let my hair down as I sprayed on my perfume. I caught a glimpse of my reflection in the mirror, noticing how the dark spot that left a scar on my face was now getting bigger. I gulped, feeling my chest tighten as the memories got to me, the past I buried. The mistake I made.

No, this was not the time to be weak. I had to go now. I combed my side bangs to the right, to hide the ugly scar as Louisa appeared at my door.

She guided me to the car, then drove me to the venue where the gathering would take place.

As soon as Louisa parked the car, I opened the door and elegantly walked outside. Guards spotted me and went on alert.

I gave them a look. "What? Am I not invited?"

The guard gulped. "Of course, you are invited, Alpha · Kamilah!" They instantly opened the door and a piece of nice slow music greeted us. It was the VIP room of the five-star hotel, the usual meeting place.

"Come on." I motioned Louisa to come inside with me but she stopped. "Oh, I am not allowed inside, my lady. Only alphas and invited guests."

I furrowed my eyebrows, not liking the discrimination the elders put here. Did they fear that I would bring myself a weapon? Tsk, they really took countermeasures against me.

"Then wait for me here, alright?"

Louisa nodded and I instantly entered the room. The moment I walked in, I saw the Elder Drucilla sitting at the head of the table while the other two alphas of the different packs were seated across from each other.

They all paused, looking at me with wide eyes as if I was not invited and a crasher at the party.

"What are you staring at? Am I not one of the guests invited?"

I said boldly, to which the elder acted quickly and stood up to welcome me.

"Oh, Alpha Kamilah! Thank goodness you finally attended!" he said, motioning for me to sit. "It has been such a long time."

I faked a smile, sitting in the empty chair beside Alpha Killian. Elder Drucilla, this wicked elder who has been attempting to kill me for the past years really irked me. He was the elder assigned to the West region for us four alphas reigning over here. He was the one assigned to restore order. In his eyes, he saw me as a threat for disrupting the balance of things, but he seemed to stop attempting to kill me, knowing his efforts would just be in vain.

Their eyes were still on me with a judgy look.

I scoffed at them. "Are all of you just going to spend the whole afternoon staring at me? I know I am beautiful," I said. "Or the thought of a female alpha alone in a room intimidates you?"

"Is the world ending or did she actually attend the meeting for the first time in decades?" Across from me, Alpha Rohan of the Dawn Pack asked the elder, which made me turn my head to him.

"You know I can hear you," I said smugly. "Why bother whispering, Alpha Rohan?"

He just huffed, now silent.

Silence fell, and the elder cleared his throat. "Now we are waiting for one more alpha… Alpha Magnus of the Bloodlust Pack."

Alpha Magnus? I shook my head. "Don't bother waiting, we all know that man is not going to show up in all of the meetings."

Suddenly, a loud banging on the door came and it burst open, the wind breezing harshly together with the deep voice of the familiar man.

"Are you talking about me?" Ah. Of course, there was no one better in a grand entrance other than Alpha Magnus. Everyone looked at Alpha Magnus in silence, even the elders who were pretending to wait for him just for tradition were too stunned to speak.

It was not every day this happened to our filthy normal lives.

Being present in this stupid gathering instantly made us the stars of the show. Alpha Magnus's eyes lingered on me as he approached me. He sat in the empty chair beside me. "It's good to see you again, Alpha Kamilah," he greeted me. "It has been such a long time since I last saw you. You surely had seen my note and yet you did not wait for me."

I just raised my eyebrows at him. "Why would I wait for you?" I asked challengingly. He was so clingy, just because he helped me last time. I turned to the elder. "He's here now. Shall we begin then?"

The elder nodded, clearing his throat to gather our attention. "Good afternoon, everyone. Thank you for attending this meeting and we are complete now for the first time in history. As we are all gathered today, we'll get to the tradition of reporting about your packs and territorial borders." I laid comfortably on the chair, sighing and looking at the elder with a bored expression. Right.

Why did I even bother to attend if I knew this was supposed to be this boring? Where the hell was Almiro? I thought he attended here for me. I could feel the hard gaze of Alpha Magnus from beside me but I chose to ignore it, not wanting to waste a single breath. But then, the bastard kept staring at me with such eyes that eventually it made me turn to him.

"What do you want?" I growled in a low voice.

He winked, and I scoffed, holding his stare, not even flinching, wanting to show him who was the boss here. But the idiot Alpha didn't back down in our little staring contest. He had this cocky smirk plastered on his face and it took a lot of restraint to stop myself from cursing him right then and there.

I had to show him that it didn't even affect me. No one could. And no one would.

I halted, suddenly remembering my plan. The other reason why I came here.

I stood up, which made the elder stop talking. "Is there something wrong, Alpha Kamilah?"

"Yes, there is," I blatantly responded. "You see, the reason I came here is to not actively participate in this gathering but the opposite. I want to stop this tradition."

"Stop?"

"Yes, each of us alphas here holds our packs very dearly and with pride. But this stupid sharing of information is just so boring. How many times a year do you hold this again? I mean I just don't care."

The elder stood up, approached me, and clenched his teeth, his fangs showing, trying to intimidate me, Alpha Kamilah, with his power. "This is what keeps us in peace from all the other clans. This helps us keep updated on our territories, you can't just change—"

I put my fingers on his lips to shush him. "Oh, I can. I managed to change the history of alpha males, why not this simple task?"

The elder was stunned at this, and I could see Alpha Magnus raise his hand in the air. "Allow me to speak—"

"No," I said to him, shutting him down. But he chose to ignore me either way as he stood up and came closer to me.

He smiled at me. "I completely agree with Alpha Kamilah's decision. I mean, coming here annually is such a hassle." He then turned to me. "Right, Kamilah?"

"No. I don't want you to back me up here," I said irritably, wanting to present this alone. "Shut your unwanted ass."

He gasped, pretending to be hurt. "Yes, hated female alpha."

I took a deep breath, not showing how it affected me. Female alpha. That was an insult that they made for me. Alpha Magnus seemed to enjoy this so much.

He leaned in and whispered to me, his hot breath fanning my face, "We're practically the same, aren't we?"

"Enough!" yelled Drucilla, breathing heavily out of anger,

which made us turn our heads toward him. "There is no use continuing this meeting with you two fighting. I'll get the higher-ups to discuss what you wanted."

I crossed my arms in front of me, seemingly happy. "Tell them if they don't give in to my request, then I'll come barging in on my own," I threatened, before walking to the door.

Alpha Magnus whispered, "Let's meet outside, I have something to tell you."

I halted, glancing at Alpha Magnus who was looking discreetly and innocently as if he didn't utter anything that offended me.

I motioned for him to meet me outside later and the bastard just smirked. Rolling my eyes, I went to the door, closed it, and waited. I tapped my foot, glaring at the door and waiting for Alpha Magnus to show up but he was nowhere to be seen. I hated waiting, yet here I was. I couldn't help but be curious at what Alpha Magnus was going to tell me. Seconds turned to minutes and minutes almost turned to an hour and I sighed walking to the exit, when my assistant Louisa came.

She bowed her head. "Is the meeting already over, Alpha Kamilah?" I shook my head.

"I decided to leave the meeting early and was waiting for someone, but let's go home."

Louisa nodded, following me we both quickly left and returned to my pack. I instantly went to my office to deal with my paperwork. My sharp senses felt something was not right. I was not sure what it was but I anxiously looked at the clock and saw two hours had passed.

Just then, my door slammed open and Almiro, my loyal personal guard, came hurrying in, panting. His blond hair fell down to his shoulders, his silver eyes staring at me and his thick eyebrows were in a furrow.

"What is it, Almiro?" I asked, looking up from my papers. "And where the hell were you earlier?"

"Somewhere… but I have to tell you something urgent."

"Go on."

"We have an intruder."

I raised my eyebrows, "Who?"

"Alpha Magnus," he replied. "He kept on persisting to see you, saying you were asking for him but we took him to the dungeon," he reported, not batting an eye.

I dropped my pen as I stood up and went to the door. "Good job, now let's see what he wants to tell me."

He kept me waiting earlier after all, for sure this alpha is up to something. He also made me wait earlier and left me hanging. I can't accept that!

I strutted on the stairs as Almiro guided me down to the dungeon. There were cobwebs everywhere and the place was dark, but my eyes were still as sharp as ever. I could see a figure of a man in the far cell.

When we reached Magnus's cell, we stopped and I looked at him. "Alpha Magnus from Bloodlust pack, care to tell me what you are doing in my territory?"

I mind-linked Almiro to leave us alone, and he nodded diligently before doing so.

"I know what you're thinking. I came here with no ill intentions, Alpha Kamilah," Alpha Magnus started. "I apologize also for not seeing you earlier as I was gathering information from the meeting. When I returned, you were gone."

"I waited, and you wasted my time earlier. What was it that you intended to tell me?" I demanded, making sure to seek dominance in this conversation and showing him who was the one in control here.

He just chuckled at me. "Quite the temper, Alpha Kamilah. You're the one who is asking for information. Is it proper to treat your guest like this?" He then motioned at the chains that Almiro put on him.

"Come on, loosen this up first, and then we can talk."

He was the strongest alpha here, and she hated to admit that, so why was he just letting himself be locked in our dungeon like this? He could have easily just knocked Almiro down for putting him on a chain, but he didn't do it.

There must be something.

I opened his cell and got inside. I leaned in. "Don't you forget that you are in my territory now, Alpha Magnus, and alone. As I've said, I am thankful for helping me during that incident decades ago, but let's put the past behind us and move on. It's time you stop bugging me," I said bluntly.

Alpha Magnus nodded calmly. "Alright, alright, now drop the threats. I have been trying to catch your attention for the past year, Alpha Kamilah. You see, I happened to hear some valuable information. Wanna know it?"

"Depends on how valuable it is," I retorted, which he ignored as he continued.

"You believe in birds that flock together, stay together? I believe that applies to us right now…" He trailed off. "But firstly, I want to ask. Aren't you tired of being hated by the elders and everyone?"

I kept quiet, letting him speak for now. "You made a deal with the powerful necromancer decades ago…." Alpha Magnus decided to drop.

I scoffed. "And? What's your point?" I had tried to hide it, and only Alpha Magnus knew of that. I guess word got out easily.

Suddenly, he broke free from the chains and held me in his arms.

I felt electricity and sparks flashing before us and flinched. I pushed him away.

"Watch your manners, Alpha Magnus."

"After a whole century, it seems you're still resisting me as your mate," he said, his tone sounding bitter. "Why? Do you really hate the idea of having me as your mate?"

I kept quiet. He still hadn't imprinted on me so there was a chance I could refuse him as my mate. I didn't want to be tied up with anyone, making someone my whole world that I forgot my goals, only to be betrayed in the end. And I was sure he would betray me someday. "I have my reasons."

"I see, so your answer is yes," he said and turned serious. "Let's set our personal things aside. The real reason I came here is to propose an offer. An alliance. A war is coming. I want you to be by my side," he said.

"War? We have been through lots in the past," I said.

"The elders are planning something big to eradicate you completely, so I want to ask if you are going to participate in this war," he explained further.

"And what does this have to do with me?" I asked, analyzing what he said. Of course, I knew how everyone wanted nothing but for me to die right now, but I never knew the elders were getting bolder day by day to think that they could just finish me off.

"You made history, Kamilah. The fact that you risked your life and became an alpha despite being a woman... is honorable. You defied the norms of the werewolf realm," he stated.

I shook my head. "I want to live in peace, Magnus. If you are planning on waging war, don't include me. If they kill me, then let them, I will fight back, but I will never have anything to do with you," I said. "But, you're telling me all of this.

What if I tell the elders about your plan and make you my enemy?"

"Oh, I know you are not that dense, Alpha Kamilah. I know you are going to side with someone strong and right now, that is me. I'm just fulfilling the prophecy after all."

"Prophecy?" I stopped at that, his hands grabbing mine and I felt electricity tingling.

Just then, he instantly bit down on my neck and I growled, pushing him away.

"You bastard!"

I held my neck, feeling blood all over, and saw Alpha Magnus licking his lips as his teeth were dripping with blood.

"I apologize, I have to show you so you'll believe me," he said, showing his sharp canines as his eyes glinted with red pools of blood. "I am the child of prophecy, Kamilah. I am the hybrid."

I blinked, feeling my heart beating fast, and gulped.

I tried to recall what the necromancer said to me last century. He said I would meet… my mate when a child of prophecy comes to me.

I stepped back, looking down and breathing deeply.

"Get out, and don't include me in all of this," I said and called Almiro through the mind-link.

"Almiro, get him out of here and make sure he never returns back to our territory."

"As you wish, Alpha." Almiro did as I ordered.

"You'll need my help soon, I promise," Alpha Magnus mouthed before letting Almiro escort him out.

I returned to my room, washed up, and stayed in the bathtub for an hour, staring at the wall blankly. What Alpha Magnus said to me shook me to the core. Millions of thoughts were running wild.

$$\mathcal{Territory}$$

KAMILAH

Alpha Magnus is back. My mate. The hybrid and child of prophecy. I survived without him for years. Why now?

There were three things to take in here.

I could kill him so I didn't have a mate left, but I knew someone who had gone nuts from killing her mate accidentally. Tamara… who was one of my subordinates, was a prime example of this. Remembering her now, I planned on visiting her.

I got up from the water and dressed, then went to eat dinner with my pack in the dining hall.

I saw Tamara's parents, Nameera and Fernando. They were the only werewolves that I saw who had true love. They were 200 years old and yet they were still together and mated as if it was just yesterday they got together.

I smiled at them. "Hello, love birds. Where's your daughter?"

Their eyes widened. "Oh, I haven't seen her," Fernando said hurriedly.

"Fernando! I asked you to monitor your daughter!" Nameera scolded him. "It's going to be a full moon later."

I gasped and instantly ran outside. I could sense her scent was not that far from here.

Well, the problem here was that Tamara had accidentally killed her mate and whenever she saw the full moon, she was triggered and rampaged on.

I had taken the task of calming her down whenever this happened as the leader of the pack. Going to the scent of her direction, my wolf instantly went on alert.

'I am picking her scent up. But some filthy smell is with her,'

said my wolf. I instantly ran to the deep wood and let my nose take me to where her scent was.

Just then, I saw Tamara who was transformed into her wolf form with brown fur. She was walking deeper and deeper into the woods… like leaving our territory.

"Tamara!" I yelled, gaining her attention.

She looked at me. *'Stay away from me, Alpha Kamilah.'*

So she still had her senses. I looked up at the sky as the moon was slowly creeping up into a full moon. The last time this happened, she had almost killed Almiro.

"Calm down, let me help you."

I mind-linked Louisa and Almiro to come to back me up, as my wolf sensed something was wrong.

'No, I'll be leaving for a while to stop myself from killing all of you!' she growled and I breathed deeply.

"Tamara, you are better than this. You are strong, do not let yourself be dragged into the darkness," I tried to coach her. She was still glaring at me, growling at me.

Just then I picked up some other scent.

Tamara was going to run away when a very dark-furred wolf came at her and bit her neck.

"Tamara!" I yelled as I saw her struggling. I transformed into my white wolf.

I pushed the wolf away that attacked Tamara, and stood beside her defensively.

I sniffed the air and spat at the ground, growling at him. One instantly grew fast in numbers, and I could count there were ten of them surrounding me.

'Rogues,' I snapped at them.

The wind blew as we glared at each other, the leader stood in front with his dark raven fur. *'Alpha Kamilah.'*

I took a step forward, not scared of them. I know I could easily take them out, but Tamara behind me was whimpering and I had to be careful. *'Who the hell are you?'*

'I'm Borris,' the leader responded, his tone menacing and cold. *'Consider this a warning, Kamilah. We're coming after you.'*

I scoffed. *'Bring it on. You rogues are no match for me.'*

In an instant, the rogues lunged at me and tried to bite me. I fought them alone and bit them, sinking my teeth to their bones. I managed to bring down five but they jumped on me again before I could catch my breath, and the leader, Borris, had a hold on Tamara's neck behind me. I pushed him off while stopping the other four, but Borris had kept up with my pace.

With one bite, he had bit down on Tamara's neck, beheading her in an instant. I howled.

'Is this warning enough for you?' he asked as he held Tamara's wolf head.

I gritted my teeth. *'I won't ever forgive you! I'll hunt you down, you scoundrels!'*

I instantly chewed on his legs and made him stumble on

the hard rock. He bit at my legs but I kicked him off and I grabbed his head.

I could smell some strange substance inside them as if they took something to make them this strong that they almost kept up with me. Rogues are not typically this strong, that they made me defenseless. And they didn't usually attack without a reason.

The four other wolves were helping him, and I roared as I grabbed his head and bit his neck, beheading him.

I glared at the four wolves behind him who watched the scene, whimpering.

I threw the head of their leader toward them and said, *'Tell this to the one behind this, fuck off. You can't just bring me down like that.'*

They nodded grabbed their leader's head and ran away from me.

I let them escape, soon they would be dead anyway. I heard the sound of the twigs and saw Almiro and Louisa.

'You two are late for the party,' I said, panting and catching my breath. I rubbed my white fur, feeling a bit drained, then transformed back to my human form. I felt the cold wind brush my skin as I laid down on the ground without any clothes on.

Louisa gasped in shock seeing Tamara's headless body and immediately went to her.

Almiro came to me to give me a black cloak to cover my naked body. He had been with me through the years so he had gotten used to seeing my naked body. Plus, we werewolves didn't feel any shame when we did this. It was completely normal.

"I apologize. We had driven out two rogues who attacked our packhouse."

I snorted. "So they sent two decoys for you not to help

me. They led me here and killed Tamara, saying they'll have a war with me."

Almiro frowned, looking at the scene that was filled with the rogue's blood. "They smell like Alpha Magnus's pack, are they his past subordinates?"

"Why would his past subordinates turn rogue just to attack our alpha?" asked Louisa.

I was silent, gritting my teeth. What business did these rogues have with me to wage war on me. It was obvious they had someone conspiring with them. Louisa and Almiro didn't know that Alpha Magnus was my mate… and I planned to keep it that way.

I glanced at Tamara's body with a sigh. "Send Tamara's body to the pack doctor. I have to think about how to say this news to Nameera and Fernando about their daughter."

Almiro came to my side to comfort me. "You did your best to help her."

"Are you going to see Alpha Magnus?" asked Louisa and I shook my head.

"No. I'll investigate further," I said. Almiro looked at me deeply and I motioned for him to go.

"Go with Louisa, I'll be fine."

He looked at my left shoulder. "But you're wounded."

"I'll heal soon. Just go and protect my pack for me." Sighing, he threw one last look at me before leaving. He grabbed Tamara's body and ran in the direction of our packhouse.

Turning to where the four wolves had left, I sniffed where they were headed and quickly ran in that direction.

I continued running for fifteen minutes, away from our pack and near the borders. I stopped, noticing that the rogue's scent stopped.

'Someone is there.'

Warned my wolf and the trees rustled.

"I can help you," I heard someone say from the darkness. "I know where they headed."

I turned to the man behind the tree and asked, "Who are you?"

He came down from the tree. I could clearly see him now. He stood 6'1" tall with long limbs and a lean body, with curly black hair and seductive red eyes. He looked around 20 years old with flawless white skin, but I could sense he was one of us supernatural's, a vampire.

He looked at my wounds, before quickly placing his mouth on my left shoulder and licking the blood that escaped from it.

I gasped and pushed him away. It was Gusev. He still looked exactly the same. Never growing old despite the time that passed by.

"Kamilah, I missed your blood. It really is too sweet for a werewolf. I normally vomit but yours is… savory," he commented, licking his lips and savoring the taste.

I glared and growled at him, and he chuckled sheepishly. I had almost forgotten about this vampire's existence. As I talked with him now, I felt like the past had crawled back to me again.

"Oh, forgive me. Did you miss me?"

I looked at him, standing on guard. "No."

He pouted. "Come on, Alpha queen…"

"What? Why do you call me that?" I snapped, a bit riled up from the little nickname he gave me.

"What? It's true. You have been famous for years, you know, so I decided to visit you again. I never truly left you that day in the hotel, but watched you grow your own pack."

He gulped and glanced at my shoulder, sniffing it. "I smell some strange substance in your left shoulder."

Oh, it seems it was not only me who noticed it. He scrunched his nose as if remembering something. "I know those things. They are werewolf steroids."

"Werewolf steroids?" I repeated. I had heard of those and never encountered someone that used them before. Why did they suddenly appear? Now? I could still feel rage from them killing Tamara right in front of me, and I swore I would get revenge.

"I'll take you to someone I know. He's more knowledge-able than I am," urged Gusev, expecting me to follow him but I shook my head.

"No, thank you. I won't go with you."

"Why?"

"I don't trust you," I simply replied and he pouted.

"Ouch. That hurts. Did you forget that I protected you? We were friends, right?" he said and sighed. "C'mon. I don't bite. I mean I just licked some of your... even though I could drink your blood all day by how tasty it is."

I rolled my eyes. "Stop talking about my blood, mosquito."

He gasped dramatically and looked so hurt. He acted as if I didn't use that nickname for him the last time we met.

He cleared his throat. "Wow, you really have grown fierce now, Kamilah. You just called me a mosquito? How could you! Then you're a dog!"

I scoffed, not feeling offended at all. He whimpered sadly.

"Fine, I offered to help you, don't take it the wrong way!"

I gritted my teeth. "Wait! Direct me to that person."

At this, he instantly smirked, then stood beside me, and pointed to the right. "Then, this way, please."

Self-Control

ALPHA MAGNUS

I was right. Kamilah still hated me. I let time pass by, letting time heal her.

It pained me to know that Kamilah still hated me. When she rejected me and vanished from my pack, I made sure to always check up on her and keep updated with what she was doing, because that was what calmed me down.

I partly expected she would come running back to me… to come to me and ask for my shoulder to lean on. But she didn't.

I did everything to be with my mate, but she hated me.

All those 150 years without her, I felt like dying. No, I expected myself to die and that I wouldn't last even a year.

I would have gone nuts, if not for Dimitri pushing me to become better for her, to get prepared for the day we met again.

Kamilah was such a strong woman. She had her strengths that only she could do, including shaking my world.

That night when she left me, she clearly misunderstood

me. I didn't even remember what happened. Good thing that Dimitri told me that Kamilah saw me with a human in my arms.

But I didn't do it because I wanted to. That night, it was a full moon, and I lost control.

Living as a hybrid, half-vampire/half-werewolf, my blood had been fighting over who was more dominant.

On normal days, I was just a werewolf who could control his urge to drink blood. But at night when it was a full moon, my vampire blood took over, craving for blood.

I did not anticipate that my vampire blood would take over, good thing that I managed to lock myself in my office and had Dimitri take over. Only Dimitri knew this secret of mine… and I planned on keeping it a secret from anyone, other than Kamilah.

My Kamilah, if only I could have explained it to you in advance… You wouldn't have left me. You would have shared an ounce of understanding with me… but then again, I couldn't blame her. It was fully my fault and I had to suffer.

Just then, my ears perked up and my body went on alert as I sniffed the air, sensing another creature coming into our packhouse.

'We have an intruder. Check it' I mind-linked my beta.

Dimitri replied, *'The security patrols are knocked out, and judging from the smell, we know who it is.'*

My fangs started to appear and I growled and howled, waiting for that creature to appear.

"Hello, best friend!" exclaimed a black-hooded figure from just outside my house.

I didn't have to check the windows to know it was really him. But something was amiss. There was another familiar smell with him…

I instantly stood up to see the window and I was right.

Alpha Kamilah was right by his side. She sensed me too and glared at me, despite the distance.

My mate...

I sniffed the familiar delicious smell of hers and licked my lips, my throat drying up and my wolf inside growling in so much anger.

But why was he with her?

I clenched my jaw, as Gusev still stood outside, clearly sensing my annoyance but feigning innocence.

"Why are you here and why are you with my mate... I mean Alpha Kamilah?" I growled at him. I shouldn't have been surprised how he did this... I knew for a fact Alpha Kamilah hated me and wanted nothing but to run away from me and my pack... and right now, she must have a reason for coming here.

Gusev smirked. "Would you not even let your best friend in? Come on, my alpha friend."

"Did you kidnap her?" I answered his question with another question.

Gusev sighed and turned to Kamilah. "He's saying I kidnapped you. Can you tell him why I directed you here?"

Kamilah looked at him with annoyance, and I was a bit relieved knowing that she hated that bastard too. She glanced at me for a second, our eyes meeting before she huffed and looked at a tree from a distance. "I want to know about the steroids," she demanded with such a cold voice.

I nodded, motioning for her to continue but when she stayed quiet, I took the initiative to answer. "Those Steroids?" I felt a bit disappointed that she came here for another reason... there was a little part of me that was hoping she would come to accept me as her mate...

I cleared my throat. "The Lycan king is investigating that."

She raised her eyebrows at me and scoffed, as if not content with my answer. "And why are your past subordinates in my territory? The rogues attacked and killed one of my powerful subordinates."

My ears perked at that, looking at her body for any sign of cuts or wounds. "Did you get hurt?"

She looked at me with an offended look. "Hurt? How little do you think of me? I killed their leader."

"But you let the rest get away," Gusev interjected from beside her, earning a death glare from my mate.

"I did that purposely, to give them a warning."

The corners of my lips turned upwards, somehow enjoying how my mate clearly hated Gusev's guts. Of course, she could handle anything, she was strong. She was an alpha. My mate. My luna.

I shook my head, clearing away my thoughts. "I apologize about that incident. Some of my subordinates didn't like how powerful I was so they left my pack. I didn't know they would become rogue."

"Tsk. You fail to keep your pack on a leash," she commented and I cursed under my breath. This was bad. I was giving a negative impression to her. Well, I broke it 150 years ago… but still…

Alpha Kamilah sighed. "If you have no more knowledge about those steroids then I have to return to my pack."

"Wait!" Gusev and I simultaneously called out.

I gave him a judging look that said mind your own business trash, but his look replied you watch your words, bastard.

"What?" Kamilah snapped at us, looking at us with an irritated expression.

I gulped, my mouth opening and closing, not wanting to say something that would offend her, but then wanting to see her face a bit longer. No, I wanted her to stay here… but I knew that she was an alpha and had her own pack.

But that thought of meeting her lips now after so long…

Have some self-control, self. We don't want her to leave again...

Secrets

KAMILAH

"What?" I asked them, more like snapped as I was irritated. I looked at my wristwatch, seeing that it was past my pack's curfew. I had to get back as soon as possible and watch over them. I knew Almiro was capable enough and my beta Louisa could handle it but just to be sure.

I tried to mind-link them but they were not even responding. Something must have happened. I felt a bit panicked inside. Gusev's teasing look and Alpha Magnus's hopeful eyes from the second floor, both looked at me with emotion.

"Nothing, just want to see your beautiful face for more than a moment, little kitten," Gusev said, and I just rolled my eyes.

"Little kitten? Wow Gusev, mosquito sucker!" I argued back, insulting him. I really hated that little kitten name. It just irked me.

But that didn't have an affect on Gusev as he grinned more."

"How about you call me baby?" he teased me.

"Gusev, stop bothering her," I heard Alpha Magnus's strong and intimidating voice ordering the stupid vampire, but the vampire just stuck his tongue out at him childishly.

Should have known that nothing good would come from following this vampire.

"I want to offer to take you back to your pack but I know you will reject me like you always do," said Alpha Magnus, then gave a small smile at me. "Take care, Alpha Kamilah."

I just gave him a look. "No, you take care. The second those rogues come after me again, I'll come after you. You better put a leash on those bastards, got that?"

He just nodded and I instantly walked away from them.

I got back to my pack and told Tamara's parents about the incident. I also ordered Almiro to arrange the funeral and left the paperwork to Louisa.

I massaged my temples, feeling tired from today. I would have collapsed if I was my past self. Thank goodness I was managing now.

The next morning, I was woken up by a familiar scent. I instantly sat upright and looked to my left to see *him*. Gusev.

"Hey there, little kitten."

In a reflex, my hand went up to his head and hit him.

"Ouch! That hurt, alpha queen!" he complained and I grabbed his throat, pinning him to the wall.

"What are you doing in my packhouse?" I hissed at him. I mind-linked Almiro and Louisa, both were not responding to me.

Tsk. What were those lazy ones doing now to have let this bug inside? And in my room?

"Chill! I wanted to surprise you, Alpha Kamilah."

"We are not someone who could be buddies, mosquito head," I yelled at him.

He tried to loosen my grip on his neck but since I was stronger, he gave up.

"C'mon! I want to get to know you now," he announced. No surprise, he knew exactly where my packhouse was and even managed to slip by my warriors...

"Don't forget you are in my territory, vampire. I could easily get you out of here."

"But you're not doing it. Which means you love my company. So I'll stay here for you and chat with you."

I sighed, loosening my grip, feeling my eyebrows were just going to get wrinkles talking to this insect. "I don't have time to deal with you."

He really was like a pest.

"Oh, I'll be quiet. I'm just curious to see what an alpha queen does in her everyday routine. You know, for old time's sake."

"Leave. I'll get ready now," I demanded and he quickly obliged.

"Alright!" He then opened the window and jumped down. I went to my bathroom, showered and got prepared for the day. I put on my black tank top and my favorite black jeans.

My schedule would be full today, training the pups, overseeing the schools, and my company.

Once I was ready, I opened the door and saw Gusev the vampire sitting cross-legged on the floor, drawing some heart shapes on the red carpet.

"Oh, you're done already?"

"Why are you still here?" I asked back sassily.

He just shrugged and dusted his pants off as he stood up.

I instantly started to walk, attempting to leave him but he was fast and instantly came to my side. "So what are we doing first today?"

"None of your business," I replied. Plus, I had to drive him away. He might be a spy.

Almiro instantly came into sight, holding a bunch of papers with Louisa by his side.

I stopped them with a glare. "Why did you let this insect in?"

Louisa raised her eyebrows, used to my attitude. She glanced at Gusev and back at me. "Oh, must have slipped from our hands as we're busy doing all your work that you were supposed to finish last week," she replied sarcastically, not even bothering to hide her irritation.

I raised my eyebrows at her and Almiro took a step forward. "I'll tighten the security next time. I apologize, Alpha Kamilah."

I nodded at him. "Good. Make sure you do that. I knew I could rely on you, Almiro."

I glanced a disgusting look at the vampire beside me, who seemed to not care about us as he looked fascinatedly at some rare artifacts on my wall.

He turned to me. "Wow! I have looked everywhere on Earth for this rare piece of the bowl. Who knew you had this one?"

I sighed and faced Almiro. "Next time, don't even let him step foot in here."

I continued walking as Almiro and Louisa parted ways from me. Gusev stayed on, following me. "You know, I still find your blood delicious."

"I didn't tell you to talk to me," I responded as we neared the training grounds I built for my pack. It was just an open area full of grass, with trees surrounding us. I would some-times hold contests and let them hunt for food.

"I couldn't help but just think of it, my personal juice box," he added.

With that, I glared at him. "Do you realize who you're talking to? Show some respect. I'll kill you if you keep on calling me a juice box and talking about my blood."

He just chuckled at me and I instantly pushed him into the sunlight.

He yelped in pain, his skin forming some wounds. He instantly went to a shady spot and cast a look at me. "Do you really think I would be killed, just like that?"

"Nope. But I hoped. At least I did some damage."

He shook his head, his arms now fully healed, and came closer to me. "You really want to kill me, do you?"

"What else? You trespassed on my packhouse, and you keep bugging me."

"You're so hard to get to. I just want to befriend you again like in the past and somehow woo you."

At that, I paused. Woo me? For what? "I am warning you this early. I do not belong to anyone. Understand?"

"Want me to change your mind then?"

Just then, our bickering was cut off by someone.

"You look beautiful as always, Alpha Kamilah," Karleen, one of my strongest warriors, commented.

Her nose sniffed the air and scrunched in disgust at Gusev beside her.

"And who's this?"

"No one, he trespassed here. Don't mind this insect. I'll dispose of him soon."

Karleen instantly got in a defensive stance as her eyes looked menacingly at Gusev. "Should I kill him?"

Gusev's eyes widened in horror and he looked at me nervously. "Alpha Kamilah! Help!"

I smirked. "Go on, Karleen," I urged her, taunting Gusev.

Gusev whimpered, giving me a puppy eyes look, but I held on. I just wanted to give him a bit of a scare.

Karleen seemed to get my hint as she joined along.

"Alpha Kamilah," Louisa's voice interjected, which Gusev was thankful for as he managed to get out of the situation.

"Yes?" I replied, noticing the big, wrapped box in her hands and a bouquet of red roses. "What is that?"

"Someone dropped this off in front of your room," she said. "It's a gift from someone, I think."

Furrowing my eyebrows, I looked at the box as Louisa placed it on the ground. I sniffed to check who it was from, but whoever gave this was smart enough not to leave any scent.

Great. What a mysterious creature to have me guess.

"Oooh, a secret admirer?" Gusev interjected, grabbing the piece of paper that fell off the box.

"Our Alpha sure is beautiful to have admirers all over the world," Karleen commented, proud of her alpha.

Gusev cleared his throat. "Dear Kamilah, I hope you find this useful. I hope to see you wearing this soon—"

Gusev started to read it but I grabbed the letter from his hand.

"Louisa, throw it away," I ordered, and Louisa, Gusev, and even Karleen gasped.

"Awe, that's such a waste! Why would you throw it?" asked Louisa disappointedly.

"Yeah, why? How about giving it to me then?" Gusev suggested. I hit his right ribs, making him yelp in pain.

"Ouch, Alpha!" I ignored his pleas and just looked at Karleen.

"How about keep it for a while? So you can track who that admirer is, Alpha," Karleen suggested.

I rolled my eyes at their complaints. "Fine, do what you want with it for all I care."

At this, Louisa smirked and left to take care of the gift.

But she only returned with a lot more gifts in her hand.

"What's that again?" I asked, confused.

Sweat was on her forehead, tired from running back and forth. "The whole living room of your house was filled with gifts."

My eyes widened and I instantly ran to see it. Boxes upon boxes were there, filling the whole space of my living room. I gritted my teeth, annoyed that I would have trouble stepping into it. "I swear whoever gave that will get punished. We don't have a place to store it. Just throw all of it."

"But—"

"No buts," I firmly said, making sure she understood what I meant.

Whoever gave that would surely be dead. Did he think that my house was a mailbox to give gifts to?

"Oh! We should do some 'unboxing videos'! I watched some humans do that on our tiny little phones in an app," Gusev cheekily said, finding this interesting. I gave him a death glare and left the house, planning on being productive for the day.

"Can I come?" Gusev asked. "I'll be a good company, I promise."

"No," I firmly replied. "Just seeing you now destroyed my day."

He pouted at my comment and silently followed me. I sighed, not having any choice but to let him. I started to train the pups for the day, overseeing the school for werewolves that I built just around my territory and managed my business.

I massaged my temples, tired, trying to relax back in my office. I situated myself on my sofa. I was too tired to even go to my room, so I'd just stay here for now.

"Want me to give you a massage?" Gusev offered, still standing by my side and not leaving me.

"No, thank you."

He didn't even listen to my answer as he came to his feet and softly put his hands on my temples. He started doing some circular motions.

"I thought an alpha queen like you wouldn't get tired," he commented, his touch now relaxing me.

I looked at him, pretending that he was not even that talented at this. Wow, who knew this vampire could even massage?

"No, it should be you who's tired. How come you still have enough energy to mess with me?"

"I'm a vampire, remember? I don't sleep. I don't get tired. I only get bored with life." That was all he answered.

He continued on until I slowly closed my eyes and did not notice that I fell asleep in my office.

But when I woke up, I was in my bedroom. The clock said it was already midnight, meaning I slept for five hours... Goodness, had I become so old that I easily got tired these days?

I stared blankly at the wall, trying to regain my consciousness and wake myself up.

Just then, a dark figure was by the window, seemingly staring at me. It opened the window and I instantly stood up.

"Who's there?" I called out. Judging by the smell, I didn't

have to feign innocence as I saw Alpha Magnus's dark eyes, staring right back at me.

Disgust, irritation, and furry instantly clouded my mind and I growled, "What are you doing here?"

He instantly wrapped his hands around me, not even being slightly affected by my hatred for him,

"I missed you... Kamilah."

"Get your filthy hands off me!" I yelled, then mind-linking Almiro and Louisa, but he was quick to stop me.

He grabbed my chin and made me look at him. "How have you been doing all these years? Do you eat well?"

"Thanks for the concern, but I don't see you as part of my life now," I snarled, keeping my distance from him.

He sighed. "Why are you so hard on me? Come on, we can talk things out. Doesn't it drain your energy every time you see me?"

It did. It drained me seeing him… so much so that I wanted to leave this place again.

"I'll make sure that you won't even step foot here. You're in my territory. You're disrespecting me every time you invade my space," I said firmly and his eyes flashed sadness.

"I apologize, but I just miss you. My eyes always crave for you. How can I gain your trust back?"

"You can't, not anymore, Alpha Magnus, now leave." I pointed at the door, "And I'll put thorns out my window so you won't get in next time."

He held my hand, looking at it. "Don't let Gusev touch you. I'll surely give you a pet that will bite off his hands whenever he touches you."

I raised my eyebrows, oh… he must have seen earlier how Gusev massaged my temples. "Why? Are you jealous that he could touch me?" I taunted.

His expression darkened and he clenched his jaw. Just hearing that, made him irritated.

But then he quickly grabbed my neck and I felt his sharp fangs on it. I was stunned, but I felt him drinking my blood. I was suddenly reminded of that night… when I saw him with a woman. My heart clenched, feeling that those past emotions I tried to bury had been making their way back to me.

He then released me, panic on his face at seeing my expression. "I apologize, I was too thirsty and smelled your blood…"

As always, he was giving me mixed signals. He was a walking red flag. I learned these terms from humans.

I tapped my foot on the ground, glaring at him, unamused. "Are you done?"

"Can we talk about what happened that night when we kissed?" he questioned me, and I shook my head.

"There is nothing to talk about, Magnus."

He nodded. "I see. Then I won't stop bothering you until you let me talk to you. Starting now, I'll be so persistent that you can't even push me away," he said, his eyes filled with so much passion and seriousness, but I knew better.

"You may push me all you want but I'll not risk losing this chance and losing you for another 150 years again. I waited long enough, Kamilah."

Just then, the door opened and a concerned-looking Louisa came in. "Master!"

We both turned our heads and Louisa gulped at the sight. "Did I interrupt something?"

"Yes," Alpha Magnus replied.

"No, you were late," I said to her strictly, annoyed at how she got here so late. My hands reached my neck and covered the bite that Alpha Magnus gave to me.

A panting Dimitri, Alpha Magnus's beta, instantly came

and leaned by the door. "Alpha! Goodness, I knew you would be here! You're late for your meeting!"

He caught sight of me and his lips instantly broke into a grin. "Oh, it's good to see you again, Kamilah."

I just looked at him, and motioned for Alpha Magnus beside me. "Get your alpha out of my pack, Dimitri."

He rubbed the back of his neck and chuckled nervously. "I'll assure you that my alpha just seemed to… lose his way. I'll make sure he won't wander around aimlessly next time."

He then looked at Alpha Magnus and mumbled, "Why do I even serve an alpha like him?"

"I can perfectly hear what you said about me, Dimitri," Alpha Magnus said and gave one last look at me. "Remember what I said, Kamilah." He then turned to his beta. "Let's go."

They started to walk away, but not before Dimitri looked back again and smiled at me. Louisa, beside me, nudged me in the arm. "So you're getting close to Alpha Magnus?"

"Shut up. Brief me, what's my schedule for tomorrow?" I ordered, but Louisa was still looking at the retreating figure of Dimitri and Alpha Magnus.

"So Alpha Magnus's beta's name is… Dimitri?" she asked dreamily. "He's handsome."

I looked at her, quite shocked. No, it seemed that even Louisa would fall off track. Goodness, Dimitri, what did my beta eat that she was staring at you like that?

"Should I ask for his number next time?" she asked me and I shook my head.

"Focus, Louisa, there are more werewolf men out there, one that is more suitable for you," I answered and she pouted.

Avoidance

KAMILAH

I watched how Darian's gentle smile turned grim as Valentina snatched him away from me.

"Darian!"

I yelled, but somehow my voice was nowhere.

I cried out in frustration, running after them but the ground seemed to stretch, and Alpha Rufus, the last alpha of the Shadow Pack appeared from behind me.

"You've been a good child. I apologize for everything. You'll know your true identity soon."

I blinked, letting what he said process. As far as I knew, Alpha Rufus was dead. Killed by Alpha Magnus 150 years ago…

Why was he appearing now?

I suddenly got a hold of things. This was a dream.

"Is this… a dream?"

"Depends on what you perceive it to be… but I've been trying to reach out to you for a long time."

He should be with the Moon Goddess by now… did he

somehow have a mission he did not get to finish in this world? Was that why his soul is still roaming around?

Millions of questions buzzed through my mind, and I watched as darkness engulfed me. I stopped trying to reach out to them, seeing Darian, Valentina, and Alpha Rufus were gone.

"Let me drink your blood," Gusev suddenly appeared and I pushed him away. No, this was a dream. Just a dream.

I started to run away into the abyss, and Alpha Magnus's face welcomed me. "Wake up, you're going to be late," he said to me.

I raised my eyebrows. "What?"

"Wake up, you're going to be late," said a voice, waking me up. I groaned, not wanting to be woken up as I wanted to melt into slumber. The harsh sunlight hit my face and I dug my face deeper into my comfortable mattress.

"Five more minutes, Louisa!" I yelled and heard nothing but silence.

"You've been saying that for an hour already."

I instantly snapped my eyes open hearing that voice. No... it couldn't be. "Magnus?" I yelled in disbelief.

Yes, there he was, in all his glory. Alpha Magnus sitting in the chair by my bedside table to my right.

I breathed in and out, trying to calm myself down.

"Good morning, baby," he greeted, his eyes glancing up at me as he read the newspaper in his hands. "You've been screaming in your sleep. I didn't want to wake you up since you've been salivating there. Must have been a nice sleep."

I pulled the blanket up further, hiding from him. "Why didn't you wake me up? And you again? I thought we settled this matter of you entering my room last night?"

He closed the newspaper from his hands and stood up. "Yes, we did... But I'd like to take you somewhere today."

I cocked my head to the side. "Who said I'll let you?"

He shrugged at my mocking. "Me… I won't stop bothering you here in your room, if you won't listen to my request today…"

I gritted my teeth. "Are you threatening me?"

He thought about it for a moment. "Hmmm… you could say that."

Standing up, I grabbed my metal hanger placed on my table and pointed it at him. "Leave! I'll get dressed now."

His eyes gazed at the hanger and up at me, twinkling with happiness. "So you'll come with me?"

I crossed my arms in front of me. "Depends if you're not going to annoy me or not."

His lips turned into a full smirk and he nodded. "Alright, I'll leave. I'll be waiting outside."

He started to walk away, using the door properly this time. As soon as he left, I immediately took a shower and got dressed quickly. I would normally go to the training grounds and instruct everyone, just as I usually did. However, I stared at the ceiling in boredom, sitting and plopping my hand on my desk.

Just then, my phone rang, notifying me about a donation to my orphanage, an orphanage I built for homeless children wandering aimlessly around the area.

Checking it, my mouth left my jaw, seeing that it was a ten million dollar donation. It was sent by someone without a name, just anonymous.

Just then, the business email I had notified me too.

"Hey, I sent a donation to your orphanage. I hope you like it."

It was sent anonymously, but I already knew it would be Alpha Magnus. Wow, he just donated ten million? That was quite a large sum, I admit.

Louisa suddenly got behind me and took a peek at my phone. "Oh, speaking of the devil…" Her eyes then widened. "Ten million dollar donation? Come on, I didn't expect him to be that crazy rich!" She shook her head at me. "You need to thank him…"

I raised my eyebrows. "Why? It was up to him to willingly do it." She cocked her head.

"Come on! Your man just did that huge amount, don't you need to do something?"

I stared at her deadpan. "He's not my man."

"Oh, yes, he will be, in the future. Mark my words, Alpha Kamilah." I just rolled my eyes, ignoring Louisa's comments. Of course, it bothered me a bit… but what could I do? He donated willingly…

Game of Hearts

KAMILAH

The next day, I woke up to Louisa's panicked face greeting me.

"What?" I snapped in frustration, pulling the blankets up me and, hiding in the covers to sleep more but she pulled it.

"Hide me," she yelled in fear, and I groaned, sitting up as she went under my bed. What was it this time? It was too early to disturb my beauty sleep. I wiped my face to remove any snot and drool from when I slept, and yawned.

Just then, I heard a knock on the door and Almiro's voice followed. "Louisa? Dimitri's looking for you."

I cleared my throat and answered, "She's… not feeling well. Why is he looking for her?"

I went under and asked Louisa, "Why is he looking for you?"

Did I miss a whole chapter? They only met once last time and I'd never seen them talk alone. Plus, there wasn't any matter that needed Dimitri to address Louisa.

She shrugged. "I don't even know!" She then scrunched

her nose in disgust. "Ew, under your bed needs some cleaning."

I rolled my eyes. "Of course it does, it's your fault for hiding there," I said and sighed exasperatedly. "Just tell me what this is about, Louisa."

Louisa cursed under her breath. "I don't know!"

I think I could finally connect everything together. Dimitri might be pursuing Louisa now...

"You started this mess, deal with it, Louisa," I teased and forced her to get up. She bit her lip and mumbled to herself, before bravely facing the door.

"Where is he now, Almiro?" she asked when we saw Almiro standing there.

"He left, he just wanted to leave something here." Saying that, Almiro handed Louisa the bouquet of purple lilies.

Louisa blushed giddily, her smile so wide that it covered her whole face. She sniffed the flowers and shrieked in happiness. "Smells so good! I have to put them in my vase."

As Louisa left to deal with her precious flowers, Almiro came to me. "You too, Alpha. Alpha Magnus has been waiting in your office with a gift."

I looked at the clock hanging on my wall, reading it was still seven in the morning. Too early for me.

I sighed. "Is it that important?"

"It is," said Alpha Magnus's voice from behind Almiro, his intimidating aura oozing into the room.

"Good morning, Alpha Kamilah," he greeted, taking in my morning look. I was still in my white silky pajamas, with my long-sleeved shirt and comfortable pants. On the other hand, he was wearing his typical white polo shirt that hugged his biceps and his denim pants. He was also wearing his usual black sunglasses.

I huffed, hiding a bit in the door. "Morning,"

Almiro left us alone to give us some privacy and Alpha Magnus smirked. "I'll wait for you in your study. I have things to talk to you about."

I scoffed. "What things?"

"You'll know later. Get dressed, I'll leave you alone now." As he said that, he walked away.

I looked at my bed, my soft mattress, and my lovely pillows, wanting to get back to sleep but remembered Alpha Magnus wouldn't stop until he got what he wanted.

Taking a shower in my attached bathroom here in my room, I put on a lovely green maxi dress that reached my knees, and I matched it with my white suit jacket. Then I grabbed my shoulder bag, and sprayed myself with perfume.

I glanced at the mirror one last time, checking my appearance, before going out and heading to my office.

As soon as I was close to my office, I saw Alpha Magnus opening the door for me and smiling. "Good morning again."

I nodded, sitting in my chair and leaving my bag on the table before facing him. "So? What is that 'thing' you wanted to talk about?"

Just then, I noticed that we had another creature there with us. He smirked, motioning for it. "Before we talk, I have to give you this gift."

I watched as the gift he was mentioning stood up and walked toward me, and softly snuggled its head on my thighs, as if already familiar with me.

It was a tiger. Its stripes up close were much visible and mostly huge. I had only seen tigers around Africa and in some zoos… but I never personally got eye to eye with them.

My wolf instincts were on alert, and I had to calm it down.

I look at Alpha Magnus. "A big cat?"

"Her name is Lumiere. We found her in the woods hiding

from humans so we rescued her. I just couldn't help but think of you when I saw her," he started to explain. "I'll give Lumiere to you so she can drive away certain vampires."

I chuckled at his reason. "Gusev? You really hate your best friend around me?"

He nodded. "Of course, I have to earn your trust... I'm jealous."

I scoffed. This was Gusev's fault. My hands reached for the tiger in front of me and gently pet its head.

"Lumiere…" I rolled her name on my tongue and the tiger instantly looked at me, purring and pushing herself against me. I grabbed my stress ball from my desk and threw it for her to play with.

I heard a phone clicking and I looked up to see Alpha Magnus's phone flashing.

"You're taking a picture?"

He shrugged. "Yes, I just couldn't help but capture this moment with our child," he replied and I snorted at the word child.

"What? I consider her as our child from now on."

I would have felt a bit triggered by that but now, I am strangely content as I watched Lumiere play with the stress ball, almost knocking down some of my vases and decorations.

"Why did you name her Lumiere?"

"It means light in French. Why? Do you want to change it?"

I shook my head. "No…it kind of fits her…" Silence fell as we watched the new pet in my office play. I cleared my throat, suddenly remembering the reason why he came here. "So? What is that 'thing' you wanted to talk about?"

He leaned on my desk to meet my eyes. "You didn't reply to my email yesterday."

"I don't have to," I said. "But since you're here, I guess I'll have to thank you."

He cleared his throat, leaning closer, so our faces were a few inches apart. "How about thanking me in another way?"

I raised my eyebrows, standing my ground. "So you want another thing from me? Fine, what is it?"

"Your phone number," he suddenly blurted out and I processed what he said.

"Why? You already know our company's email? You could contact me there."

He sighed, withdrawing from me and standing tall now, leaning on the wall behind him. "You could ignore my message or delete it there. I want to text you or call you."

I nodded, getting his point but asked again, "Is that all that you wanted from me, that you came here so early in the morning?"

He nodded, staring at me with a serious look on his face. His dark eyes gazed at me, waiting for my response.

I grabbed my latest model of phone and rolled it in my hands. "You could get my phone number from Louisa… why bother coming here personally?"

He shook his head. "No, getting it from her and getting it from you personally is different."

"I see…" My hands then waited for him to pull out his phone. "Okay, give me your phone."

He did as I ordered and instantly put his phone in my hand. I unlocked it, surprised that he didn't have any passcode. His wallpaper was a picture of him and his whole pack, with him smiling wide and Dimitri beside him.

I then clicked the phone icon and typed in my phone number, handing it back to him when I was finished. "Done. So? Can you leave now? I have work to do," I said harshly, lying a bit since I had already finished all my tasks for the week.

"Did you get enough sleep?" he suddenly asked.

I looked at him, confused about why he was changing the topic. "Uhm, yeah?"

"Want to go to town?" he offered, making me breathe deeply, clenching my teeth in annoyance.

"Will you please leave? While I'm still asking nicely?"

He looked a bit hurt at what I said and nodded. "Alright, if that's what you want then… I apologize for bothering you." And with that, he started to walk away, his feet heavy and dragging with each step.

I bit my lip, feeling guilt swarming up inside me. He really just wanted to spend time with me and earn my trust. And how could he do that when I'm not opening my doors? I had built this tall wall around me, to protect me, and I have no plans to let anyone destroy it.

"Wait." Before he could open the door, I spoke up.

He turned around and looked at me with hopeful eyes. "Yes?"

It won't hurt to give him a chance…right? Just this once…perhaps he'll stop whining and bothering me.

"Fine." I muttered, "Let's go."

Magnus's eyes instantly lit up, "Really? Are you sure about this?"

I rolled my eyes, "If you keep on asking then I'll retract my words."

"No! I'll make sure you'll enjoy this!" He exclaimed, and led me.

He led me to his car, and he turned it on before driving away. I don't have any clue on where he'll take me, but after a few minutes, he parked his car just near a tall building. We were greeted by humans lined up and a bouncer waiting by the entrance.

"The line is at the end, did you have a reservation?" the tall man, an inch smaller than Alpha Magnus, asked, his eyes trailing to my dress and to Alpha Magnus.

"No, but I have this." I showed him my special card and he gasped in surprise when he saw it and cleared his throat, trying to regain composure as he bowed a bit,

"A… VIP? Oh, I apologize, Miss Kamilah," the bouncer stuttered and offered to lead the way. "This way please."

I smirked, hiding my VIP card in my bag. I was not a partygoer a few decades ago for nothing.

Alpha Magnus pulled me behind him protectively and leaned in to whisper, "To a bar?" He gave a look at me, not expecting me to do this.

I shrugged. "I mean, you can choose not to follow if you don't want to."

He gritted his teeth, glaring at the bouncer in front of us who had been waiting. "Are you planning on looking for another man?" He gritted his teeth. "Then all more reason for me to come with you. I have to guard you, so if anything happens…"

I followed the bouncer and Alpha Magnus sighed behind me, also tailing behind me.

The music blasted through the speakers and sweaty people dancing around the floor welcomed us. I scrunched my nose in disgust and the bouncer led us up the stairs where the VIP area was, which was much calmer. There were a few people already here, some higher-ranking human officials, chilling around the area.

We sat by the bar as the bartender made drinks. As time went on, Alpha Magnus was on alert, scrutinizing everyone and watching their every move.

"Tequila, please," I requested to the bartender and as soon as he gave it to me, Alpha Magnus grabbed and sniffed it before passing it on to me.

I raised my eyebrows. "Why?"

"I check it for any poison…" he whispered and I sighed. He still looked uneasy and was protective… He was really keen on his role of being my bodyguard for today.

Lost in the Rhythm

KAMILAH

"Come on, relax. I trust this bar in town here," I said, sipping on my drink. We didn't even get drunk, but I loved the taste and smell of the drinks. It was intoxicating and tickled my brain.

"You'll never know when Drucilla might come. We must be relaxed but not too much, we still need to be on our paws."

"I dare him to," I said, gritting my teeth at the thought. Alpha Magnus finally gave in and drank with me, ordering a whiskey for himself.

I stood up, starting to dance as the sound of loud music boomed in the background, losing me in the beat. The taste of tequila on my lips stayed and it made my world a bit hazy but exciting. I didn't even mind the stare I got from Alpha Magnus as I came here to let loose, not to impress or think about his opinions.

Alpha Magnus stood up. 'I'll go to the comfort room," He informed me and I just nodded.

Left alone, I continued on my own and heard someone

calling me. "Hey, beautiful," said a human in front of me, earning my attention.

Judging from the slight accent he had, I was guessing he came from the northern region. I offered a small smile and continued dancing, used to being flirted with. Hmm, I was over a hundred years old now but these cute little humans still hit on me.

I smirked, of course, men were weak against beautiful women.

"Let me buy you a drink," the guy offered as if I was not rich enough to afford one. I was sure that I could even buy this whole guy's life, and my inner feminism wanted to fight back but I fought the urge.

Instead, I nodded. "Go ahead." The stranger then, eyeing me with a hungry stare. As I sat, I thought that he surely had his looks, but he was obviously a womanizer.

The man then cleared his throat and offered his hand. "I'm Lukas, by the way."

"I'm Rose," I lied, not wanting to reveal my identity.

"What a beautiful name for a beautiful woman like you." I grimaced at that, hearing that overused line a million times now. Couldn't they be creative and think of another pickup line? Men really had the same brain cells.

The man, I mean Lukas, then inched closer, starting to make his move. "So...you alone?"

I just shrugged.

"Well then, let me accompany you throughout the night." He decided we'd have a nice little chat to 'get to know me', except for him talking about himself mostly.

It was quite boring as I knew exactly the reason why the man came to me in the first place. He wanted what every man would want from me... my beautiful body.

"So? What about you?" he asked.

I raised my eyebrows. "What about me?"

His eyes trailed down to my lips. "You can tell me anything about yourself."

"Well, I don't really like talking about myself," I answered honestly.

His dark brown eyes stared directly at me, as if trying to read my expression and he seemed to sense that I was not in the mood to open up so he stood. "The night is getting livelier now, how about a dance?" Lukas offered his hands to me, waiting for my response.

I ran my hand along my dress that fell on my knees and accepted his offer. "Sure."

The beat changed into something livelier and got loud enough to distract my wild thoughts.

I followed my body's rhythm to the dance floor and before I knew it, Lukas directed me to the center. Everyone was cheering for me, and the man came to whisper to my ears, "Everyone's staring at you."

I smirked at that, not needing him to inform me about that fact. "Good, I'm glad I got their attention."

"Whoa!"

"Get those moves!"

"Damn woman!"

Different cheers came from different people who were looking at me. I swayed my hips sexily and grabbed my hair. This night was made just for me. So I owned it.

Instantly, Lukas then grabbed my thighs and followed my moves. The people cheered even more and they continued, his hands trailing on my stomach and before they could land on my breasts, I instantly pushed him away.

"What the—"

"Don't touch me!" I yelled and the crowd went silent.

Lukas scoffed. "Why are you acting like it's my fault,

bitch? Things were just getting good. You were asking for it with that dress."

I gasped at what he said. The nerve! Give a man a chance and he acted like it was you who followed him. Really, they needed to realize that things didn't revolve around them. My hands instantly slammed on his face, earning a slap. The man glared at me, not expecting it.

"Be grateful that I don't hit a woman," he snarled, gritting his teeth.

But I am not just a woman. I am an alpha.

I wanted to say that in the heat of the moment but I stopped myself.

"Oh yeah? What a sexist comment. If you're up for a fight, I'm on." Instantly, I felt strong hands slide on my waist, grabbing me and I felt my nape getting tickled as the breath of the stranger hit it.

"That is enough," said the stranger who grabbed me from behind, his tone dripping with malice. My heart stopped beating for a second, biting my lip. It was Alpha Magnus. Tension suddenly filled the room, and his intimidating aura oozed, scaring almost everyone.

"I was just gone to take care of a small matter and you're making some mess here, baby," he said to me, his tone was filled with so much anger, directed at the man in front of us.

"Who are you? This hoe's mine, dude. Back off," Lukas replied, wanting to fight back. A few men came behind him, and I was judging it was his friends.

Alpha Magnus arched his eyebrows as if what Lukas said had triggered him. "Oh, she's mine. So back off before you lose teeth, bastard."

I glared at him. "I'm not yours."

Lukas scoffed, mocking Alpha Magnus. "Oh? So you're just some assuming guy then? Know your place, dude."

"It's you who should know your place." his husky voice thundered. "And you're a stranger she just met at the bar. I had her, while you are still here trying," he retorted. "So who's the real winner here?"

Lukas gritted his teeth, glanced at me, and spat on the floor before silently walking away. "My father will hear about this."

"And? Who's your father?"

"Drucilla, know him?" he blurted out, and I sniffed the air, wondering why I didn't sense that he was a werewolf too. If he was able to mask his scent like this, he must be strong… or they came up with some weird innovation to hide our werewolf scent.

Alpha Magnus groaned, hissing at Lukas, and looking at me. We exchanged glances.

"What? What did you say?" Alpha Magnus said, instantly in a defensive stance and instantly mind-linked his pack. I also did the same, asking how Almiro and Louisa were doing at my pack.

'Prepare yourselves, Drucilla is starting now,' I said to them but didn't receive any reply.

I gritted my teeth, trying to remain calm. I wanted to sprint right then and there and see what was happening at my pack, but Lukas, Drucilla's child, was right in front of us. A chance to kill him.

He smirked. "Silly, Alpha Kamilah. You keep enjoying life here, with Alpha Magnus protecting you there. Don't you fear what will happen to your pack now?" He then paced around and whispered in my ear, "You're in terrible danger. You must scam off to your pack before it's too late."

"You bastard!" My lips were shaking with so much anger, I pushed him so hard that he immediately hit the wall.

Everyone saw the scene and yelled, and humans began to scatter off.

Lukas laughed, blood everywhere and he growled, yelling orders to his men to catch us.

I wanted to beat him to death, have my own hand wrapped around his head, cut it off, and gift it to Drucilla, but Alpha Magnus grabbed me and started running away from the bar.

"We caused unnecessary trouble here, let's go back to your pack. Drucilla must have planned to divert you today and touch your pack."

He didn't have to tell me that, but the thought itself scared and angered me so much that my wolf inside wanted to shapeshift. I waited until we reached the woods and in my territory before shapeshifting, and sniffing the air to have some news.

But all I could smell was the fire from my pack's direction.

Just then, I could sense fear from my warriors.

I instantly ran in the direction of the fire as I kept my ears perked up and I focused my senses on my surroundings.

I lost sight of Alpha Magnus. He must have gone back to his pack to check too.

Seeing that the fire was in our chicken pen, I breathed a sigh of relief.

I saw Gusev and my other pack members as they threw buckets of water into the fire.

Gusev caught sight of me. "Where were you?"

I ignored his question and looked around. "How's everyone?"

"Still intact. You?"

"Where's Almiro and Louisa?"

"They left to secure the place as soon as they heard some

rogues howling nearby," he explained quickly. "Thank goodness I came here in time and saw the fire. If not, your pack's coop would have been burned down."

I sighed in relief. "Thank you, Gusev."

He just nodded. "Anytime, I'll always be here to help."

We managed to put the fire out. Just then, my leader warrior Karleen showed up.

She saw me and instantly apologized. "I'm sorry, Alpha—"

"It's alright. Things like this happen, we must prepare for worse to happen," I said, interjecting on her apology.

I started to explain to them. "This is no other than Drucilla's doings, hating me so much that he'll risk this. We actually saw his son Lukas earlier at the bar in town."

His eyes widened, grasping the situation. "So it's really starting."

Just then, I looked to my right as a harsh wind came to blind me, along with a filthy smell. It was all too quickly as a shadow came and a pair of fangs suddenly bit my left arm. I gritted my teeth, pushing the object harshly as it fell to the ground.

I glared as I saw it was a creature with long hair, her eyes all red and veiny, a dark aura surrounding her.

Karleen instantly stood beside me and Gusev hid at my back, startled too.

"Do you know this creature?" I asked him and he shook his head.

"I'm famous to women but not this kind of… woman," he attempted to joke and I mind-linked Louisa and Almiro about the situation.

'We're tracking down every Rogue in the area. They're surrounding us,' said Louisa.

'How is everything there, Alpha?' asked Almiro and I bit

my lip, grimacing and feeling the harsh pain from the woman's fangs that were buried in my arms.

'A strange creature appeared and attacked us. But I can handle this, I just need you two to make sure that other rogues won't come here.'

'Roger that. Be careful.' said Louisa.

I then cut off our mind-link as I focused on the enemy in front of us. She then snarled at us.

"Who are you?" I demanded, glaring at the foreign one.

She started to attack Gusev. He was about to launch when I stopped him. I grabbed the woman's throat and avoided her sharp teeth.

"Speak, or I'll kill you."

I never smelled anything so strange in my entire life. She was not a vampire, nor a werewolf. And I could only guess what she was.

She's both.

No, if I was not mistaken, she seems to have some blood traces coming from a werewolf, vampire, and witch.

A tri-blood.

Hybrids are one thing, but seeing a tri-blood in front of me, it's another level. I had always thought they only existed in legends, but seeing one in front of me now removed my doubts.

Just then, arrows came at me from my right and Karleen was quick enough to grab it. "It has poison. Careful!"

The tri-blood managed to get out of my grip and attacked everyone. Some of the pups and some of my trainees were still at the grounds so I instantly mind-linked everyone.

'Everyone, evacuate. We are in a state of emergency. Those who can fight, protect your pups,' I ordered, then I ordered Karleen to protect the pups too. Almiro and Louisa appeared from the woods, then we all transformed into our

wolves, grabbing the arrows and letting the pups evacuate from the place.

Gusev stayed, watching everything silently.

Just then, his eyes widened, and he pointed. "Behind you!"

I didn't have to look up and saw the woman getting beaten up by a tall figure.

Alpha Magnus.

He transformed into his wolf, black fur and a size bigger than me, He cast a glance at me. *'I apologize that I'm late, Kamilah,'* he breathed out, looking at me, and pointed at the filthy creature in front of us.

'This is a tri-blood that Drucilla released. This time, they are seriously coming after you. We need to leave for somewhere safe.'

I creased my eyebrows. *'We? What do you mean we? Why are you dragging me with you?'*

He looked me dead in the eye, his gold eyes shimmering against the sun. *'They only want you, Alpha Kamilah. As long as they know where you are, they'll attack you. Staying here will only endanger your pack members too,'* he explained. *'I'll get some of my pack guards here for extra security. But you need to come with me. I know somewhere safe for us.'*

I looked around, looking at my whole pack which was now in disarray. Looked like almost everyone had evacuated.

Realization suddenly hit me. Alpha Magnus was right. I needed to leave in order to protect them. I gulped, feeling emotional as I had to leave my pack, the most precious thing in my world. The world I worked so hard to build for decades. It took me a whole freaking century! And it will take only one night for them to destroy it! I can't let that happen.

I nodded my head, and Alpha Magnus took the lead.

"Are you just going to leave me here?" Gusev asked us.

Alpha Magnus rolled his eyes. *'You can run faster than us.'*

"But the enemy is a tri-blood! I stand no chance!" he complained.

'Then that's your problem,' Magnus replied and looked at me. *'Say goodbye to your members. We might be gone for a few weeks there.'*

Alpha Magnus then stayed to the side to give me space.

I called my trusted warriors.

Karleen, Almiro, and Louisa instantly appeared in front of me.

I cleared my throat. *'It's me that they want. They won't stop until I leave this place. I leave the pack to you, my subordinates. Don't worry, Alpha Magnus will deploy some of his members here for added protection.'*

'Is this a temporary goodbye?' asked Louisa, her eyes a bit teary.

I shook my head, trying hard not to let my tears fall. *'We'll see each other again soon.'*

'I'm going to miss your orders,' said Karleen, wiping her snot, as tears fell from her eyes.

Almiro looked at me with a serious look, understanding the gravity of the situation. *'Please keep safe, Alpha.'*

I nodded, giving them a hug and throwing one last look behind me, before facing Alpha Magnus who was waiting to the side.

'I'm ready,' I announced to him and he nodded.

Just then, Dimitri and some of his men came. Louisa saw Dimitri and avoided his gaze.

I wanted to tease the two but this was not the right time for it.

Looking at them, there were around ten of Alpha Magnus's men here.

'*But what about your pack?*' I asked him and he shrugged.

'*They can handle it. And Drucilla is after you, not me. I also have planned ahead in case something happens.*'

I nodded, somehow feeling a bit comfortable and relieved. He was really willing to help me.

Honestly, if he wasn't here, that tri-blood might have taken a toll on me, and worse, my pack would have fallen.

'*Keep your senses clear. We don't know who our other allies are,*' Alpha Magnus warned as he started to guide me away from the pack. Glancing behind to check for enemies following us periodically, we ran side by side.

'*How did they find out where my pack is?*' I asked in frustration as we were slowly leaving my pack borders.

'*Don't tell me that it's Gusev?*' I asked, somehow clicking it all together.

'*No, that mosquito is dumb,*' he reassured me. '*It must be my former members. Those rogues must have joined forces with them. Just as I suspected.*'

I gritted my teeth and quietly followed him. I didn't trust Alpha Magnus in the past but with the recent encounter with him, my inner wolf has told me now that he was right.

'*So where is this place you're taking me?*' I asked.

'*I'll tell you later. Someone might be following us and hear it,*' he answered, then continued running. We had been going on two hours, with a few missed attacks from other rogues and having to distract them so they wouldn't know our final destination.

We were completely out of my territory and his, nearly reaching the Lycan king's territory.

A howling from a distance came and I could smell a familiar scent. Lukas is here.

'He's here,' I announced and Alpha Magnus nodded calmly.

'So that bastard chose death.' He smirked, getting angry.

"Hey, love birds! Do you mind if I ask where are you two going?" he asked mockingly, keeping up to our pace as he had two of his men behind him. He shifted into his wolf, having gray fur, and continued taunting us.

We stopped running and decided to face him, stuck in the woods.

'That lovely white fur of yours is indeed pretty, Alpha Kamilah. But I'm afraid it will get full of blood soon.'

'Blood? Mine or yours?' I asked, fighting back.

Alpha Magnus put his hand on my shoulder. *'He's distracting us. It's best we ignore him.'*

'And risk he'll follow and find our destination?' I arched my eyebrows and scoffed. *'It would be best to end his life right here and now,'* I said menacingly. *'Isn't it good manners to cut his head off and gift it to his father?'*

A smirk played on Alpha Magnus's lips, agreeing with me. *'Good idea.'*

'Are you sure about that? Kamilah, you seem to be underestimating me.'

'It's you that is underestimating me,' I responded. Let's see how this goes. Let the games begin, Drucilla. You messed with me, and I won't back down. Since you started this, I think it would be fitting enough for me to start with your weak son.

Sacrifice

KAMILAH

I instantly launched at him. His two men behind him came to his defense but Alpha Magnus came at them. *'Na uh, I'll take care of you two.'*

I smirked, knowing that he was letting me fight alone. Good, because I wouldn't be merciful in killing this man in front of me.

I watched as Lukas in front of me took a step back, but tried to stand brave for himself.

He sent a chilly smile to me, his tongue licking his upper lips. *'I won't get easy on you, babe.'*

I scrunched my nose in disgust at the word babe.

'Good, but why are you shaking now?' I taunted, pointing my muzzle at his legs that uncontrollably shook.

'Come on, you can back down now if you know that you can't handle this.'

He seemed to be triggered by what I said as he didn't waste another moment but got his paw on me. He tried to bite off my neck but I jumped and threw him to the ground.

"Is that all you can do?" I teased, biting his neck. Sure, he's much bigger in size but just like my other enemies, my speed and strength overpower that.

He pushed me off and I stumbled a bit. Growling, he launched and tried to bite my shoulder and I lost balance, suddenly feeling the pain from the hybrid bite from before.

'What about now?' he retorted, eyes focused on me.

I could sense Alpha Magnus's hard gaze on me, making sure I was okay and preparing himself for any backup I might need. I knew he completely trusted me on this, but the look of worry flashing in his eyes couldn't deny how he was ready to kill Lukas for me with just one snap.

I appreciated that, but my pride wouldn't let him do that. This was my business so I had to complete it on my own.

'Make sure one of them is alive,' I reminded Alpha Magnus behind me.

'Sure, but why?' he asked, confused a bit. *'I already killed one though.'*

I looked behind, checking to see that he had indeed taken down one of them—he was lying on the ground, blood all over the woods. Goodness, we'd have to cover the smell as soon as possible. This would only gain attention. Lukas saw his men on the ground and breathed deeply, anger running in his veins now.

'Then leave the other one. I'll have him deliver Lukas's head to his father, of course.'

With my response, he immediately agreed.

I caught sight of the only one left and I smiled at him.

'Make sure to stay alive for your master,' I reminded him and he gulped, panic and fear in his eyes. He tried to open his mouth but his voice wouldn't get out.

I faced back to Lukas and cooed, *'You should have brought more of your men.'*

I found the right timing and I instantly chewed on Lukas's legs and made him stumble on the hard rock. He bit at my legs but I kicked him off and grabbed his neck.

'Any last words?'

'Fuck you!' he roared, completely at my mercy, knowing he was done now. I could sense fear flashing in his eyes now and his two men behind me were already taken care of. He was all alone now. No one could help him. No one. Tsk, leave it to egoistical creatures who would never beg for our lives. They were too arrogant that they would choose to die, rather than beg for their lives.

The thought even excited me. Call me psycho or whatever, but situations like those always gave me some unknown motivation, remembering my past when I was too weak as an omega. I felt like it was really my time to shine now.

But look at us.

How fast time flies by.

'Awe, I wanted to let you off, I'm kind after all. But no, I want your father to experience hell for messing with my pack.'

I continued, *'I guess you could call this a sacrifice?'*

'You'll pay for this, you'll be dead soon anyway!' he threatened and gritted his teeth, trying to fight back but I had pinned him down already. Alpha Magnus watched, grabbing Lukas' subordinate and making him watch the scene.

I didn't hesitate a minute and grabbed his neck and bit, and in a snap, his subordinate watched as I beheaded him and whimpered. Lukas's howls were so loud that Alpha Magnus instantly stood beside me.

'We need to be quick, their men might have caught on to his cry for help. We don't want to waste more time here.'

I threw Lukas's head to his subordinate and said, *'Tell his father I said hi, okay? He can't just bring me down like that.'*

He nodded, trembling as his hands grabbed his master's head and ran away from us obediently.

I smacked my paws together and noticed Alpha Magnus's hard gaze on me.

I faced him with my arched eyebrows. *'What?'*

'It's the first time I watched you kill someone in front of me…' He trailed off, letting out his thoughts to me.

Hmm… You thought I really wouldn't kill someone?' I asked.

'Honestly, yes…' he admitted and I just shook my head.

'Come on, let's go now.'

I let him take the lead and followed him to our destination, noticing how eerily quiet it was now. Too quiet that it was strange. Magnus noticed it too as he glanced at me, giving me a signal.

We roamed around until we made sure we were not being watched. Just then, Alpha Magnus stopped at a cave.

I looked around, sniffing the air and sensed neutral energy from here.

'This is the least dangerous place right now. I made preparations for this day to come. But now we have to seek shelter here.' We shifted, then he looked at my arms and his eyes widened, seeing the blood still gushing forth from the wound.

I looked at it, remembering that I was bitten by the tri-blood earlier. It was pretty deep, I admitted.

But my healing abilities should have taken care of it. "It should be healing by now…" I trailed off.

He clicked his tongue, looking angry at the thought of me hurting. "It must be because of the tri-blood's fangs. We need to treat that as soon as possible before it spreads in your system."

I gulped. "If not?"

"Haven't you heard of the tri-blood's legend? Their saliva is poisonous enough to paralyze someone."

I sighed. "I really thought they were only legends."

"I thought so too. But didn't the humans think that we are only legends too?"

He has a point. I nodded, and he immediately led me inside the cave, where an old man was waiting. The inside of the cave looked very messed up and had some ancient items. It looked like the mage was living here on his own. He was wearing a long robe that dragged on the floor and his beard almost reached the floor too. He carried a long wooden staff to assist him walking.

"Alpha Magnus!" he exclaimed in happiness and Magnus put his hands on his lips to silence him.

"Oh, haha, I apologize. I already prepared everything." He rubbed the back of his neck awkwardly and looked at Alpha Kamilah's wound.

"Treat her wound," Alpha Magnus ordered.

I raised my eyebrows. "Who is this?"

"He's a mage. Don't worry, he's my most trusted one," he assured me.

"It's a pleasure to meet you, Alpha Queen Kamilah. I am Zefren, a mage," he introduced himself and I silently nodded.

"Please take a seat and don't mind me. I'll heal your arm." I did as he told me and sat down. He then grabbed my arm and touched it.

I glanced at Alpha Magnus who was standing beside me.

He gasped. "It's a poison that is spreading quickly in your body! It also contains a spell to track you."

He then whispered some incantations and closed his eyes. A bright golden light came and he put it on my arm but a flashing light came out from my body.

He blinked and looked at me curiously.

"What is that?" asked Alpha Magnus impatiently.

"Let me try again." He then cast some spells, this time the light was much stronger and it blinded me, but then, as if a strong magnetic field stopped him, his spell fired back at him and he was pushed harshly against the wall.

Zefren looked at me with a scared look.

"Tell me what is happening, mage," I demanded, feeling a bit nervous at this.

"It-it's the first time that I met someone rejecting my magic...." he trailed off. "Y-your body is rejecting my powers."

"What? What does that mean?" I asked.

"I-I'm sorry but I can't heal you like this."

"What? I think he's a trusted one."

"Zefren. You know that one mistake and I'll kill you."

"Yes, master! But I really couldn't. Please give me a second. There must be a way!"

He instantly ran inside to get his books and I was left with Alpha Magnus. I awkwardly cleared my throat but grimaced when I felt the sharp pain spreading all over my arm.

Alpha Magnus instantly noticed my discomfort. "Are you alright?" He hesitated to run his hands on my shoulders to comfort me, but decided against it.

Zefren was running and pacing around, looking for books, still searching. "No... no... Aha! I need a vampire's blood!"

We both looked at him.

"I have some. I am a hybrid after all," Alpha Magnus offered.

Zefren gasped, whispering to him, "Oh... master does she know about..."

Magnus nodded, speaking very loudly for me to hear, "Yes, Zefren, she knows I am a hybrid... but that's not the point now."

Zefren gulped. "Ohh… right… I appreciate your offer, master. What I need is the blood of a pure vampire…"

Just then, I could smell the sudden change of air and Magnus also noticed it. He glanced at the small opening from the entrance of the cave and instantly grabbed the person outside.

"Magnus! I really won't forgive you! You left me there! They almost got my head! Yikes, that tri-blood almost got me!"

I blinked, as there, in all his noisy splendor, was Gusev the vampire.

"You found us? How?" I asked.

He smirked. "Well, thanks to my extraordinary nose."

Magnus instantly tightened his hold on his throat. "You followed us here and someone might have followed you too!"

Gusev raised his hand in surrender. "Yes, but I managed to lose them."

Alpha Magnus's throat clenched. "Are you sure about that? If not, I'll be the one aiming for your neck, Gusev."

Gusev looked at me with a pout, like a little boy complaining to his mother. "Kamilah, he's threatening me again!"

I just put my hand on his face. "Na uh. You put yourself in danger, Gusev. You shouldn't have come to my packhouse in the first place."

"Alright! It's my fault! But at least I get to be with you now in this cave." He raised his eyebrows playfully, and Magnus growled angrily from beside him.

"Back off, Gusev."

Just then, Zefren came in between them and grabbed Gusev's hands. "Aha! This one is a vampire. Come little one, let me draw some blood!"

Gusev looked at us with a confused look. "Wait, who is

this lunatic? Magnus, help me. I thought I was the one who should be drawing blood here but eww, oldie, your blood stinks! I'm a vampire with class!" he rambled on and on, struggling as Zefren the mage got his blood.

"Magnus!" Gusev yelled in despair and we only watched him get his blood taken. Zefren was happy now and Gusev laid down dramatically as if he lost all his blood.

Zefren then looked at me. "Now let me go again and heal you."

As Zefren tried again, my eyes drooped and the last thing I could see was Magnus's panicked face, calling my name out.

"Kamilah!"

A Great Escape

KAMILAH

"Wakey, wakey."

I felt something ticklish on my nose and I scrunched it and sneezed, feeling like there was a feather tickling my nose.

My eyes flickered open and saw the very closed-up face of Gusev.

"Hi, baby doll."

My hands instantly came up and hit his face as a defense and he yelped in pain.

"Goodness. Waking up seeing your face for two consecutive days is irritating," I commented, rubbing my eyes to wake myself up. I looked around and saw I was still in the cave. I saw the mage sleeping and Gusev was beside me.

"Why do you keep hitting me whenever you see me?" he asked, grabbing his face.

"Why not?" I asked back.

He smirked. "I wouldn't mind seeing your face every morning by my side for the rest of my life."

I rolled my eyes, seeing he was being weird again. "Eww."

He's really doing it on purpose to irritate me more. He really likes to get on my nerves.

I put my feet on the floor and tried to stand up but fell, and Gusev stood up for support.

"Careful, you just woke up five hours ago. The poison got to you, but your blood as an alpha is strong. This is just the after-effects, don't worry," he said and tried to sit me down.

"Oh, and thank me."

"Why?"

He shrugged, pointing at his veins. "For my blood. Without my blood, the poison would have taken you over and paralyzed you."

I sighed. Oh right, I could remember that. "Yeah, yeah. Thanks."

He leaned in and pouted his lips. "Then give me a kiss."

I just blocked his lips with my hand and asked, "Where's Magnus?"

"You're awake." Instantly, Alpha Magnus came with a bottle of water for me to drink and I downed it.

I took a second to look at him. He was all dressed up and prepared.

"Where are you going?" I asked.

He sighed. "Drucilla. He also found out I was a hybrid and planned to overtake my pack knowing I was gone. I have to be there. I am going to contact my beta."

He gave a look to Gusev. "Give us some space."

"What if I won't?" Gusev teased and Alpha Magnus just gave him a cold stare, enough for him to shut up and leave us alone.

I furrowed my eyebrows, wow. So if they got to Dimitri, they would know they are in my pack. And if they did, my pack will be the one who's most affected by this. "But you said it's dangerous. And I'm surprised they only found it out now." How come Alpha Magnus lived all his life hiding it? How did he manage to hide it? Our world is cruel, and a hybrid almost never survives. But he…stood at the top as an alpha.

"Well, thanks to Zefren. He was the one who managed to mask my blood's scent into a full-blooded one," he responded. Really, this discriminating world doesn't just balance the weak from the powerful. As if the hierarchy of power is not enough, the hybrids, tri-bloods, and all are treated like slaves and the lowest of status, lower even than the omegas. They could easily be discarded.

And with Alpha Magnus's power and masking his identity, this might have angered even our neighboring packs from other regions.

He then took a peek at the small opening at the entrance. "I have to get going now. Gusev, guard her." Gusev instantly appeared.

I stood up. "Why are you treating me like a kid? I am an adult, an alpha woman. We both know I am stronger than you," I defied. "I'll come with you."

He shook his head, caging me on the wall. "No. You just recovered from that tri-blood's poison. That is why I am going alone. You're precious, Alpha Kamilah. Once they get you, they'll win. But with me, they can easily discard me. I am just a mere hybrid after all."

I gritted my teeth. "Really? Or are you just scared that once they get me, you'll lose your mate?"

"That too…" he admitted.

I sighed. "Then there is no point arguing now. Let's fight together. Combine our strengths together."

I chuckled. "This is funny. One alpha is chased because

he's a hybrid. One alpha is chased because she's a woman who broke the norms and changed her fate. How cruel."

Alpha Magnus nodded, and couldn't help but chuckle bitterly at this. He removed his necklace and kissed it.

"This has protection conjured by Zefren. I'll leave this for you to return it to me later, when I get back."

"No, I won't accept that. I'll come with you," I said stubbornly. "I don't want to miss out on something fun."

Alpha Magnus blinked and said in a low voice, clearly irritated, "This is a serious life-and-death situation, Kamilah. You were almost paralyzed earlier and if I didn't get there in time, they would have gotten you."

He quickly leaned in and kissed me.

I froze. Then he quickly threw the necklace at me. "I'm sorry but you need to stay here."

He instantly ran away from the cave.

"Magnus! You bastard!" I yelled out.

Gusev came in. "Whoo, that alpha has guts," he commented. "So how was the kiss? Was it good?"

I glared at him and he chuckled, running away from me before I could even hit him.

I'll never forgive that man for what he did today! How dare he leave me, and give me a kiss!

"You liked it though," my inner wolf commented.

I shook my head, clearing away that thought.

I stared at the wall blankly, wondering what to do now.

Looking around, I waited for the opportunity to escape and go after Alpha Magnus. As I was just outside, Gusev instantly grabbed my arm.

"Stop being naughty, alpha queen, I have to keep you safe here," Gusev said, and I rolled my eyes and was escorted back inside.

My second attempt didn't go as planned either because as

soon as I stepped foot on the ground outside, Gusev's cold breath whispered to me, "You can't beat my senses."

"Just let me go, Gusev. I need to fight too," I stubbornly yelled.

He snorted, softly grabbing my shoulders. "Yeah, and that fighting includes you staying here."

I crossed my arms, and stopped to face him. "What must I do to get you to leave me alone?"

Gusev chuckled at me. "Hmm, are you seriously going to bribe me?"

Kamilah nodded. "Yep."

"And you're announcing it proudly…" Gusev gulped. "Fine, your mate might kill me the moment he returns."

"I'll find a way around that." Screw Alpha Magnus and his overprotectiveness. I could handle myself.

"Alright, but let me come too." He finally gave in and I smiled.

As we walked along the woods, I personally chose the track where I was sure it would be secluded. It was a shortcut and a mage's territory… so a few wolves wouldn't even bother going here, not unless they had a death wish. Throughout the whole duration of our journey, Gusev did nothing but continue poking around.

"So what's your plan?" he asked me, repeating the question for the millionth time now.

If someone paid me a dollar every time he asked, I'd be a billionaire in no time. Well, I was already rich but that was not the point.

I sighed, mustering patience and trying not to snap at him. "I'm not telling you."

He pointed at me as if that would even have an effect on me. "Come on, the least you could do is spill it. I risked my life and let you go out, remember?"

I stopped walking and completely faced him, having had enough of this. "Okay, so here's the plan."

He instantly nodded and leaned in, directing his ears to me. "Alright, I'm listening."

I whispered in his ears, "The plan is not to have a plan. I'll just check my pack, and before Alpha Magnus notices I left, we'll return."

"Sounds like a good idea. At least you have the conscience to return to him. But what if he manages to get back to the cave in no time? And sees you are not there?"

I shrugged, now continuing to walk as I grabbed some pretty stones. "Then I'll blame it on you."

He shrieked, "Come on! So whatever happens, it would still be my fault! Come on, just kill me."

I gave him a 'really' look. "You're already dead, Gusev."

"Right. But still!" he complained and sat on a rock, grabbing a stick and drawing heart shapes in the mud. "I won't leave here until you say that you won't blame it on me."

I rolled my eyes at his childish ways, not even entertained at this point. "Fine, enjoy staying here."

Then I looked around. "It's a mage's territory, stop being so fussy," I warned, completely aware of how dangerous it was.

I continued walking, just letting him have his tantrums like a child, as he continued yelling in the middle of the woods.

I was not here to babysit some lonely vampire. I had to get to my pack as soon as possible.

"Fine, you're on your own now!" I heard his steps walking away and I didn't bother to turn around, ignoring his pleas, and just continued on my way, knowing he would give in soon and it was just his tactics.

Then, silence fell.

My ears perked up, my arms suddenly felt goosebumps. I instantly widened my senses to see if enemies had somehow picked up my scent. I was sure my scent was hidden… who could dare to be in this secluded area now?

Gusev's scent was gone now.

I instantly turned around and noticed Gusev wasn't sitting there anymore.

My breath hitched, waiting for any movement and preparing myself. I couldn't shapeshift now as this mage's territory is somehow close to humans and I wouldn't risk being discovered and harming our clan.

Just then, a branch of a twig snapped and Gusev's scent reappeared.

I instantly felt his presence beside me as he whispered, "Hey there babe."

I jumped, feeling that he moved suddenly. I looked at him clearly, seeing that his usual smirk was playing on his lips.

Clearing my throat, I hid the goosebumps on my arms. "Where did you go?"

He was holding something, hiding it behind his back. He then gently placed it in my hands. "I left to give you this."

There were white daisies in my hand now and he looked at me expectantly, waiting for my reaction.

I sniffed the flowers, smelling them nicely. "Where did you get these?"

He pointed at a nearby tree. "I was about to leave you but I found these lying there."

I chuckled, ruffling his hair, and sighed. "So you're not going to complain now?"

He pretended to think about it and shrugged his head. "Fine, I won't. Let's go now, your pack must be surely waiting for you."

He tried to lead the way, and I walked slowly, looking at

his back and around the place. My inner wolf was sensing something, but I couldn't depict what it was.

Maybe we were being watched? Glancing at my surroundings, I noticed it was still the same. Gusev hummed a tune as he walked as if nothing happened. Really, I had to give it to him for being so bipolar. His mood changed so fast.

He looked back at me and yelled, "What are you waiting for? Let's go now!"

I rolled my eyes. "Yes, yes, stop being impatient."

We crossed a river and a few more woods, not even stopping once. Gusev and I even raced, betting on who would get their first. Being my competitive self, I made sure to go full speed while conserving my energy in case something happened.

Amidst the silence of our walk, Gusev gazed at me. "What are you thinking now?"

I kept silent, still thinking about my pack and our safety. How I wished I could talk to them now while being far away... I could use my phone, but Alpha Magnus had confiscated it to avoid being tracked.

"Come on, talk to me. I am the master of solving problems," Gusev said, still pushing the topic. I decided to stay quiet. He sighed exasperatedly, leaving me alone with my own thoughts.

"You know, you need to be careful once we get there. Alpha Magnus had given me a pet to chase you away," I warned him, remembering Lumiere. Due to my situation, I believed I had completely neglected her. I wondered how my pet was doing? I hoped Louisa and Almiro took care of her. Also, the most important question. How was my pack? How were they protecting it from there?

Gusev pulled me from my trance as he scoffed. "I knew he would do that."

"Yeah, so you need to be careful there." I chuckled, then watched as Gusev laughed.

I blinked, hearing the slightly varying tone of his laugh. I had heard his laugh enough that I completely memorized the way it would rise and fall. This time, it was completely different.

I cleared my throat. "You remember, that time 150 years ago…"

He looked at me curiously. "Yeah? And what happened?"

I blinked, knowing he would fully know what happened that time as Gusev never missed a beat. He was always there at every stage of my life. And he was a vampire, he would never forget anything.

"Sorry, I just lost track of that since I lived for a thousand years…"

Seemed understandable. But I had to test him, see if he somehow remembered it… even a bit.

"When I escaped Alpha Magnus pack…"

He nodded, motioning for me to continue, "Yes, you were alone."

Alone? Ah, looks like he took the bait. With the way he answered, I instantly knew this creature beside me was not Gusev…

I immediately grabbed his neck and hissed, "You played Gusev well, but Gusev knows me so well that he knows I had someone with me that time. Try to guess who it was and I'll decide your fate."

"Louisa?" he asked, dragging my beta in this and I laughed at this silly creature. He should know I was with Owen at that time! He was even angry about how Owen left me at that moment!

"Stupid, you should have known my past well before playing Gusev." So that was why the air changed and he didn't even remember anything about me, not even flirting and having his playful ways.

The man in front of me raised his hands up in surrender, chuckling at me. "Alright, I surrender. I should have done my research."

He pushed my hand away from his neck and pulled off his face as if it were a mask and revealed himself.

I gawked at the sight, watching as his evil smirk played on his lips.

"Hello, Kamilah, miss me?"

The elder Drucilla greeted me and I was halted on the spot.

Instead of fear, anger filled me and I clicked my tongue. "Well, well, well, what do we have here? My enemy, right in front of me, decided to show up."

The Fowlers

KAMILAH

Guess I didn't have to chase him all the way. He made it easier for me to kill him.

"I have to say you were keen and know Gusev very well. You tested me a lot and ruined my surprise. You should have stayed quiet until we reached your pack," he said. "But it was nice walking with you."

"Where did you put Gusev?" I calmly asked.

"Don't worry, he's in good shape."

He paused, pacing around me. I waited for the perfect time to launch at him, knowing I had the upper hand here. He was old enough that his abilities had weakened and I knew that he only relied on his subordinates now.

"Yes, can't wait to kill you. You made it easier for me to find you," I retorted, to which he replied with a smirk.

He shook his head, his hands put on my lips to silence me, "I have to say that gift you gave me brought tears to my eyes. You killed my only child, my heir to my position. I was heartbroken." He then paused, his eyes glaring at me. "Since

I'm very much a kind creature, I have to return the favor. I have a present for you too."

Whistling, I stayed alert as I heard the bushes shaking, until a few creatures appeared.

It wasn't another of his werewolf subordinates, or vampires, or even mages.

Instead, what stood before us were humans.

Not just any humans but the human hunters that we called "Fowlers".

I gritted my teeth at Drucilla. It was not that humans were tough, it was just that they were persistent in sending backup, using tricks, and traps laid everywhere to their advantage.

They killed any creature they found, from mermaids, witches, vampires, and others of our clans. Even worse, they sold us to other humans in high bidding auctions. They were that greedy.

They were wearing various human weapons from high-technology guns, bows, arrows, swords, daggers, and even bombs that contained a special type of liquid, enough to wipe us out.

Drucilla then caressed my cheek and walked away. "I hope you enjoy it! See you soon!" He waved at me, and winked. "That is… if you survive."

Now left alone, the Fowlers snickered at me. "Looks like you're alone now," said a man with a strange hat.

A girl with a lollipop grabbed her gun and pointed it at me. "Shall we start then?"

"Wait, let me talk to her first," said another guy. "She looks pretty for a dog."

I gritted my teeth, listening to their conversation. A dog? Leave it to some bad humans who felt the need to insult our kind. Their minds could not even ponder what I could do next.

One of the men in his twenties started to approach me. "You're the very first female alpha, right?"

I stayed still, growling at them, deciding when to attack as he continued on with his comments. "We'll get a good dollar for you."

I saw them dropping a big cage, intent on catching me.

The man then pointed at the scar on my face. "I see you must have experienced a lot."

Before his filthy hands could even get near my face, I instantly gripped it hard and bent it over, making him yelp in pain.

"Get your hands off of me!" said the man, groaning in pain and I snapped his arm, making him yell and drop to the ground. He tried to walk away from me but I held him hostage.

"That was unnecessary. Just go with us so we don't have to hurt each other," said the old man with a hat, I somehow sensed he was their leader.

'No, you leave," I growled, threatening them all. "Or I'll kill him."

Their leader sighed and stopped his subordinates. "Back off, she's a high caliber!"

I instantly got to each of them, breaking their bones and throwing all their equipment away. The girl had managed to pierce a bullet in my stomach and blood poured out of me.

"Don't fire at her!" hissed their leader, irritated. "We need her in full health to gain a higher price!"

But my adrenaline kept me going and I grabbed their leader's arm, wanting to cut each limb but he was quick and pushed me away.

Just then, he grabbed a tin can and opened it, and a green smoke suddenly filled the air, engulfing the area.

I instantly prevented myself from breathing, keeping my

senses clear as I knew whatever the hell that can had was made to harm me.

However, as much as I prevented myself from breathing it. It was all useless as the moment it had contacted my skin, I could no longer see clearly, my mind hazy and I felt dizzy. All of my senses faded… my sense of sight, smell, and hearing.

But I could see them a bit as they covered our faces with a mask, grabbed the big cage they had, and walked over to me.

"Sleep well, alpha queen," said the leader as he grabbed my body. I attempted to fight, managing to break his nose but they were quick to put chains on me. They even placed a big metal necklace on my neck and I winced, feeling it scraping the skin around my neck.

"Try to escape and this necklace will cut your head off," he whispered, and I felt my body being dragged inside the cage.

I tried to fight back and gain my senses, but it stung my eyes so much that all I could see now was darkness.

No… it blinded me. That gas was a poison to weaken a werewolf's senses. Dammit.

Those Fowlers were trained enough to deal with us super-natural's with all our types of equipment, knowing everything.

That damn Drucilla, he must have spilled everything about us werewolves, betraying us.

He was so keen on destroying my existence that he was willing to make these filthy Fowlers become his allies.

I howled, groaned and struggled inside the cage as I felt it moving. They had put me in the back of a car, and I was feeling sleepy but I fought it, memorizing each turn they took.

I'd have to stay still and regain my energy to escape.

With each second, the poison gas overtook me, worsening my condition that I couldn't even see anything besides darkness.

I counted each second in my head, and they finally stopped the car for around thirty minutes. I was guessing we must have reached the outskirts of the town.

They slowly grabbed my cage and put me on a cart to deliver it inside.

"Slowly, please. Make sure not to even graze her! Her value decreases with each wound!" I could barely hear the leader saying that, but I forced myself to make out their words.

I felt a door opening and I could feel them unloading me into the room before locking the door after them.

I stayed still, still trying to regain my senses.

"So they also got you?" I heard a man speaking from the other side of the room.

I went into the sound and rested my back on the wall. "Who's there?"

I could feel the man sniffing the air and chains rattling. "So you're a werewolf too."

He must be one of our captured. Those damn Fowlers.

"How long have you been here?" I asked, trying to get information. I put my hand on the wall and felt everything for any clue since I couldn't even see it now.

"A year ago... they got me from the North West," he answered.

So he was part of the Lycan king's territory. But then it hit me... the voice, it was strangely familiar. He had a faint accent but I knew that voice in the back of my mind. No, it had to be someone I knew. His name was in the back of my mind but my brain knew it.

"Owen?" I called out and instantly, I felt the chains rattling as he neared the wall.

"Kamilah?" he responded and I couldn't help but chuckle. "Wow, what a small world."

He laughed, his same damn laugh from 150 years ago. "No matter where I go, we met, huh?" He then cleared his throat. "I advise you to stay still though, the poison gas they gave you has a toxic substance for us werewolves."

"How could they develop that?" I asked. Humans were smart creatures, but I still couldn't process how exactly they had an idea that we were somehow weakened with a certain substance.

"Through me. They did experiments on me the whole time. There were some more werewolves here but they got so much substance that their bodies failed… it's only me who's alive here now," he explained and I shuddered at that. His voice had somehow become a bit raspy and sounded weak now… the human experiments must have taken a toll on him.

I scoffed. "So they will do that to me too?"

"I don't feel that… you're a rare breed. They know your value so they will sell you at auction."

Silence fell, and I gulped. I had to somehow recover from this poison and think of a plan soon. "When?"

"Tonight."

I breathed deeply. "We'll both escape from here. I'll—"

"You can't," he interjected. "Not unless you want to get your head blown off with that thing on our necks."

"How do you know it will?"

"Because I watched a friend of mine get blown apart while attempting to escape," he said, panic and fear were in his voice. "I guess this will be our fate now. We have to accept it."

"No, Gusev and Alpha Magnus will find me," I firmly said and he chuckled. "How can you be so sure?"

I stopped. Alpha Magnus was busy dealing with the trouble in his pack. If he… truly valued me… he would. I knew it. He would come to me.

The Owen I knew is someone who never gave up easily and hearing him say that now, the experiences he had here must have broken his soul.

Footsteps suddenly arrived and a nasty voice spoke. "How are you doing there, fellas?" he asked, mocking us. "Werewolf bonding, eh?"

I hit the door, and he clicked his tongue. There was a sound of metal grazing against the cold hard floor. "I know you hate us, but you need to cooperate with us, dear." He then continued, "I apologize for having to dull your senses, it's for your own good."

He then left after not getting a reply from me.

"Eat that, you need it for later," Owen spoke up after a while.

I shook my head, trying to sniff it but couldn't. Stupid senses not working now. "It may have poison."

"Better than you starve to death," he said. Being the prideful woman, I chose not to eat and just stared at a wall blankly, my mind racing with how to escape this hell of a place. I would rather starve than having my body get weaker and unable to fight back.

What bothered me the most was the chains attached to my hand and the stupid metal necklace on my neck. I yelped in pain feeling the cold metal scrape against my small hands that have open wounds now.

Silence fell, it felt like it was only me now. I felt my hands regaining a bit of strength, so I instantly looked around and tried to break free from my chains but no luck.

I didn't even know how many minutes had passed with me doing nothing but waiting to get sold in the auction. Since it would be tonight, it might only be three hours left now. Any moment, someone would come to me and direct me to the auction. That would be the perfect time for me.

By now, my senses have improved a bit and I could now see a little, just a bit blurry.

Another person came and grabbed me from the room, directing me to another room to see a very attractive woman.

She had shiny blonde hair that reached her shoulders and striking blue eyes. The beautiful woman stared at me with a fierce gaze, almost studying my whole being.

"So? What do you think? We hit a jackpot, right?" I heard the leader from the Fowlers team ask excitedly.

"Just stay still, werewolf woman. Your body is numb right now. We'll treat you later but you have to endure for now," he said, trying to calm me down but I gave him an icy stare that made him shut up.

The girl with a lollipop emerged from beside her." She's fiercely strong, she even broke our arms!" she said proudly, squealing.

The younger man appeared too and snorted. "But that beauty is such a waste. If only she were a human, I would have asked her to be my girlfriend."

The girl just shook her head. "Yeah, you and your playboy skills. You never pass any woman in every creature." She then looked at me. "I wonder what her fur color is when she shapeshifts?"

She then approached me, "Blue? Black? Brown? Oh, and can we experiment on her first?"

The beautiful woman who was just watching everything in silence now stood up and the air changed. Everyone got quiet as no one dared to speak up. The level of her authority was so bizarre.

"Speak," she ordered, and I ignored her. No one could order me like that. I would never let anyone do that.

She hummed a tune. "She's fierce and has a face," said the woman, walking around me and grabbing my chin to make me look at her. She then gave me a crooked smile. "I hope we can work together as a team."

Instead of replying, I spat on her face and smiled at her. "This place will be burned down to ashes soon."

The leader and the other members of the Fowler gasped. "Madam!"

The woman stopped them, and grabbed a tissue to wipe her face. "It's alright. She's cute."

She then glanced at the wall clock hanging by the door and called on two men and ordered, "Looks like it's time. Take her now."

I blinked, knowing they would put me out now. Meaning, my perfect time to escape. The two men then put a mask on my face and I let them direct me outside the room.

When they grabbed my chains, I quickly sunk my teeth into the men's arms and they yelped in pain. I jabbed their stomachs and weakened their knees. It didn't affect them much, as the men then put a cloth on my mouth and eyes and dragged me out of the room.

I could barely even feel my feet now. I realized that I might be drugged enough that I couldn't even dare to run away.

From afar, I could hear the yells of people and their excited cheers as we got nearer.

Biddings

KAMILAH

"Ladies and gentlemen, this is our last and most special item for today!" I heard a man speaking from a stage.

Just then, the two men who were dragging me removed the cloth from my face, and I was met with a hundred people in front of me.

I realized I was on the stage along with the emcee beside me—I was now officially in the auction. A spotlight flashed on me and I adjusted my eyes at the sudden brightness.

"Representing to you, a very rare creature. Are you a fan of fantasy novels and supernatural movies?" The crowd yelled in answer and the emcee laughed. "Well then, you must be aware of the werewolf's appearance and this woman right here, is a she-wolf! But, what's more important, this woman right here is an alpha. The very first female alpha in our world!"

The crowd gasped, some even started whispering.

"I know, you guys are doubting how the hell a woman could be an alpha. Normally, werewolves have men as their alphas, but never a woman. What you are witnessing is a woman who made history. A woman who defied her fate and came out on top."

I gritted my teeth at his sickening words. How I wish I could cut them off right now.

"Don't believe me? Then this mark on her face is the proof!"

They all went silent, staring at me until they all cheered again.

The emcee gathered all the screams and announced. "The bidding starts now!"

I watched everything in horror with only one thing in mind. I want nothing but to burn down this whole building, along with its people. My fists clenched tighter and I gritted my teeth.

"$1000," a man yelled.

"$2000."

"$3000."

It went up and up, rising as the humans raised their bids on me.

That damn Fowler. That damn Drucilla.

"So, anyone higher than five hundred thousand dollars?" the emcee asked when ten minutes had passed and the bidding was still ongoing.

I had experienced more dangerous situations in the past than this, but this made me sick to my stomach.

I could go through bullets raining down on me, have werewolves fight with me, but not this kind of bullshit.

I noticed the crowd were all wearing masquerade masks with suits and ties, so I figured it was an auction for the rich people. For politicians, for those in higher ranks.

"Higher than eight hundred thousand?" asked the emcee again as the bidding went higher each minute.

I stood still on the stage, wanting to kill everyone in sight out of range, but I held on. I had to take this calmly and escape as soon as possible.

"Nine hundred thousand!"

"One million!"

"One point five million!" said old men who were ravaging me with their eyes. I looked at them disgustingly. I couldn't help but think how stupid everyone looks. Are rich people nowadays so lonely that they pay a literary million just to have me?

No offense to them, but I know I was worth more than any gold or diamonds combined. I was priceless. No money would ever be worth it.

"Okay, last bid for tonight? Two million?"

"Two point five million!"

"Three million!"

"Five million!"

Looking behind me, I saw the door close and there was no opening. With my hands still tied in a chain and my feet not regaining any feeling, I was about to run when I heard someone yelling from the crowd.

"Ten million," Said a dark and husky voice. Gasps came from the crowd and even I tried to look for who said this. I squinted my eyes and I managed to see, in the middle of the crowd, a man holding a glass of wine.

I couldn't make out his face as he was wearing a black masquerade mask and he stood up for me to see him. He didn't look that old. He had a smirk on his face as if teasing me.

Wondering who this person was, I gritted my teeth. Knowing who the man was not important. I really needed to get out of this place as soon as possible.

"Fifteen million," said another one, from the front line of

the crowd. He was a tall and masculine man, and unlike the other man, this one was looking me straight in the eye, completely focused.

"Forty million," interjected the man who was smirking at me earlier.

"One hundred million."

Looking at the back and forth, I could see the tension filling the entire room as both of the men dared each to go higher.

At this point, they were not just competing for me, but competing for their egos and pride, to see who would rise higher than that. Pride.

"One billion," said the serious man, still looking at me with a focused look. The smirking man's jaw dropped and he cursed under his breath, now utterly lost.

The emcee from beside me grinned and announced, "Okay we got our last bid for tonight, ladies and gentlemen! Only the best for this lovely creature here!"

People began to leave and the emcee motioned for me to wait in the waiting room in the back. Two men in suits approached me and guided me back to where I was held captive earlier. Except now, the room was empty. They had already removed the chains from my hands and my feet were starting to feel okay now.

"Wait for the man who bought you tonight to come," one of the men instructed.

I nodded and waited for them to leave.

When I heard the door click, I forced myself to run to the door and planned to escape. I struggled against the doorknob, fumbling with it.

Damn, they must have locked it.

I smacked the keyhole, destroying it instantly. I grinned in victory and pushed open the door to get out. I had to go to the room where Owen was and get him out too.

I dragged my feet and tried to quicken the pace while looking around me, checking for any bodyguards. When I saw that the area was clear, I continued with my plan. The outside was dark with only dim lights around. The room I stayed in felt like a prison cell more than a waiting room.

"Awe, you escaped already?" a voice said in the silence. I gasped, not bothering to look behind me as I sprinted away in a hurry.

Dammit! I cursed under my breath. To think that I would be caught this soon as I wasn't able to reach the end of the hall.

"That's not where the exit is," The voice spoke up again, now chasing after me.

I took a quick glance behind me and gasped. Now that he was closer, I could see his figure clearly. To be precise, he was the serious man who bet on me earlier, still wearing his masquerade mask.

"I bought you with my one billion. Shouldn't you thank me, Kamilah?" Hearing his voice clearly now, I instantly knew who it was.

The man took off his mask for a few seconds for me to see before he returned it to his face and I gasped at the sight.

"Was my cover so good that you didn't recognize me?" Alpha Magnus said.

So it was Alpha Magnus who bought me tonight.

Relief washed over me. A tear escaped my eyes from seeing him, and pure relief washed over me. "What took you so long?"

My voice broke and tears after tears fell like waterfalls. He was here. Finally here. I instantly let my guard down as all I could feel was happiness. I knew he would come for me.

With one scoop, Alpha Magnus's strong hands carried me bridal style and I could feel his anger with the way his sharp jaw was clenching.

"I apologize for arriving late. I'll make them pay. They really have a death wish for messing with my mate."

He broke the chains I had on my hands and feet, and carefully slid a key into the metal necklace on my neck. As soon as I was free, I felt my feet going numb and I almost fell to the ground, except Alpha Magnus caught me.

He pulled me to him in a hug, as he whispered in my ear, "You're safe now, baby." He then scooped me up in his arms and started to run, with one hand carrying me.

He entered each room, his hands shifting into his sharp claws and he rampaged on every man he would see. Security was instantly alerted, deploying armed men but Alpha Magnus's hand just scratched them, killing them on the spot.

"I may not be able to stop so hold on tight," he whispered to me and I smirked.

"Go on, show me what you got."

He nodded, still in rampage mode. When we reached the Fowler's room, they fired some strange weapons on us but Alpha Magnus was quick to crack their bones and kill them.

Everyone was almost dead, except the old man, their leader. "You killed enough of my men, bastard!" he yelled in rage, pointing his machine gun at us and started firing.

But Alpha Magnus's skin felt like it was made out of stone as it didn't even have any effect on him. He blocked every bullet and instead, grabbed a bullet to fire back at him. The bullet pierced straight into his heart, knocking out his life.

"Let's leave this shitty hole now," muttered Alpha Magnus, but I stopped him, remembering Owen. "We have to save someone. Owen."

Alpha Magnus's expression changed the moment he heard the name. "So the Fowlers caught him too…" We went to the room where I thought Owen was. And when we entered, I could see him looking blankly at the wall.

His eyes had completely turned black as if infected with a disease. He was wearing no shirt, just the worn-out denim pants and the necklace on his neck.

Dirt was all over his body, but he was thin, weak and pale, so he must have lost a lot of blood. When he noticed our presence, he called out to me, not believing I had made it out. "Kamilah?"

He then glanced at Alpha Magnus beside me and nodded at him. "So he really came for you."

Magnus gulped, seeing his past subordinate. "Owen…"

Silence fell and I cleared my throat. "We have a lot of things to talk about, but let's get you out of here first."

Alpha Magnus destroyed the cell's lock and even got the key he used on me earlier on Owen. Once he was finally out, Owen coughed blood and stopped. "Don't touch me further. I might spread the disease I have gained from the series of experiments."

Alpha Magnus nodded, understanding it. "Then follow us. We'll get you treated by my pack doctor."

He nodded. "Just lead the way."

We somehow got outside the building and another familiar creature appeared.

"Hey," Dimitri greeted us warmly, wearing sunglasses, and looked so chill as if he was on vacation.

He spotted me in Alpha Magnus's arms. "Long time no see, Kamilah."

I nodded. "Same to you."

"By the way, I was the other man who had bid on you,"

he said, pointing at the masquerade mask he had. I snorted, shaking my head at their tricks.

"What a great way to buy me," I joked, now having the energy to do so. I felt my energy slowly coming back a bit, but not enough that I could run and attack anyone.

Alpha Magnus noticed my discomfort. "I'll let Zefren heal you and fight off the poison gas's effects."

Dimitri noticed Owen's presence as he nodded at him. "Great to see you, Owen."

Alpha Magnus cleared his throat. "Let's leave the catching up for later. For now, we have to shut this whole building down."

Dimitri then threw a remote control to me and I raised my eyebrows at him. "What is this?"

"The bombs I placed in their building. One click and they'll be gone," he explained and I nodded, smirking.

"Good job, Dimitri," I complimented, eyeing the remote control. When we were a far distance from the building, I clicked the button, and a loud bang echoed throughout it. Smoke and fire came out, along with the smell of gas, and dead bodies being burned.

"Let's go," Alpha Magnus said, still carrying me.

I suddenly stopped him, remembering something. Seemed that I forgot something.

Oh yeah... Gusev... I wondered where he was?

Death Wish

KAMILAH

As soon as we got back to Alpha Magnus's pack, Dimitri immediately called the pack doctor to get Owen treated. Owen was hesitating and I couldn't even blame him as he once left this pack.

As for Alpha Magnus, he brought Zefren here to his pack to cure me of the poison. They took me to the packhouse, then to Alpha Magnus's house.

"You're lucky you're still alive. One more day and you would have been dead already," Zefren commented, making me drink the brewed tea.

Alpha Magnus resented that, clenching his jaw but staying quiet as he watched me drink it.

"It would take more than just a mere poison to kill me," I said proudly, slowly gaining my senses. "I have to go to my pack now."

Alpha Magnus instantly stood by my side protectively, seemingly not agreeing with my wants. "You can't do that. You need to rest first."

Zefren excused himself, giving us some privacy.

I rolled my eyes. "I'm fine now."

"If you're still worried about them, I already settled everything. I made sure Drucilla won't bother them."

Despite what he said, trying to reassure me, it only made me overthink more. "No, I have to see them."

"I'll video call Louisa later for you then," he offered.

I nodded, giving it up. "Fine. fine, I'll rest."

"Promise? You won't escape again?" he asked, making sure I wouldn't do it again… fully knowing my stubborn self. I just stayed silent, not wanting to make promises.

I suddenly thought of Gusev. "What about your best friend?" I asked.

Magnus bit his lips. "I couldn't contact him, so I'm guessing Drucilla took him," he said. "He did not watch over you, so I'm not going to go after him, he needs to have a lesson."

I blinked, remembering how Drucilla tried to copy him last time. "That time when Gusev gave in to my request, Drucilla attempted to copy him. Thank goodness I caught on early."

Magnus nodded, gazing at my eyes as he listened intently to me. He leaned in. "He had gathered more troops to fight you. He even used the humans this time."

I scoffed. "Seems to me he's just getting desperate and intimated by me, knowing I only have my pack… and now you."

Alpha Magnus blinked, surprised a bit, his dark eyes turning red. "So you're saying you're fully accepting me as your ally now, right?"

I sighed. "Of course, I sacrificed everything, and even accepted your help. Why would I back down now?"

A smirk suddenly played on his lips. "I knew you would

eventually… thank you for trusting me." His hands reached for my own and he kissed the back of one. "I won't fail you."

And with that, he smiled at me. "Then I'll let you on your own so you can rest. If you need anything, call Dimitri. But if you want, you can ring the bell, and I'll come to you," he reminded me. "I'm just next door."

I nodded, letting myself relax as I heard the door closing. I settled deeply into the soft mattress, breathing in the familiar comforting scent that I could smell from Alpha Magnus.

My days passed by with Dimitri delivering my food and offering some company to me and Zefren checking up on me once in a while.

Alpha Magnus stopped by and gave me a phone to contact Louisa.

"You can use this," he said meekly before leaving the phone on the table and leaving me alone.

Video calling them through an app, I saw how my pack had missed me.

And I missed them so much.

Nothing had changed for them, instead, they looked happier now. "Alpha Magnus has done a lot of things for us!" she exclaimed happily. "So when are you going to accept him as your mate and come back here?"

"Louisa…" warned Almiro behind her.

Louisa just giggled. "What? Your mate had been so considerate to us that he protected us from Drucilla, and gave us food every day here. Ahh, what a bliss!"

I scoffed at her. "Don't get too used to those gifts, and don't be too dependent on him."

She gave me a look. "Hmm are you sure we're the ones who are too dependent on him? Who's the one who's with his pack now? Hmmm?"

Clicking my tongue, I replied sassily, "I got in trouble because of wanting to check up on you, and show some respect to your alpha, Louisa."

"Alright, alright."

We exchanged a few updates on our life, how Louisa was still being courted by Dimitri and Almiro's training with Alpha Magnus's men, wanting to get stronger. And, some of my pack members were falling for Alpha Magnus's men.

But anyway, I was just glad to see them well and happy. That was all that mattered to me now. At least I could rest easy. I ended the call and stared blankly at the wall.

I wanted to visit Owen as we didn't have a proper talk last time in the Fowler's building, since the events that happened.

When Dimitri came to give me my usual meal, I instantly dropped the question. "How is Owen?"

"Recovering. Looks like his body received major trauma, physically and emotionally. He doesn't want to talk to anyone now. Not even to Alpha Magnus."

I nodded, understanding his side. The experiments those humans did on him really affected him a lot. It was just sad to see how the once lively, dependable, and trustworthy Owen had changed into this… new personality. But I had to be considerate enough and not judge him.

"When he's ready, please take me to him," I said and he nodded. "Sure, but you'll have to quickly recover, or our Alpha might go nuts."

I arched my eyebrow at him. "Alpha Magnus? Why?"

He looked around and instantly leaned in to whisper, "Don't tell him that I told you, but he's been asking for updates from me about you every second. What you're doing, what you're eating… He can't concentrate. He doesn't even attend meetings and the papers. I'm the one who does every-thing now."

I chuckled at his complaints. "Then quit being his beta."

He scoffed. "I wish it was that easy… if it was, then I'd be enjoying my life a long time ago."

I patted his back. "Don't worry, Dimitri, don't you have your new source of happiness now?"

He blinked, confused.

I gave him a look. "How's Louisa?"

He immediately turned meek and stuttered, his cheeks flushing. "W-what?"

"Louisa… aren't you interested in her?"

He rubbed the back of his neck. "She's interesting, but why are we talking about her now?"

"Why? I want to know what is happening between you two." I said, diving in further.

"Well… she's feisty and hates me, just unusual for me," he admitted, now in a trance.

"If only you knew," I mumbled and his ears perked. Louisa might hate me for this but I am rooting for them so I guess this can't be helped. Sorry, Louisa.

"Knew what? Come on tell me. You're keeping secrets from me, I thought we were best friends?"

I playfully stuck my tongue out at him. "I never told you you're my best friend. It's between me and her, so you'll have to work harder and pursue her."

He just chuckled and shook his head. "Alright, enough about me… I have to go and do something so see you later."

Leaving me now, I stared at the window to see the night was now entering. I just nodded, letting him off the hook as he made an effort to give this to me. Plus it was night, so if he goes to town, the shops might have closed by now. I returned the ice cream to the table after a few scoops, still wanting it to be chocolate flavored.

Despite what Dimitri said, Alpha Magnus didn't visit me

as usual… except for giving me the phone coldly, this makes me wonder what happened.

Standing up, I quickly ring the bell. The door opened, and I saw Alpha Magnus's panicked face. "You called for me?"

I nodded. "Yes, I did. You didn't visit me today… Why?"

His gaze on me felt different. He was avoiding my eyes as if hiding something. "I have some other business."

I gave him a look. "Much more important than me? Or are you getting tired of taking care and pursuing me?"

"No, it's just—"

"Alright, you're avoiding me," I interjected, which made his head turn and he grabbed my hand.

"I would never, Kamilah. Never… it's just tonight… is the full moon," he said with so much intensity, his warm hand gliding over me.

"And? What if it's a full moon?" I asked further, still looking at him and forcing him to gaze at me. Was he keeping a secret from me? I didn't know, but something from him now looks…. sexy. I gulped, feeling intoxicated and the thing between my inner thighs was heating up.

His eyes trailing to my eyes and to my lips. "So Dimitri must have never told you…"

"Told me what?"

"This." In a flash, his soft lips came crashing down on me. I was taken aback, feeling sparks whenever our hands touched, but I let him for a minute and he stopped to whisper in my ear, "I can't control my vampire instincts every full moon. and your blood is so… tempting."

His eyes looked at me, waiting for my reaction. Expecting me to hit him. I looked him in the eyes, burying into his soul, and kissed him back.

He groaned, and I could feel his groin. He must be battling his inner demons now. He was acting as if he wanted to push me, but his hands and lips were completely attached to me. He let out a moan and mouthed my name breathlessly, "Kamilah."

I rested my hands on his shoulders, grabbing his soft hair and called back, "Magnus."

Hearing me call his name seemed to excite his member even more. I could feel it throbbing. His eyes looked at me with a heavy expression, looking intoxicated, pale, and cold.

I bit my lip, staring at him. "Magnus, fuck me."

He paused, taken aback at what I said. "What?" Something seemed to wake him up now as he shook his head and looked at me before shaking his head. "You're killing me. You're in heat."

I chuckled, feeling my wolf taking over and I let her. "I'm in heat and you can't control yourself. Take this chance. I might not let you next time."

Alpha Magnus gulped, tempted that one wrong move and he'd risk it all. "Don't say things that you can't take, baby."

"Or what? You're the one who wants me here…." I said, sliding my hands on his back and he suddenly pushed me against the wall, caging me in and putting my hands above me.

"If I'm ever going to fuck you, then I will gladly do so. So much that I'll mark and claim you all night and you won't even handle standing the next day. I want to do it when you're completely yourself, not in heat, so you will be aware of every single moment when we do it," he said intensely, breathing hard as if he would ravage me any minute now. "So, I'll have to stop now. Only the Moon Goddess knows how much I yearn for you. I'll leave now before my vampire blood completely takes over."

Before he could leave me hanging, I grabbed his hand and

replaced our positions, so I was the one who was caging him in, with his back against the wall.

"You're not going anywhere," I smirked, feeling like I just dominated him. Alpha Magnus looked at me. I couldn't bear the heat between my thighs now. Never in my life did I expect to be seduced like this. So much so that I was the one pushing Magnus. I couldn't even think straight, my mind hazy and running with dirty thoughts.

Goodness, I knew I would do something that I would regret but fuck that. Tonight was important.

"Don't blame me tomorrow." Instantly, his lips grabbed mine and he reversed our positions again, grabbing my body and throwing me on the bed.

He leaned in, and whispered, "You're so addicting, Kamilah. So much that I want to drain you, in and out."

"Then do it."

He instantly devoured my lips again, removing his shirt slowly while grabbing my two crowns. He played with them for a while before tearing my shirt apart and my pants, so that I was only in my underwear. He paused and took in the view.

His lips then tickled my face as he kissed the scar on my cheek, my insecurity…

"You're beautiful."

Instantly, his fangs came out, digging into my neck and I let him drain me. I felt the heat rushing out as his cold hands touched everywhere.

He seductively whispered into my ear, changing the mood, "I'm done draining your blood now. I'm craving for something else, baby."

"And what is that?" I asked, pretending not to have any idea what he was referring to. Knowing this man, he was referring to doing it.

He carefully ran his hands on my arms, trailing some

patterns slowly, and had this small smile on his face. "Oh, I know that you know exactly what I'm referring to."

"Is his related to quenching your thirst?" I teased, trying to just let him in for the ride.

He nodded. "Yes, but this one involves more action and less talking…" And with that, he was quick enough to claim my soft lips again and I watched as he closed his eyes, savoring the pleasure. I could taste my own sweet blood.

I didn't know why they were hyping it up so much, since it was ordinary for me, but I guess each had their own preference. He sucked on my lower lip, nibbling on it, then biting it slowly. He parted my mouth, his wet tongue asking for an entrance. He was teasing me and taking my breath away all the time.

Removing his pants, I tried to breathe but Magnus was sucking on my lips. His hands were cold and he was gripping my hair, almost like he couldn't get enough of me. He was only in his underwear and I could see his member throbbing, pulsating against the material.

He broke the kiss and looked into my eyes. "You don't know how much self-restraint I've had, baby. That I didn't even get laid waiting for you. For 150 years."

I tilted my head to the side, feeling a bit dazed by the kiss. I didn't even stop him from kissing me, not feeling guilty about it.

"Hmm… really? Never had a fling when I was gone?"

He shook his head. "No, there's no one who compares to you, baby. I didn't even try looking for any girl because I knew you'd come to me again."

I bit my lip, feeling my heart beating rapidly in anticipation. Our noses bumped each other, my body turning hotter each second and him remaining cold and pale, with his vampire blood. He breathed deeply, looking at me with heavy emotion in his eyes. He looked red, fierce and hot.

He was quick to respond because, in a minute, his hands were now massaging my two crowns while kissing them and back to my lips.

I trailed my hands on his hard abs and as always, I felt him shivering at my touch. He just smiled against our kiss and trailed soft kisses from my lips to my neck, and down to my collarbone.

He was an animal in front of me. His eyes were looking at my eyes while glorifying my body, his lips now sucking on my pearls. I let out a sound, and that urged him to continue what he was doing.

With his lips still sucking on my two crowns, his hands were doing wonders between my thighs and I felt myself getting wetter with each passing second.

He smirked as if reading what was on my mind. He paused to look at my body, which was still in my lacy under-wear, looking up and down just to admire it proudly. He trailed his hands on my body, and I trembled. He gulped, looking at me with heavy emotion. "Any final words before you hate me after this?"

"I don't, and I won't hate you." That was all I answered.

That made him stop. "You're really accepting me as your mate?"

Putting my lips on his to shush him, I said, "Just stop talking and go on."

His hands went to my breasts and massaged them. He then kissed my neck as he announced, "There is no way I'm going to let it end like than, not now when I have the chance to enchant you,"

As his tongue found its way into me and tormented my clit, he prepared my pearl. He made my body squirm by sucking, caressing, and massaging my clit. I was frantic, and I moaned with delight. Later, he began to insert his fingers inside while teasing me, causing me to expel some sticky material.

Suddenly, I remembered how loud I was screaming and how every wolf's senses were sensitive to sounds. I panicked. "They'll hear me."

Magnus paused. "Yes, and what's the problem? It's my packhouse, and everyone knows you are my mate."

He thought that everyone in his pack would know this night and hear every scream I'd make. It embarrassed me, but the pleasure itself outweighed it.

And with that, he put his pulsating member inside me, and I released a shaky breath, as he continued to bite me on the neck, my collarbone, and my breasts. I was sure it would leave a mark tomorrow. He was marking and claiming every place where it was visible.

He grabbed my cheek and whispered, "Scream all you want. So they'll know you're mine."

"You're so tight, baby," he started again. "I'm guessing we were on the same page and didn't get laid." He thrust inside me with one long, deep stroke. I rolled my eyes in pleasure as he continued.

As our bodies collided against each other in the dark night with only the moonlight offering light, it was cold, but the heat coming from our bodies made us sweat frantically. It was a quiet night with a few howling outside, but all I could hear was the ragged breathing and soft moans of each other.

I could feel the hot liquid coming out from him and entering me, giving me pleasure and satisfaction. He then settled himself on top of me, waiting for every drop to get inside me, and when finished, he laid beside me, gazing at my face.

We panted, catching our breaths and I wanted to close my eyes, but I felt his strong arms grabbing me and carrying me. We were both still naked…

"The night is still young, baby. Let's continue in the bath —I mean let's bathe together?" he asked, a lopsided grin on his face.

I gulped, knowing where it would lead to. "Your stamina is not running out?"

"No. I want more," he said, not even ashamed of it. "Are you tired already? Aren't you in heat?"

I smirked, not wanting to back down. "Who said I'm tired?"

He nodded. "Good, we'll save lots of water if we bathe together," he said and I agreed.

He had a point. For the rest of the night, I couldn't even catch a wink of sleep as Alpha Magnus continued on and on, even when the sun was up. He didn't even get tired. Neither did I.

I groaned in my sleep, loving how my dreams were so peaceful as I felt the morning sun hit me. I grabbed my pillow but felt some hard stone and hardwood instead of the soft texture.

I halted… noticing the smell. Wait a minute—

As soon as I opened my eyes, I saw a naked Alpha Magnus, along with his smile as he sat upright.

"Good morning, baby," his morning, deep voice greeted me. "Well, it's already afternoon."

I instantly sat upright, noticing I was naked too so I grabbed the blanket to me, which revealed his body to me and I instantly closed my eyes.

"What are you doing in my room!" I yelled. "Stay away from me."

"It's my room," he interjected and sighed, standing up as

he grabbed a pair of pants and threw them on. "And I knew this would happen."

I muttered a curse, what in the hell happened? My mind suddenly remembered what happened to me... to us last night and the flashback made me puke.

No, it was just a dream, right?

But the whole pain from my body, especially the thing between my thighs, just disproved it. And the marks all over my body too.

The marks that Alpha Magnus made.

I swallowed hard, taking it harshly. So it really happened. Damn it. Why was I so horny? I swear, I'll target the Moon Goddess myself and make her remove the "in heat" thing for us females.

I blamed my inner wolf, but she was still sleeping inside. Damn it. What now?

And worse, I could remember everything, except the part about how in the hell we arrived at his room.

Alpha Magnus smirked at me. "That was a peaceful night for me." Between us, he was the one who looked so refreshed. He seemed to enjoy what happened too much.

I hid my face from him. Now the whole pack will know that I was… marked.

"This is your fault," I roared angrily and he clutched his chest.

"My fault? Baby, you practically threw yourself at me last night. I held on and on but since it was a full moon, you couldn't blame my vampire blood."

I gritted my teeth. "You… drained me!"

I realized the words that left my mouth and he chuckled.

"I...apologize."

He then offered a glass of water from the table, but my pride wouldn't accept anything that he offered.

Just then, the door opened and a shocked Dimitri walked in.

"Alpha, you're late to the meeting…" he stopped, seeing me in his bed, and looked at the standing alpha, before darting his eyes back and forth between us and gulping. When he realized what was happening, he mumbled a curse, "Oh shit."

He instantly closed the door and yelled, "I didn't see anything!"

I glared at Alpha Magnus. "Great. Your beta saw us. Couldn't you mind-link him and warning him about not entering your room?"

He rubbed the back of his neck. "I… forgot."

I instantly wrapped the blanket around me and ran to my room, which was just next to this. Last night was something I never imagined I'd do, but my inner wolf seems to look forward from letting it to happen again.

Burn It

KAMILAH

"Good morning, Alpha Kamilah," Dimitri smiled at me and turned to his alpha, "And good morning, Alpha Magnus."

I had already showered and Alpha Magnus kept on gazing at me, which I've been ignoring. He forced me to sit in the dining room beside Dimitri, awkwardly.

I just glanced at Dimitri before glaring at the plate in front of me. Tension filled the room. There was nothing I wanted except to get eaten by the ground right now.

That was it. I'd leave.

I started to stand. "I'm not in the mood to eat—"

"You need to eat to regain your energy after what happened to us last night," Alpha Magnus said, stopping me from leaving.

Dimitri gulped. "I mean… I'm going to pretend I don't know anything and this is a relationship mate thing, but why am I seated between you two?"

Alpha Magnus clasped his hand. "Let's talk about earlier. You didn't see anything right?"

Dimitri nodded. "Yes! I promise!"

Alpha Magnus gave me a look. "See? He didn't, so I assure you—"

"Stop playing nice now. Everyone in this pack has heard that you already marked me last night. It's normal for the mate's thing, like you said," I said firmly, now accepting the harsh truth bitterly. "So let's move on."

Alpha Magnus nodded, his lips had formed a smirk, clearly enjoying this. "Alright." He then turned to his beta beside him. "What's my schedule today?"

Dimitri opened the tablet in his hands and started to enumerate the list of his schedule. "We're going to visit your company and instruct your new human employees, then we'll fly to the North West to have a business meeting with the Lycan king and discuss the Drucilla matter and imbalance in werewolves, along with—"

"Cancel everything," said Alpha Magnus, staring at me directly. "I'll spend my time on the most important thing for now."

I rolled my eyes. Starting to eat now, I tried to focus on the food as Alpha Magnus and Dimitri continued conversing. I was a bit glad that Dimitri was here to make him distracted and to ease off the tension between us.

After that, Alpha Magnus got a bit too clingy for my liking. I would walk around his pack and try to avoid him, but he would find a way to call for me.

'Kamilah, baby, I know you're avoiding me,' he said through the mind-link.

Yeah, mind-link. Stupid mind-link. After he marked me, we somehow had this connection that he could mind-link me now, just like 150 years ago when I was a member of his pack but severed that connection.

Damn it, I was not even enjoying the situation. I felt suffocated, but then my inner world would always find a way to gaslight me, saying I was reacting way too much.

'Don't tell me you hate this whole connection thing 'cause you know you can't escape this,' my inner wolf taunted and I rolled my eyes, ignoring her.

Alpha Magnus would then come every night to me, not to mark me again but to sleep beside me.

"Sleep on your own," I responded, and he stayed leaning on the wall of my door.

"Come on, I already marked you. We're tied now. Why are you so embarrassed when you were so aggressive to me that night?"

I gulped, avoiding his gaze. "That was... a one-time thing."

He sighed, disappointment in his voice. "You mean a one-night stand? If I knew this would only make you angry, then I shouldn't have let my instincts get to me that night." He paused. "But you hate me so much as your mate. If it's not about me being a hybrid, then what is it?"

"You don't understand," I answered, still remembering that night. I felt a bit traumatized... cementing my doubts about him.

He grabbed my hand. "Please explain it to me so that I can understand."

I turned to him. "One hundred fifty years ago... you remember? The night that I left you."

He blinked. "Yes?" he urged me to continue, wanting to be enlightened.

"I went into your room and saw you... drinking from a human."

He gasped. "That was a… full moon… my vampire blood took over. I wanted to drink your blood so badly but I didn't want to harm you, so I found the closest thing I could find."

I looked at him incredulously, processing his response. "That's it?"

He nodded. "Yes. I am telling the truth, you can ask Dimitri about it."

I couldn't help but chuckle. "You talked to me, saying you would treat me kindly but I had doubts, knowing your reputation as womanizer… And after seeing that, my doubts cemented. I knew I couldn't trust you as your mate without getting hurt."

As silly as it might sound and as shallow as it may appear, I could still feel that thing. I've been traumatized by men, I admit. I was scared of them, but I wouldn't tell that to Magnus.

"Forgive me for what I did in the past, Kamilah. If only I had known about this… I should have been better. I promise to be better for you if you'll let me…" he asked humbly. "I'll leave and let you think about it for now."

He then walked away, closing the door behind him and I breathed in, not knowing I was sucking in the breath I was holding.

But hearing him say that, I felt a bit pathetic and stupid for my reason. He was a hybrid, a rare occurrence and even he might be confused to understand himself sometimes. As a werewolf, it was hard for me to adjust growing up, having to learn how to survive and fight.

Alpha Magnus had it harder. He had to live his life a werewolf most of the days and a vampire every full moon, his blood fighting for dominance every time, craving for blood even when he tries his best to reject it.

I gulped, sitting in my room, looking at the window. Just

then, the door opened and a panting Dimitri showed me a piece of paper.

"What?"

He breathed deeply and let out, "I have news."

He breathed deeply and let it out. "I have news… Owen, he's gone."

I tilted my head to the side. "What?"

He cleared his throat, handing me the paper. "He left this paper in the room with your name on it."

I sensed Owen's smell on the paper and instantly opened it to see a letter inside. My eyes slowly grazed each letter, feeling a pang of my heart hurting.

To Kamilah,

Thank you for helping me, once again. I'll make sure to return the favor next time we meet. I'll be on my way now.

Take care.

-Owen.

I sighed. Problems after problems. But it was alright, Owen must have felt suffocated here and really wanted to leave again. We have to respect his decision as it was his life after all. But I didn't get to say goodbye to him.

I guess we'd see each other soon… who knew?

"Oh, and someone wanted to surprise you," said Dimitri, taking me away from my trance. The door opened and a familiar scent followed. Glancing at it, I saw the tiger, Lumiere, who jumped happily at the sight of me.

"Lumiere!"

I chuckled, feeling her tongue licking me.

"She's happy to see her owner," Dimitri commented.

"Awe, you must have missed me?" I asked, pinching my tiger's cheek and throwing a ball for her to play with.

I faced Dimitri. "How did she get here? I almost forgot about her!"

Dimitri smirked. "Well, let's just say someone wanted to make up to you."

I nodded, not even having to guess who it was. Of course, it had to be the someone who gave Lumiere to me… it was Alpha Magnus. I guess he thought it was a way to cheer me up.

Days passed by, with me killing time with my pet Lumiere and still not talking to Magnus. But I woke up one day with her not by my side anymore.

I instantly called Dimitri. "Where is Lumiere?"

He shrugged. "I don't know, I was out the whole day."

Just then, a patrol guard assigned came to us. "I saw your pet tiger getting caught by the humans."

I gasped. "What?"

"But Alpha Magnus has already gone to save her," he said and Dimitri gulped.

"This is bad, he gifted it to you, Kamilah! I know how angry he'll get now, he might burn the whole town trying to get the tiger," Dimitri shrieked. "Last time something like this happened, I barely even saved the humans. He'll probably listen to you, Kamilah."

I instantly ran to town, following Alpha Magnus's scent, and was directed to the local zoo. I watched as my lovely pet was caged and Alpha Magnus ran and spread gas everywhere. He took Lumiere out from the cage and had a match in his hand.

"Magnus!" I yelled, stopping him and grabbing Lumiere. "You're going to burn the whole place?"

He nodded, gritting his sharp jaw. "Yes, they keep messing things up. I want them to suffer."

"No, stop this, right this instant," I yelled, ordering him. "It's alright, Lumiere is fine."

Yes, I was angry at the humans, but I didn't want the whole town to suffer. I might have hated the humans, especially the Fowlers, but it was not enough for all of them to suffer. It was not all the humans' fault for the way they treated me. I thought about the innocent children and women who would be affected. I didn't want that to happen.

I instantly removed the match from his hand and hugged him. "Please, Magnus, let's just go back."

He seemed to somehow calm down and let me direct him to the pack. With Lumiere by my side, he walked behind me slowly.

He put his hands in his pockets. "So you're talking to me now?"

I sighed. "Depends on what you'll do."

"But you already hugged me."

I rolled my eyes, he sounded like a kid with how immature he sounded. "I'm tired, let's just head back."

As soon as we went back to his pack, I put a leash on Lumiere so she wouldn't wander around anymore. I laid on my bed, thinking of something to do. I felt so bored here, besides Lumiere keeping me company and I was sure Alpha Magnus would only bother me, and Dimitri would follow his orders.

I mean, what was I waiting here for? Some miracle? Drucilla might pause for his attacks now, and I was wondering what my pack was doing now since I'd been gone for weeks.

I was about to close my eyes when Alpha Magnus came into my room. "What is it?"

"I don't want you not talking to me. I can't sleep, Kamilah," he said, his voice filled with so much sadness.

I turned around. "Then sleep on your own."

"How about a thank you for saving your pet?" he asked.

"Yeah, thank you," I said tiredly and still kept my eyes closed.

Instantly, I felt him closer. "Then pat my head."

"Huh?" I asked, confused.

"I want you to pat my head," he repeated without blinking. Sitting upright, I did as he said since I didn't have the energy to argue anymore.

"Again, please." He pointed at my hand. "I want another pat on the head."

"What are you, five?" I asked, finding this weird but a bit... adorable.

He had a small pout on his lips. "No, but I want your touch. It's relaxing for me. Please, Kamilah?"

Clicking my tongue, I placed my hand on his head and patted him for a bit.

"Done, can I sleep now?" I asked, feeling so tired and wanting nothing but to sleep.

"Will you not avoid me tomorrow?" he asked hopefully.

I yawned. "Depends, Magnus, Depends."

He nodded. "Alright. Goodnight."

I was playing with Lumiere one morning when she suddenly hissed at the door.

"Lumiere? Is there something wrong?"

The door opened and a familiar scent appeared. "Did anyone miss me?"

Judging from the jolly voice and stingy scent of a vampire, I didn't have to turn around to see it was Gusev.

My eyes widened, seeing him alive and well. "Gusev!"

I instantly flung my arms around him without hesitating. "I'm glad you're alive."

He held my hair, slowly stroking it. "Seems that you

missed me so much, and of course, I'd always be alive." He then broke our hug. "You… smell different."

I blinked. "What?"

"Your blood… I mean, nothing happened to you after Drucilla had taken me, right?"

I nodded, slightly lying. A lot had happened without him, but he didn't have to know that.

Lumiere hissed at Gusev and Gusev jumped, closing the door and yelling, "What is that thing!"

"A tiger," I answered, wondering why Lumiere was hissing still. Then I remembered the reason. Alpha Magnus had gifted her to me the last time to push Gusev away from me. I chuckled, petting Lumiere. Vampires had a long history with big cats, but why is Lumiere still hissing at him?

"He's not an enemy, Lumiere." I soothed her, trying to calm her down. When she didn't, I just tied her leash to my bed frame and went outside, closing the door behind me.

Gusev gave a look at me. "I don't even have to ask why. I know Magnus gifted that to you…" He pouted. "He's so harsh to me!"

I just directed him to the living room and offered him tea. "So, how did you even get away from Drucilla?" I asked, changing the topic as he rambled on and on about Lumiere.

He scoffed. "Oh, I have my ways, but I couldn't forgive him for trying to confuse you and attempt to copy me. Did he think I was lowly like that? Hah. No one will ever be successful in copying me 'cause I'm born unique!" he said proudly then cleared his throat. "But I'm glad you're fine. I should have protected you, and I swear I will make him pay for that."

His eyes then darted behind me and he grinned brightly. "Hi best friend!"

Alpha Magnus's voice thundered behind me. "So you're here."

Gusev pouted. "Awe, aren't you happy that I'm finally here?"

Alpha Magnus instantly grabbed him by the throat. "No, how would we know you're really Gusev and not Drucilla again?"

Gusev rolled his eyes, seemingly not affected by his threats. "Yeah, be gentle with me, will you? I have gone through hardship! They tortured me there to spill some secrets about you but since I'm loyal, I didn't even dare!"

Alpha Magnus narrowed his eyes at him but then loosened his grip.

Gusev just stuck his tongue out at him and faced me. "Come on, I have a lot to talk to you about."

He motioned for me to follow but I felt Alpha Magnus's hands stopping me. "No, I need to talk to Kamilah about something."

I raised my eyebrows at him. "You do?"

Gusev crossed his arms in front of him. "And what is that? Is that more important than my news for her?"

Alpha Magnus gave him a look. "'Yes it is, now, Kamilah, let's go." He grabbed my hand but I pushed it away.

"I'll listen to what Gusev has to say first," I answered, and he breathed deeply, seemingly irritated.

Gusev gave a teasing look at him. "See? She likes me more than you. She must have gotten sick of your attitude, best friend. You need to change that."

Never in my life did I imagine that I'd prefer Gusev's company over my own mate.

As Gusev pulled me away from the house, he decided to let me walk around as he gossiped to me. "Did something happen between you and Magnus? The air is just different this time."

I shook my head, not wanting to answer that since we're kind of in a hot and cold type of relationship now.

"What were you going to say to me?"

He shrugged. "Nothing important. I just want to see his reaction. I miss teasing him."

We spotted Dimitri by Alpha Magnus's office, working. His eye bags were deeper and darker than usual and we decided to stop by. So that's why he did not come to me today.

He must have been too busy, taking over the alpha's tasks.

"Hi there, Dimitri!" Gusev yelled as soon as we opened the door.

"If you're here to disturb me, please leave. I did not get any sleep," was the first thing he said, not even moving his eyes off the piles of paperwork in front of him. Then his eyes saw Gusev and nodded at him. "Oh, Gusev, you're here."

"Wow, seems my best friend is pushing you hard enough you became a robot," Gusev commented. "And everyone's reactions here are so boring. I thought you'd miss me since I've been gone for a long time."

Dimitri scoffed. "What? You want us to throw you a party?"

"Yes!"

"Nice thought, but no,." Dimitri replied, and then looked at me. "And please don't stress out our alpha as I'm the one doing all his work now."

"That's not my problem anymore," I said teasingly, and he sighed.

"What did you do, poison our alpha? He's not so sweet like this," he complained.

"Want me to call Louisa?" I threatened, and his lifeless eyes suddenly brightened up.

"That would be amazing, but I don't want her to see me tired now."

Deciding to give him a break, Gusev and I just left him and walked around until he raised his eyebrows playfully to me. "So he finally marked you."

I blinked, wanting to ask how did he learn it but it was a bit obvious now, with the marks that Alpha Magnus made still not leaving my body.

He smirked. "You're wondering how I even learned it aside from it being obvious? Well, it's everywhere, I could hear everyone here is talking about it."

I gritted my teeth, feeling embarrassed but I guess I have to get used to it. It was not like I could turn back the time.

Gusev's smirk turned into an evil smile and he leaned in and whispered in my ear, "Don't worry, since I'm here, I'll make him jealous. See if he cares enough."

I cocked my eyebrows. "What are you planning now?"

"Oh, it's a secret."

Beg for me

KAMILAH

That was what Gusev said, but I shouldn't have trusted him.

He was acting all lovey-dovey on me, purposely grabbing me from Alpha Magnus every breakfast and only returning me late at night.

This triggered Magnus so much that he didn't make it past three days. "You're hanging out with Gusev lately," Alpha Magnus said, dropping the fork as he looked at me during our breakfast.

Any minute now, Gusev will come. Just then, Gusev appeared with his usual grin as if nothing was happening. "Hey, Alpha Magnus, I'm going to borrow Kamilah—"

"That's it. Leave, Gusev. Now," Alpha Magnus cut his sentence off before he could finish. Gusev and I exchanged looks.

"Awe, why? You're no fun!" Gusev complained but Alpha Magnus stood up.

"You're talking away my tie from her purposely, I let it pass last time, but it's enough now."

He then faced me. "As for you, let's talk." I stood up, wanting to fight back as Gusev waved at me and I glared at him.

Great, things were not even good between us and Gusev is making it worse.

"So tell me, did you enjoy being with him?" he asked, making me sit on the bed.

I gulped, this is the first time I came to his room after that… night. Feeling a bit nervous, I stood up and tried to mask it. "Let's talk outside."

He grabbed my hand and pushed me to the wall harshly. "Why not here? Are you scared that I will do something again?" He smirked. "Don't worry, it's you who will beg for me. I won't even do anything, other than punish you."

The look of horror on my face was evident and Magnus was clearly enjoying this. I gulped, not sure of anything anymore. But worse, why was I looking forward to the thought of it?

No way, Kamilah.

"I was controlling myself this day, Kamilah. I've been patient enough to give you space, but you're still avoiding me," he said. "I can't wait any more. No one will help you if you scream, princess."

I scoffed at that. Sure, I was clearly scared of it all, in this state and the way he was advancing at me but damn... my eyes slid to his broad shoulders and up to his lips, knowing all too well how they taste.

"Then what are you going to do to me? You're all words, Magnus," I said, daring him. "One moment you're weak and cute to me, and next you're advancing at me, threatening me."

His eyes, looking all challenged, didn't look like he was expecting me to say that.

"Do you want me to be honest?" he asked me with the thought of having no problem being honest, knowing things could lead to something more.

He was making it seem like he was giving me the choice to back away from this conversation, now, before he revealed exactly how impure and worldly a man like him was around a pure woman like me.

"Yes," I whispered, peering up at him.

He smirked, wanting me to hear exactly what he was going to say, so that I understood how serious this all was. I was still looking up at him with interest, with slight curiousness and daringness.

"Fine, then. I've wanted to fuck you again after that night," he said, watching me. I was surprised at his blunt lewdness. Since he was still caging me in, I couldn't even do anything except suck my breath as his breath tickled my nose.

"I was desperate to have you here in my room again. I can't stop thinking about pushing your pants down to your ankles and nuzzling into your flesh until my face smells like you. I want to bite your crowns through that white shirt."

Hearing all that, my lips part but no sound comes out. My eyes were wide and searching his, and I was breathing fast, so fast that he knew for sure that I was hearing and understanding every word.

Magnus continued, "Yes, I loved to be around women, baby. I love to give women pleasure. I love to see their snug little flesh, I love to taste them and push my big member into them until they stretch. I love feeling a girl's ass clench around my finger as I tongue their pleasure zone. But most of all, I love to do it all to you. Right here, right now."

My cheeks reddened so much with all those words he uttered. This was the first time I had heard a man saying this bluntly and to my face. I swallowed hard, my thoughts encircling my imagination. I couldn't even think of a proper comeback, still stuck with words in my brain and how fast my heart was beating.

Magnus then unbuttoned his black shirt, and sat on his bed, parting his thighs so I could see exactly how urgently he wanted it. Wanted me?

"Oh," I breathed out, my eyes dropping to the thick outline in his trousers.

I couldn't stop staring at his erection, licking my lips as I looked.

He then mind-linked me as he gazed.

"I couldn't stop thinking about how those lips would give and mold under my member. How they would yield to my teeth, stretch around my organ as I carefully, tenderly slid into the back of your throat."

Hearing his words in my mind, did nothing but scare me. I struggled to drag my eyes back up to his face. My cheeks warm again, possibly in embarrassment or arousal, or some combination of the two. I couldn't even control my own body now.

"The problem is you being turned on?" I took a step forward, my hands back in my pockets as I approached him until I was completely in front of him.

He traced a line down the point of my chin, dropping to finger the starchy collar of my shirt. "The problem isn't that I want to enter you. The problem is that I want you to beg for me Kamilah and I can't control you anymore."

"That seems strange," I murmured, my breath catching as his finger went slightly lower than my collar and started toying with the chain of my necklace. "Why are you stopping yourself? Drop your pride, Magnus," I ushered, daring him.

I didn't know where all this courage came from, but I sure as hell had no plan of giving up. I knew Gusev was still outside, he must have heard every word. I could also feel Dimitri had come to take him away, probably on Magnus's order.

The way my lips creased ever so slightly as I talked, the flick of my tongue as I shaped my words. His member is painfully aware of how close it was to me—just a few inches more and he could press right into my belly, grinding away the ache I gave him.

"About that night…" I dared to bring it up, not wanting this heavy tension around us anymore. "Did you enjoy it personally? Or you enjoyed it because I am your mate?"

He shrugged. "Both."

His body responded before his mind, his heart hammering quickly and his memories whirring like a merry-go-round, bringing up half-forgotten feelings. Feelings of magic and mystery and moreness, as if I spoke a language I only heard in dreams, I pretended I didn't dream. I carried a shadow of his past, his childhood. Young, carefree, and so alive.

Magnus jerked back as he realized what he was doing, how close he was to me… How close he was in grabbing his own member just to rub at the throbbing need.

Since my pride was taking over again, and my inner wolf was fully awakened now, all my courage was from there. I knew I was fully sober, not in heat now. I knew perfectly what I was doing.

So I wouldn't have any other reason to say anything to him next time if I regretted doing this.

Since the situation has come to this, I didn't have a choice.

My eyelashes fluttered and I put my hand flat on the middle of his chest. And then I slid it down his stomach.

"Kamilah," he grunted and cursed under his breath, noting how his member was practically drilling a hole through his pants, begging for it. Begging for me. And this gave me power.

Maybe it was not so bad after all.

"What? Didn't you say you want me to beg for you? What's happening now?" I smirked at him.

My hands moved down to his thighs and to his layers of clothes and I murmured, "Huh? Talk to me, Magnus."

Magnus seemed to pause, thinking how did I suddenly get all the power. Him trapped in a trance. How did I end up taking control and how did he end up trapped and feebly protesting? "Magnus?"

Hearing me call his name, Magnus knew it was over, it was done. His control snapped like a cord and he groaned before he yanked me into a searing, burning kiss, lost balance, and ended up laying on top of him.

I couldn't even bring myself to smack him away and actually enjoyed it.

I could feel his cold hand grazing me as he trailed his eyes up and down. There was lust, eagerness, temptation, and hope, all bottled up in his eyes.

In an instant, he slammed his lips on mine and said in between breaths, "If you don't like what I'm doing, then tell me to stop,"

I chuckled lightly and shook my head. "No, continue."

Magnus smiled at that as our lips intertwined. Instantly, he grabbed my clothes.

He pulled on my clothes, slowly undressing me as he trailed small kisses on my ear, neck, down to the collarbone, then paused until I was in my underwear. He stared at the sight, admiring the view. "Wow."

I didn't know what to feel but I felt hot all of a sudden, feeling all the wet trails of kisses he left. He then removed his shirt too, showcasing his bare chest, and water droplets trailed from his sharp jaw to his chest and down to his chiseled abs.

It was not like a bare-chested man was new to me, but it was more the person. I just smiled as he continued on, his hand grabbing my butt.

My lips met with his soft lips and I watched as he closed his eyes, savoring the pleasure. He sucked on my lower lip, nibbling on it and biting it slowly.

Magnus parted my mouth with his wet tongue, asking for an entrance. He was teasing me and taking my breath away at the same time.

I tried to breathe but he was sucking on it. His hands were cold and he was gripping my hair, almost like he couldn't get enough of me. As if he waited for this all this time and now, he was engulfed in every second of it.

Panting, he still savored the taste until he ran out of breath and broke the kiss.

He breathed deeply, looking at me with heavy emotion in his eyes. He looked red, fierce and hot.

I bit my lip, wondering what just happened. He seemed to be waiting for any reaction and he spoke up. "I can't take it anymore, Kamilah. I can't resist you."

Same. I hated to admit it but now, I was too busy thinking of his lips. I couldn't help but want more…

More of Magnus.

I never thought things would turn out this way. I'm tongue-tied and lost in bliss. It might be because he had already marked me and I just easily gave in to him.

The way Magnus looked at me tempted me to initiate the

move now. He wanted to ask for permission, if we should continue, scared it would lead to me avoiding him again, but he was afraid so he kept quiet.

I stared at his lips, and at his dark eyes which were circled with beautiful golden hues… they looked so beautiful now… gazing at me and waiting for me to make a move.

Oh, screw it. Just for today.

Leaning toward him, I instantly slammed my lips on his and grabbed his hair. My hands made their way to his chest and I touched his hard abs. I felt him shivering at my touch, but he smiled against our kiss and he trailed soft kisses from my lips to my neck, and down to my collarbone.

Magnus looked like a raging animal who couldn't be stopped. He was breathing hard, and he was staring at my body intently.

With his fully exposed abs and me in my underwear, he took in the sight and released a shaky breath at my beautiful figure.

He missed my touch. He mumbled a curse under his breath.

I smirked at the sight in front of me. A shirtless Magnus, begging for me, craving and lusting for me. I hated the thought of him touching me before, but why couldn't I hate him now?

The light was a bit dim as he had turned off the lights earlier, setting up a romantic vibe all over the place.

At this point, I felt like I had control over him.

Magnus released a chuckle. "Goodness, you're really tempting me," he said, now planting a soft kiss on my forehead. "You taste so good, Kamilah... I want to taste every inch of you. Slowly so I'll savor each time."

His hands were on my breasts now, and I felt myself feeling wet from his touch.

Suddenly, he paused and gazed into my eyes. "I don't think I could stop if I continue."

I shook my head disappointedly. "You should have thought of that before kissing me."

He then laughed. "Right. My mistake."

And he continued kissing me like there was no tomorrow. He rubbed his thigh on me, and I could feel his hard-on grazing against my skin.

The two of us kept on teasing each other, with his mouth now nibbling on my breasts, his hands touching my pearl, and me stroking his erect manhood up and down. They stayed like that, as his hands prepared my insides for him.

Magnus watched me get turned on, then put his fingers on his lips and licked them. "Damn, and I could taste this forever."

My cheeks flushed red and I felt more turned on now.

And with that, I looked at his hard erect member. Damn, I couldn't remember how big it was since I was in heat… but looking at it now in front of me, I gulped.

He didn't put it inside but instead, he teased my entrance. He slowly put it inside and I groaned both from pain and pleasure. I couldn't think straight as my desire overcame me.

He was now on top of me and thrust deep inside me. My waist danced to the rhythm too, as we gazed at each other.

<h1 style="text-align:center">To the Rhythm</h1>

KAMILAH

I smiled as he clasped his hand on mine, still thrusting on top of me. He teased his erect manhood in me and I couldn't help the moans that escaped my lips.

"Ugh, Magnus."

He leaned in to whisper to me, "You've been calling my name many times now." Despite the dim light, I could see the proud look on his face and I bit my lip.

I wanted to retort but my voice was busy yelling in pleasure.

He put his hand on my mouth. "I know I have amazing skills in bed..." he teased.

Good thing that the bed was stable as I was afraid that he might destroy the frame.

"Well, just kidding. You can scream all you want. Scream my name louder, Kamilah. It's only me and you."

I went red at that. And adding on to the teasing of me, he went faster and harder until I couldn't take it anymore.

As I released a liquid, he still kept on going.

I stared at him and he just smiled at me. "What? The day is still young, my dear."

Day? Goodness, to think we did it in the middle of the day.

And with that, I just let him do what he wanted. The pleasure was too much to bear and we kept on going until night time came.

As if he couldn't get enough of me, his strong hands carried me and put me in different positions. He kept on thrusting like there was no tomorrow and he groaned.

Too much of him thrusting, made the bed frame break. He paused and looked at the bed. "I'll just buy a new one next time."

I chuckled, finding it funny. The heated and sexy tension that lingered in the room turned to light. This passionate night would surely have a safe place in my mind. And as we finished more rounds than I could count, he laid beside me, holding my hand and gazing at my eyes.

Never in my life did I imagine getting excited and content like this. He didn't say anything, but his eyes held a heavy emotion.

"Why are you staring at me?" I asked.

"It's just… I'm thinking of how I should have done this sooner," he simply responded.

I curled an eyebrow. "Like getting me in bed?" I said in an attempt to lighten the atmosphere and he just chuckled lowly.

"I mean, confronting you." He didn't say any retort other than that and stood up, revealing himself naked and showing his oh-so-glorious 'thing'.

I sat upright. "Where are you going?"

"I'll go grab some towels to help you clean up," he

replied and disappeared. I couldn't shrug away the feeling of hollow emptiness settling in my stomach.

What now, Kamilah? I asked myself. I knew this wasn't my first time with him, but it was the first time that I enjoyed it like this.

Did I regret it?

No.

Did I enjoy it?

Definitely yes. He was surprisingly gentle with me… opposite of his usual aggressive and intimidating self. It felt like he was treating me as if I were a delicate flower, with so much care, and gentleness.

When Magnus returned with some tissues, he wiped me clean and stayed beside me. "A… cuddle. I want a cuddle with you."

I gave him a look. "I didn't think you would be asking me that."

"Please?" His eyes looked at me hopefully and I sighed.

"Alright, come here." I pulled his body near me until I could feel his breath fanning on my face, his nose only a few inches from me, and I glanced at his lips before pulling his head to my chest, embracing him. He sighed in relief, looking at me with a smile.

He then grabbed me and wrapped his arms around me, spooning me from behind, inhaling my scent. "I want to stay like this forever, Kamilah, baby."

I just smiled, feeling comfortable with his touch and closing my eyes to relax. Somehow, I was surprisingly relaxed in his arms.

Again, in Alpha Magnus's arms. The alpha that I dreaded a long time ago, the alpha I ran away from, and the alpha that I kept on pushing away, was now lying beside me after he planted his seed in me.

Well, I officially accepted that I couldn't get Magnus to push me away from his life, so might as well do something about it and seized the moment.

I hated to admit how my relationship with Magnus was slowly developing. I felt like I was losing the strong and independent woman who didn't need a man. Alpha Kamilah was what I'd been trying to project. But deep inside, I knew too well how I'd been craving someone's touch. No, Alpha Magnus's touch.

'I like his wolf,' said my inner wolf suddenly. *'Don't run away from him anymore, alright?'*

'You're finally falling for your mate,' my inner wolf teased and I rolled my eyes. Falling? No, that was another matter to think of.

Thank goodness Louisa was not here, cause if she was, she wouldn't let me breathe, teasing me. I had enough with my inner wolf poking fun at me. We didn't want another one to add to it. Plus, Gusev clearly knew what was happening so I didn't even know how to face him now. He was going to be making fun of me for sure.

ALPHA MAGNUS

"Magnus," I heard my father calling me. "You need to focus."

I looked at him, same old eyes, same black hair and his thick mustache, his tall and intimidating stature.

I looked around, noticing we were on the training grounds. Seeing I was shirtless, I already knew I was training with him.

"You need to get stronger than anyone else. Do not trust

anyone. Not even your own mate," he warned and I heard some voice calling me.

"Magnus, love, rest first, don't listen to your dad." I looked at my mother's graceful smile, brightening up my day like usual. With her pale white skin and her usual red eyes, she avoided the sun, hating how it hit her skin.

And my father scoffed. "If he wants to be like me, then he has to train hard early on." My father then grabbed her waist and kissed her on the lips. "Right, babe?"

I rolled my eyes. We had been living in the mountain area, away from anyone else.

But then, a bright light came from the woods. My father's ear perked up and he grabbed both of us to pull behind him. Squinting his eyes, my mother gasped, her keen senses alarming her about something. "They… found us."

My father's eyes widened in alertness, and this was the first time I had seen him so scared as he looked at me with determination. "Magnus, look at me. I need you to use the skills I taught you."

"Why? What's happening?" I asked, confused.

My father gulped, glancing at my mother who seemed to already know it. "What's happening, Father?"

He kissed me on the forehead and pulled us into a hug, "Remember, I love you. It's just I had made a selfish mistake that I can't reverse. But please protect your mother."

And with that, he gave a long kiss to my mother as my mother's tears fell endlessly. "Be careful."

"We'll meet there. I'll just make this quick," my father reassured us and instantly shifted into his huge wolf, running to the forest where the light was.

My mother then grabbed my hands. "Let's go. It's dangerous here."

But I stopped her, still watching Father's figure. "But what about Father? We need to help him, Mother."

My mother just smiled, feigning happiness but I could see the sadness in her eyes. "We'll meet him at the meeting place that we agreed on."

But then, as soon as we got to the lake, we were surrounded by more rogues. And the elder, Drucilla.

My mother hissed, protectively pushing me behind her. "So you diverted my husband's attention to corner us here. How original, you bastard."

Drucilla, smirked at us. "Why correct, vampire." His filthy gaze then trailed to me. "It's not him that I want. It's you and your little hybrid."

My mother's grip tightened. "If you want me, then let our son go. He's innocent."

I knew my mother was strong, her strength was up to par with my father's, but being surrounded like this caused a disadvantage to her.

Drucilla puckered his lips, mocking my mother. "No, he's the product of your selfish decisions. We need to eradicate anything like that."

My mother, knowing what would happen, glanced at me and yelled, "Run, Magnus!"

I could hear Drucilla's laughter, but my mother shoved me away, and my feet instantly knew what to do. I ran away, not even glancing back, just praying to the Moon Goddess to help us. For my father to appear.

But that was the last time I prayed to the Moon Goddess. The last time I had hope left because I lost faith in her. In everything. However it was all too late as I could hear my mother's loud rage and cries for help, and tears stung in my eyes.

I felt a sharp claw grabbing me. Some of Drucilla's men had caught up with me but I still continued running away.

"Poor, little pup. Where's your almighty coward father, eh?" They mocked me, but in an instant, I caught a whiff of my father's scent.

"Magnus, where is your mother?! Tell me where!"

My eyes flickered open instantly, sweat all over my face and goosebumps over my body. I glanced to see Kamilah, my mate, sleeping peacefully and I let out a relieved sigh.

That was a dream, I reassure myself. Just a dream and I was in the present now. Looking back, I hated a lot of creatures, but what I hated the most was Drucilla. I was suddenly reminded of the past, how my mother, my loving mother died because of Drucilla's schemes.

My father, the past alpha of this pack, had fallen in love with my vampire mother and changed their fate, making my mother pregnant. Since it contradicted the balance of the world, a mere hybrid should not be alive. It was a taboo topic for everyone.

My mere existence itself was a sin, created by my selfish father who went against the nature of the world.

As soon as I was born, my father had willingly given up his role as the leader of the pack, betraying the whole pack, his parents, and his own origin.

He was that willing and ready to give up everything he owned just to live with my vampire mother. At that time, our clan of werewolves and the vampires didn't have a harmonious relationship. So being together like what my mother and father did was a curse already.

Drucilla, the elder, heard of this and killed his mother. My mother got killed by Drucilla, and my father arrived, trying to protect me. After losing his loved one, my father was driven by revenge, seemingly losing himself that he trained me to death.

He would be so harsh on me for years, every day nonstop, blaming everything on me, until there came a time when I had enough.

"It's your fault! I am a hybrid! I'm tired of being hated!" I raged in anger, glaring at him with so much hatred.

"That is why you need to get stronger and kill them all! For what they did to your mother!" my father responded, pushing me to the tree and his fangs showed.

I gritted my teeth, tired of hearing that every day. That was my driving force every day, somehow engraved in my mind. After pushing me to my limits and making sure he endorsed my values, my father suddenly lost his energy and became bedridden. He then stepped down from his position, with his last words, "Remember, revenge your mother."

I felt Kamilah's hand grabbing mine, cutting me off from my thoughts as she tried to get my attention. "Hey."

"Hey." I smiled at her, pecking at her lips and stealing a kiss.

Days had been such a bliss for me. Kamilah stayed by my side and did not escape, letting me roam around her body whenever I wanted to.

I never wanted this concept of mate thing in my entire life, except now that I experienced it myself.

I had never felt at peace until now.

"A… cuddle. I want a cuddle with you," I asked her and she gave me a look.

"I didn't think you would be asking me that."

I pouted, looking at her hopefully. "Please?"

She stared at my eyes and watched my expression before sighing. "Alright, come here."

I smiled in victory as I pulled her body near me until I

could feel her breath fanning on my face, her heartbeat, and her nose only a few inches from me. I glanced at her lips before pulling her head to my chest, embracing her.

I sighed in relief, looking at her with a smile and contentment.

I then grabbed her and wrapped my arms around her, spooning her from behind and inhaling her sweet scent. "I want to stay like this forever."

She just smiled, feeling comfortable with my touch and closing her eyes to relax.

I gazed at her relaxed face. Who would have expected that we'd be in this position, 150 years ago?

She left me, she ran away from me, and she hated me to the core 150 years ago.

Those were the hurtful moments I had but now, I wouldn't mind going back in time and experiencing that pain again if I knew that I'd get to experience this happiness now.

"You're just so beautiful," I whispered in her ear, tickling her with my breath, "Have you had a good night's sleep?"

She nodded, replying to me honestly, "The best sleep I had in a while."

I nodded, now grinning like a fool, and asked again, "Do you have plans for today?"

She thought about it and shrugged. "Hmm… I think not…"

"So you're going to see Gusev again?" I asked, making sure she learned her lesson. Or else I'd have to punish her again. Harder than last night.

The thought itself brought excitement to me.

"I've been punished enough last night… I don't think I will."

"I see… then it's my privilege," I replied and she closed her eyes and relaxed again when she suddenly stilled.

She chuckled. "Something hard is poking me."

Hearing that, my body stiffened and I quickly backed away, not realizing I had a hard-on again.

Kamilah chuckled even more at my reaction.

"Oh, I'm sorry, I wasn't... I mean—"

"You're hard," she stated, teasing me even more. "We're just cuddling you know... Or are you thinking of something else?"

I shook my head, wanting to deny it but it was already too late. "No, I mean... it's just my morning wood."

Well, thoughts have been running in my head, honestly. With her by my side, not just random thoughts but... thoughts including all the positions I could put her in for the whole night.

Important Guest

KAMILAH

The fresh and cool breeze of air wrapped around me. Fluttering my eyes open, I got the best sleep I ever had in my life in his arms. This had been very surprising for me as I had always been tense around him in the past, but now… it was different.

I usually had nightmares from my past, from Darian, Valentina, to Alpha Rufus, or the rogues attacking my pack again, but now, nothing. I glanced around to see I was in my own room now. He must have carried me to my room… and beside me was empty. After staying in his bed for a week, this was the first time I got out of his room. It felt strange to be in my own room now.

I bit my lip, thinking about it. Getting up and preparing for the day, I saw a tray of food on the bedside table carefully prepared by him. I went to it and saw a handwritten note written on a yellow pad of paper in black ink.

I know you'll wake up by lunch so eat this, beautiful. I'll be in my office - Magnus

I smiled at the way his handwriting looked on the paper. The food was also cold now but I ate it without hesitation.

Then, the door opened and a grinning Gusev appeared. "After a week, you're finally out."

I looked at him. "I'm surprised Magnus still left you alive."

He smiled. "Well, I'm his best friend, he can't just kill me... So, how's your honeymoon phase?"

"What honeymoon phase?" I acted innocently.

"Don't bother hiding it, your face says it all," he said, teasing me. He then pets Lumiere from the corner.

"And update, we're buddies too!" Gusev said as Lumiere went closer to him.

I gave him a look. "You tamed her? Good job."

He beamed at me. "Yeah, since I was the one who fed her to stay alive while her owner had the TIME of her life," he said purposely, emphasizing the time.

"I'll buy another pet that will drive Gusev away," I heard Magnus say from the back. He kissed my temple and Gusev scrunched his nose in disgust, watching his action.

"Ew. I think I'll die because of the sweetness of you two." Standing up, he went to the door. "I'll leave now, I have work to do."

As soon as Gusev left, Magnus leaned into me and whispered to my ear, "Let's go to my room."

I rolled my eyes, knowing exactly what would happen the moment we went to that place. "C'mon, haven't you had enough?"

He pouted. "Please, baby?" I was about to reply when Magnus's ears perked up.

"What's happening?" I asked and he shook his head.

"Dimitri just sent me a message. We have a visitor."

I gave him a look, "Who?"

He shrugged. "An old friend of mine."

My phone then rang, and I opened it to see it was Dimitri. Magnus's expression stopped. "Don't answer it."

But I did answer it even against his wishes. "Hello, what's wrong, Dimitri?"

"Can you ask Alpha Magnus to follow my request? His guest is waiting here outside the borders."

I glanced at Magnus who was crossing his arms in front of him. "What request? That guest has paws and fangs, he can perfectly come here on his own."

I could hear Dimitri's stress as he sighed through the phone. "See? He's always like that! Ignoring the important etiquette! The alpha of the pack should always welcome the important guests but here am I, doing it for him! Please convince him to come here now, Kamilah."

"Tell me who that guest is," I ordered, still giving a weird look toward Magnus. Who makes him feel like this?

"It's Lycan King Ace."

As soon as Dimitri said that, I gasped and yelled at Magnus, so it really was an important person!

I smirked, he could be a big help to us for us to kill Drucilla.

I dropped the call and gave a lopsided grin to Magnus. "Looks like you really made an important friend, Magnus. Come on, we need to greet him according to the norms."

Magnus stomped his feet stubbornly. "Why did he come here anyway?"

After a few pleas and coos, I managed to convince Magnus to go to where Dimitri was and we ran fast to get there.

After nearing the borders, I sniffed the air and smelled an unknown and strange scent. Strange scent but a commanding aura. Just like Magnus.

I could see the sweat on Dimitri's forehead leaving as soon as we arrived at the place.

Standing face to face with the tall and brooding man in front of us, I watched as his serious and stoned face changed into a small smile as he greeted, "Magnus."

He had dark emerald eyes with his raven hair. He stood the same height as Magnus as they faced eye to eye. Tall, brooding, masculine as his tanned skin glowed in the sunlight, his thin white shirt almost hiding his six-pack abs and hard muscles.

He had two of his men behind him, the same height as Dimitri but also intimidating like their alpha.

Magnus scoffed. "Why did you come here?"

Dimitri's eyes widened and signaled to me. I lightly hit Magnus in the ribs and he let out a strangled noise and cleared his throat to cover it.

The Lycan king smirked. "Aren't you going to greet your old friend?"

Magnus crossed his arms in front of him and snorted. "You just come here every time there's trouble".

Lycan King Ace released a chuckle. "Right. Let's end this little chitchat and get to the reason why I am visiting today. Because I heard the news, and I have a different reason."

The Lycan king glanced at me, looking at me up and down and I stood my ground, not even intimidated by him.

Dimitri offered to let them settle in the pack first before directing them to Magnus's office to have a meeting.

Before going inside, Magnus and Dimitri pulled me aside to have a little conversation. "I hate the way he stares at you."

I rolled my eyes. "Are you jealous?"

Dimitri pushed Magnus's head. "This is not time for that. If you need a victory, we need the Lycan king on our side. I already arranged the documents that you planned out."

Magnus cocked his head to the side. "Oh? I changed my mind. We can handle it without him."

Dimitri sighed. "Alphas and their pride. Just do this for Kamilah, will you?"

I nodded, looking at Magnus.

He bit his lip, contemplating until he gave in. "Fine."

Smiling in victory, Dimitri high-fived me and started to enter Magnus's Office.

I decided to join in as this was also a bit about me. The Lycan king glanced at me, which was the first time he had done so the entire time.

He offered a polite smile. "So you're Kamilah, Magnus's mate."

I nodded, not even bothering to deny it. Guess my popularity is increasing so much these days. Good job, Drucilla.

"I believe I am, Lycan king," I answered.

"Call me Ace. Lycan king is too long," he offered and I nodded.

"Alright, Ace."

I could sense Magnus glaring at him and he cleared his throat. "Speak, Ace."

The Lycan king turned to him. "My area, the North West, has been wreaking havoc. I noticed something strange going on. I came here today to inform you about the werewolves smuggling in the werewolf steroids, under Drucilla's men. They seem to be so keen on eradicating you two."

I gritted my teeth. "A few months back, my pack member Tamara was affected by this. She was killed by rogues who digested the steroids."

"It was my past members who invaded her territory, because of Drucilla's orders," Magnus chimed in.

Lycan King Ace nodded. "A few days ago, I discovered a factory containing steroids and destroyed it. But I believe there are a few more factories located in this area."

Dimitri then grabbed a paper. "We had investigated the area and found a few more."

Lycan King Ace leaned back. "Why didn't you destroy them?"

Magnus stood up and smirked. "Because I believe it's your job. We are too preoccupied with killing Drucilla ourselves."

The Lycan king closed his eyes, and sighed. "And in exchange for this information, what's the deal you want?"

Magnus clasped his hands together. "Join us in the war."

Two of the Lycan king's men stood up and were about to attack us when he stopped them. He calmly stood up. "This is out of my area."

"No, this is also your area. Drucilla covers the whole of West while you cover North West. What if all the elders from other continents join hands and eradicate him? You all know that Drucilla has been the problem all these years and yet you did nothing but let him rule over you."

The Lycan king smirked at that, acknowledging his defeat. "You're still the same. You planned this all out pretty well."

Magnus nodded. "And I did a huge favor for you last time. Why not return it back? Aren't we friends, like you said?"

He stood up. "I'll think about it."

They then left the pack instantly and promised to come back to help us.

<h1 style="text-align:center">The Perfect Time</h1>

KAMILAH

The day went by, with Gusev visiting for a second.

Since Dimitri and Magnus went out, I was left with my pet Lumiere and Gusev looking at me distantly.

"Is Magnus away?" he asked, there was something different to him today—I knew it was him and not others posing as him—it was just that his behavior changed. Even Lumiere hissed and stood beside me protectively as Gusev stepped forward to me.

"Do you really love him or do you just love him because he's your mate?" he asked and I widened my eyes. What is he asking me?

"You're acting strange, Gusev," I replied, now a bit nervous.

He smiled sinisterly. "What if I kill him? Will you love me then?"

"Be careful what you are saying, Gusev," I warned him as he continued on.

"Oh, well, I guess I have to reveal it now. My feelings for

you are growing, Kamilah," he said, staring me dead in the eye. For Gusev to act so seriously, this is a big deal. He was never serious.

I shook my head. "Why are you telling me all of this? I have Magnus."

"Just to get it off my chest. I could woo you and be patient, I have a long life after all, but your heart has already chosen Magnus."

I gasped in shock. "Does Magnus know this?"

He shook his head. "I'm not that dumb to risk my life."

I breathed deeply, my head hammering with so many thoughts now. I have a lot going on in my head and this one adds to it. Ugh.

Biting my lip, I gulped. "Leave, Gusev. I know that feeling is just temporary."

He smiled bitterly at me. "Yeah, temporary. Like the humans I fell in love with. I thought I would have a chance 150 years ago when you left Magnus." He walked away after saying that.

I knew that was the last time I would see him. I felt an empty space in my heart, but Gusev had to do that. If I knew he would get attached to me like that... then I should have stopped it.

I was left alone in the house for a few more minutes when I heard Magnus's voice in my head.

'Kamilah, did Dimitri came home?' My eyebrows creased, *'No, He wasn't here. I thought you were with him?'*

'We were, but a black smoke blocked us, and Dimitri was gone. I couldn't even mind-link him.'

I gritted my teeth. *'It must be Drucilla.'*

He sighed. *'I'll take care of this. Stay there.'*

'Too late for that.' I instantly ran and tried to follow their

scent. Wherever Drucilla was, he might have kept Dimitri alive.

Stupid schemes. He always got the person close to us, knowing he couldn't get near us.

Just then, I stopped, feeling like I was getting sucked into a black hole.

"There you are, Kamilah!" A sarcastic familiar voice exclaimed. Drucilla. I felt all my senses going weak and I had to force myself to see. But there was only blackness.

"What an original plan there, Drucilla," I sarcastically replied, referring to the last time I was kidnapped by the human Fowlers.

"Missed me, Kamilah? It's been a long time," he said. "I have my men surrounding you."

I sniffed the air and faintly knew it. I could tell it, there were around 200 of his men around the area from various clans.

I chuckled at what he said, still, my senses were weakened. "Wow, what a pleasure. You're taking many precautions. Scared I'll get away again?"

He scoffed. "Stop pretending you're strong, dear. This will be your last breath living."

"No, you mean your last? We have you surrounded now," I heard another voice chiming in. I didn't have to see it as I instantly knew it was Magnus, with his own men. We had around 300 of us, but I couldn't deny all the power we had. Quality always overpowers quantity. I could feel him approaching me and kissing my neck. "Did we arrive late?"

"Just at the perfect time," I said. "This will be fun." Magnus then carried me and I felt him taking me to Dimitri. "Take care of her."

I shook my head, forcing myself to stand up as I felt a bit dizzy. "No, I'll fight too."

"You're weak now," he argued. "Let Zefren heal you."

I felt Zefren approaching me, muttering some words and I instantly recovered.

"Alpha Kamilah!" someone called from the crowd and I saw my pack members standing behind Magnus.

"Louisa! Karleen! Almiro!" I yelled as they were standing in front. They waved to me and I also spotted the Lycan king in the crowd.

Magnus, who was standing in front winked at me and gave a mocking look at Drucilla. "So, what now? Make your next move, Drucilla."

Drucilla gritted his teeth. "So you chose death. Well, then, it's good that I can kill you both now."

I instantly ran and stood at Magnus's side. "Bring it on."

"Kill them all!" Drucilla yelled and his men started to move.

Lycan King Ace instantly came in front. "I'll take care of them. You two go and kill him," he said and Magnus pulled me to the side. We ran to Drucilla, who ran to get protection from his men.

"What a coward, Drucilla. I thought you wanted to kill us?" I mocked.

Some wolves tried to get in between us and slow us down.

"Hey, Kamilah," I heard a high-pitched voice greeting me. Looking behind, I saw Serena, Magnus's past fling, the woman who bullied me from his pack was here. I kind of forgot her existence ever since. After all it was 150 years ago. Unimportant creatures tend to leave my mind.

I glanced at Magnus. "I thought you killed her last time?"

"She managed to get out and her family fled. I forgot to mention it." She was like a poisonous plant, appearing out of nowhere. "Years have passed and you never changed," I commented.

"You two," she said, giving a glance to Magnus, whose hands were on my waist.

"What's your feeling now that this is your last day?" she asked. I sighed, we were wasting time here. Dimitri came and yelled at us, "Just let us handle these low goons. Go to Drucilla!"

"Thanks, Dimitri!" I yelled after him then realized it. "Wait, weren't you looking for him earlier?"

Magnus smirked. "Yeah, well that's part of the plan. I had to make you believe that so Drucilla would fall in our trap."

I pouted. "You should have informed me."

He shrugged. "Yes, I thought of that. But having you not know was better."

I just let it slide. I looked at the battlefield and saw how our side was at the advantage and Drucilla noticed it too.

The werewolves who protected him instantly backed out, knowing it was Magnus that was after them.

Drucilla was the only one left now and he gulped. Magnus instantly pinned him down. "Of course, you won't be dead instantly. You have to experience pain, slowly and surely." Magnus then harshly grabbed his limbs, making him yell in pain.

I grabbed his head. "It was fine while it lasted," I said.

Twisting his head felt so satisfying as the memory of all the hardships I had to endure because of him flashed back. I had always dreamed of doing this and having it now, it was a bit overwhelming.

After that, Magnus lit up a fire with his match and threw it onto his body.

"That is for killing my mother," Magnus hissed.

"Let's go. If I knew he was that easy to kill, then—"

I was stopped when I heard a yell from behind and Louisa's body flying.

"Kamilah! To your left!"

I gasped in shock, seeing Louisa's head unattached to her body. Everything seemed to stop as I tried to process it. Louisa… my beta is dead. I howled and fury instantly covered me. I rampaged on the lowly wolf who killed her. Not even showing any mercy.

I couldn't even hear Magnus's words as I attacked each wolf I saw, blinded with anger. I saw Dimitri crying over Louisa's body, and I closed my eyes, imagining the pain he would be feeling. The two never even got to have more time with each other, not even knowing if they were fated.

I cried for Louisa's fate. Damn it! If only I knew this would happen! I felt all the energy surging within me, and a bright light came out of my body, leaving me. Feeling dizzy, I blacked out.

Aftermath

KAMILAH

The hollow darkness suffocated me, and I tried hard not to scream. I was back at my pack as if nothing happened. And I tried hard to search for something but I didn't know what it was.

"It's finished, you did so well," I heard someone saying and I looked up to see Alpha Rufus. I blinked, now aware this was a dream. My eyes fluttered open and I was faced with an asleep Almiro.

"Almiro," I tried to call out but my throat was dry and the sharp pain in my mind was too loud.

I flinched, and Almiro woke up, his eyes widened, and exclaimed, "Alpha Kamilah!"

He offered me a glass of water which I downed in one breath, too thirsty right now. Lumiere, my pet was here, cuddling with me and licking my face.

When finished, I looked around, trying to look for someone.

I noticed tubes were on my hands and a machine was

running beside me. I raised my eyebrows. I was back at my own pack? In my pack's clinic?

"What... happened? Why am I here?" I asked Almiro, who avoided my eyes.

"I'll let your mate explain it to you," he answered and stood up to call Magnus who instantly appeared in a hurry. Almiro left us to have our privacy.

As soon as our gazes met, tears began to fall like a waterfall and he slowly approached me, pulling me into a hug and muttering. "Thank you, thank you for waking up."

I gave a confused look at him, not remembering anything that happened. "Why are you acting like I just died, Magnus? What happened to me? And where's Louisa?"

He gulped. "Louisa... was killed on the battlefield. You suddenly went on a rampage and killed every one of our enemies, and after that, you were covered in so much blood, even lost some of your own and blacked out." He paused, letting me process it, and continued, "It's been a month since you slept here, in a coma. You almost died! Zefren couldn't even heal you! You broke some of your own veins and your healing powers couldn't even work," he explained.

A lump formed in my throat, and I let myself break down. I was in a mess, screaming and crying for my beta. I never imagined losing her like this. If only I would have not let her fight, if only I could have protected her, but it was too late. She was gone.

"I should have protected her," I muttered. "I should... have."

All the while, Magnus stayed by my side, trying to comfort me. He just sat still and patted my back, whispering comforting words to me.

"It's alright, it's going to be alright. I'm here for you."

The rest of the days made me a mess. I tried hard to keep

myself alive, I even came to the point where I wanted to kill myself, but every time I did that, Magnus would always come to me.

"You know, I'll be the one who'll wreak havoc and kill everyone if you're dead, Kamilah," he threatened one day after delivering me my lunch, wanting me to live. "Please live, babe, for me. For us, for our pup—"

"Our pup?"

His eyes widened, looking as if he just said something he shouldn't have. He chuckled nervously. "Oh it's nothing, we'll discuss it later—"

I shook my head, grabbing his shirt and forcing him to look at me. "No, tell it to me now. You know something."

He tried to look me in the eyes but gulped "I-uh-I-"

The door opened and a familiar vampire entered the room. "Wow, you didn't tell me you're pregnant, Kamilah!"

Both of us looked at Gusev, the vampire who just walked in and yelled at me excitedly.

I thought he would leave and distance himself after confessing to me last time. Why is he here now? Magnus glared at him and Gusev bit his lip. "Judging by that reaction, I think you still don't know—"

Instantly, Magnus grabbed him by the collar and yelled, "You and your nosy mouth! I swear, I'll have to cut that mouth off—"

He shrieked in fear. "Ack! Magnus! I apologize. I didn't know—"

"Magnus!" I yelled as he was busy yelling threats to Gusev. His head turned to me. "Yes, baby?"

"Is it true? Am I really…" I trailed off, not even able to complete the sentence as I looked to my stomach, gulping nervously.

His nervous expression turned into a happy one as he

confirmed it to me. "Yes, yes, my love. You are pregnant right now."

He instantly embraced me in a hug and I felt like tearing up again. "I'm going to be, a mother?"

He nodded, patting my hair softly. "Yes, dear. You are. And I'll be there to guide them too."

The thought itself gave me mixed feelings. I had never been a mother. And I never experienced having a mother. Knowing that I was expecting a pup right now both scared and excited me.

After hearing the news of Louisa dying and then learning that I am pregnant, I feel like my head is breaking into two. What if I'd be a bad mother to them? What if I'd end up killing them? Or harming them? What if—

I felt Magnus kissing my cheek and caressing my stomach. "It's going to be alright. It's both our first time as parents. But I'll be here, we have each other."

I nodded, biting my lip.

"Uhm… excuse me but I guess I'll leave now." Gusev scrunched his nose, disgusted at our little moment. "Ew, I'll just come back here when you have the baby. I love babies."

Magnus turned to him and smiled evilly. "No, Gusev. You can't just leave like that after ruining my plan of telling the news to my mate."

Gusev wanted to run away but he couldn't as Magnus dragged him outside and gave him his own punishment. I chuckled, feeling a bit lighter now after coming back to this. It felt like things were going back to normal, with only Magnus now finally in my life, along with our adorable upcoming baby in my stomach.

I smiled, feeling so blessed. So that was why all those pregnant mothers were so happy about this. I finally understood the feeling.

Although the news that Louisa, my beloved beta, is dead, I wanted to think that she was reincarnated as my child and this is her way of coming into my life, reminding me to live on.

The door opened, then I saw Dimitri, who looked like hell had just fallen on him. His eye bags were worse now and his beard was all over.

He smiled at me. "Congrats. You're going to be an amazing mother."

I nodded. "Thanks, Magnus. I hope you'll stay with me." I knew that I wouldn't be able to survive this without Magnus. I need his help raising our pup.

Magnus kissed my forehead and muttered, "Of course, baby. I'll never leave you. We'll raise our pup together."

I gulped, wanting to bring up Louisa but he seemed too depressed to even mutter anything after that.

"About Louisa—"

He stopped me. "I know you're pitying me right now, but I'm just busy with work. I am sad about her death, that's all."

I nodded, letting his excuse pass. He might still be in denial, knowing that his lover has died. He then left the room. I felt sorry for him, and how their relationship would have progressed further by now. They didn't even get the chance to love each other for a long time...

Goodness, the guilt was eating me up but what could I do? It was not like I could reverse time...

They arranged Louisa's funeral from my pack. I buried her in the special place, and we've lit candles and visited her.

I was sad, too sad that I couldn't move unless Magnus guided me. I was walking around with my eyes looking lifeless and my head empty, no thoughts forming inside. I felt like something died inside me and I could never recover that missing piece in my heart. My red and puffy eyes couldn't even release tears anymore as I cried everything out already. I became numb.

Louisa became my family after all. Almiro came to me, his eyes bloodshot. I hugged him, comforting him.

"Alpha Kamilah," he muttered. "So she's really gone, isn't she?"

I nodded, feeling sad for him too. They were closer in age, and treated each other like siblings. Almiro must have felt dead without Louisa.

When we finished burying Louisa, I stayed for a bit, and I caught sight of Dimitri, with a blank look on his face as he silently watched Louisa's grave.

I wanted to come and talk to him, but I figured it would be best to leave him alone for now. Like me, he was shocked and needed some time for himself.

I felt Magnus's gentle hands holding mine and mumbling, "Let us go, Kamilah."

I looked at his face quietly. I can't deny it but the thought of killing myself after hearing Louisa's news came to my mind. However, looking at Magnus's face now, and feeling his presence all the time, I couldn't bear the guilt of leaving him alone. If I died, he would be devastated and might lose his mind.

I might have been staring at him for a long time as he suddenly asked me, "Is there something on my face?"

He then continued, "I know I am handsome, you can even make a portrait of me if you want."

I chuckled, and he stared at my lips. "There we go. Smile for me, I missed that."

I tilted my head to the side. "If I die, would you miss me?"

I seemed to have took him by surprise with that question.

He frowned. "Kamilah, don't joke about things like that. Not now when you are carrying our pup."

"Oh right." I instinctively held my stomach, my mind was so busy grieving for Louisa that I forgot about that.

"I know it was too hard to accept Louisa's death, and I respect that. But please don't even think about killing yourself, Kamilah. You still have me, don't forget that," he reminded me, kissing my forehead. "Now let's go back inside before you catch a cold."

I let him guide me inside, and watched his black figure. I appreciated his patience with me, and he was right. I still had him. It might take a long time for me to recover but I would try.

For Magnus and for our pup.

<h1 style="text-align:center">New light</h1>

KAMILAH

The grieving period took me a full month to recover. It was still hard, knowing that someone special died.

But today, I woke up with a pair of big warm arms wrapped around my body. At this point, waking up every morning in Magnus's arms didn't feel strange at all. If anything, it felt... like home. I looked at Magnus's thick eyelashes as the sun gleamed on his skin, making his now olive skin shiny. Really, what did this guy put on his face? His skin was smooth as sin, with no pores visible. His nicely cut dark hair showed that he really maintained himself well. Plus, he slept shirtless. I had somehow gotten used to seeing his abs every morning. His lean and muscular body was showing. I could feel his morning wood always poking my pregnant belly. It had been two months in my pregnancy journey and my belly was aching from carrying all my pups. Other pregnant wolves got their morning sickness, but I was here chilling and enjoying myself, eating everything I wanted, whenever I could. Standing up, I was going to the bathroom to pee, strong hands stopped me. I looked at Magnus, who still had his eyes closed, but his hands were on mine.

"Where are you going?" he asked. I smirked and rolled my eyes before answering, "I'm going to pee. "I'll just be gone for a minute, Magnus. I won't leave you," I said and tried to push away his hands. Magnus was quick enough to grab my small waist and put me onto the soft mattress. He then attacked me with a hug and I just let him.

I knew that no matter how I'd fight against him, he'd still win anyway. Magnus opened his eyes and looked me in my eyes without saying anything.

"What?" I asked, suddenly feeling suffocated, both from his hug and the way he stared at me. I gulped at the intensity of his gaze.

"You're so beautiful," he said, then caressed my stomach. "And sexy carrying our pups." He bumped his nose into me and I chuckled. Just then, he stopped and ran to the bathroom. I chuckled, knowing he'd vomit there. Well, it was not me who has morning sickness. I somehow passed it onto him so he was the one enduring it.

Lumiere, my lovely pet who still stayed alive after every-thing that happened to me, had come to snuggle with me. I pet her, stroking her fur and kissing her.

Alpha Magnus appeared after a while and came to me.

"I just disappeared and you are kissing her more than me." He said with so much jealousy.

Lumiere seemed to understand him as he flicked his tail to Magnus.

Magnus gasped, "How dare you abandon your owner! I was the one who discovered you and gifted you!"

I chuckled at his childish antics, enjoying the company of Lumiere. Lumiere then left after teasing Magnus.

Magnus then turned to me, "How are you feeling?"

"Like hell." I answered, and he chuckled, looking at my stomach.

"It will be worth it. I promise, Kamilah." He assured me, "I promise to protect you and our pup until my last breath."

I smiled at him, appreciating his words now. It may have been a month that passed but my mind and body are still in a mess, but having him beside me and assuring me that everything will be alright is comforting me. Magnus stroked my hair and let me lean on his broad shoulders. He was quiet, letting me immerse in my thoughts.

I already accepted him as my mate, already marked and mated with him too. Soon, this pup is going to come to the world.

I believe it's time for us to officially be one. As partners for life and announce our oaths. Join our packs and lead together.

I finally decided it. I was still overwhelmed with all the things around me, and having to think about another matter might be stressing me out. However, I appreciate Magnus beside me, and I believe it is finally the right time to let him enter my life, especially since will be raising our pups together. Forever and for eternity.

I looked up at Magnus, stopping him from stroking my hair.

"Magnus." I called out.

He looked at me attentively, "Yes, Kamilah?"

"Isn't it time?" I asked.

He frowned, confused at my words, "Time for what?"

"For us. To announce our vows and join our packs together."

He froze, gawking at me with a shocked expression.

Magnus caressed my cheeks carefully, "Kamilah, do you

hear yourself right now? Are you aware of what you are proposing to me?"

I smiled at him, nodding my head.

He broke into a smile, squeezing my hand as he mumbled, "I've been waiting for this, baby. So much."

Tears fell on his eyes and I chuckled at his expression, I never seen him cry before, and seeing him melt under me and letting me see his true self was refreshing.

He then kneeled down. "I figured this would be proper to ask you now. Kamilah Ziraili, Alpha of the Dark Crest Pack, I, Alpha Magnus of the Bloodlust pack, would like to ask for your hand and commence our exchanging vows ceremony."

I grabbed his hand, "Yes, Magnus, I agree to your proposal."

He instantly embraced me. "I love you, Kamilah. This is the best day of my life. I will treasure this forever. I will not fail you, baby."

I smiled at him, "I know you won't. But relax, stop proving yourself to me because you had already captured my heart."

"Am I dreaming? This day is too good for me." He muttered happily, laughing. I can't wait for things to happen. I was just in a dark period last month, but I know that light is going to come soon for me. This marks the new dawn. A new beginning for the both of us.

Oath

KAMILAH

I never imagined I would be in this place right now. If someone were to ask me a few years ago that I would be tied with Magnus like this, then I might have laughed in his face and called out how absurd that was.

With the new moon hanging on the dark sky, and the cool breeze of wind, I stared at Magnus, my mate. I could not believe that I was carrying our pups.

And right now, I couldn't believe that we were taking our vows to each other and having me as his Luna.

We were now at the open field as all of his pack, mine included, were witnessing a once in a lifetime event. A hybrid binding his vow to me, the only female Alpha.

Magnus gazed at me, his hands tightly holding mine as if I was going to let go and disappear any minute. "Do you remember the very first day that we met? You were on patrol duty that time for your past pack and you even reported me, thinking I was an attacker." He chuckled as he held my hand. "Then you were rampaging on the Blood Moon night in your

281

past pack. They wanted to kill you but I saved you that night, and I never regretted it." After saying that he paused. He was looking at my eyes as he said that.

"Kamilah Ziraili, my beautiful Kamilah, you have made me the happiest man in the world today by agreeing to share your life with me. I promise to cherish and respect you. I promise to care for you and protect you. I promise to comfort you and encourage you. I promise to be with you every day. I promise to love you loyally and fiercely. Forever and for eternity."

I smiled at that, feeling tears in my eyes. It was now my turn. I cleared my throat. "I chose you and promise to choose you as my husband every day we awake. I will love you in word and deed. I will laugh with you, cry with you, scream with you, grow with you, and craft with you." I paused, reliving the moments with him.

"To be your kin and your mate in all of life's adventures is all I could hope for in the world. Loving what I know of you and trusting what I don't yet know, I give you my hand. I give you my love. I give you myself. Forever and for eternity."

Ending my vow, Magnus's face was flooded with tears. Wiping it, he breathed in and out to calm himself down.

Zefren went and cleared his throat, turning to Magnus. "Magnus, do you take Kamilah as your forever luna, to live together in holy matrimony. To love her, to honor her, to comfort her, and to keep her in sickness and in health, forsaking all others, for as long as you both shall live?"

Magnus stared at me. "I do."

Zefren nodded and now looked at me. "Kamilah, do you, take Magnus, as your alpha, to live together in holy matrimony. To love him, to fight with him and your pack, for as long as you both shall live?"

I smiled at Magnus. "I do."

The mage then said to Magnus, "Repeat after me."

"I, Magnus, take you, Kamilah, to be my forever luna, to have and to hold from this day forward. For better, for worse. For richer, for poorer. In sickness and in health. To love and to cherish, forever and for eternity."

Dimitri, who was looking so adorable in his suit, was now holding the two boxes of rings in his hands.

He was looking red and flustered. He handed them to us before running away and I chuckled at him.

"You may place the thorn of crown on her head and repeat this: I give you this crown as a token and pledge of our constant faith and abiding love."

As he said that, Magnus gently held my hand and put the rings on my hand.

Zefren then asked me to do as he had told Magnus, and I did.

"By virtue of the authority vested in me under the Moon Goddess, and to the Dark Crest Pack and Bloodlust Pack's alliance as we witness their alpha's bond, I now pronounce you, bound by the permanent oath. May you never break your oath with each other."

Putting the crown on Magnus's head, Zefren then smiled at Magnus.

"You may now kiss your luna."

Magnus grinned at that, sighing in relief. "Ugh, finally."

Magnus drew a heavy breath before clashing his lips to mine. Everyone in the crowd cheered, and I could hear my pack laughing happily.

I closed my eyes, savoring the moment, and when I knew we had been kissing for almost ten seconds, I took the initiative to break it.

Magnus seemed disappointed but I gave him a look. He winked at me, mouthing, "I can't wait for the honeymoon."

I gasped at that, turning to him with wide eyes. He just pinched my nose, a smirk playing on his lips.

And as if he couldn't wait anymore, Magnus then carried me through the place, now covered with flowers.

The crowd continued cheering as Magnus opened his car door and made me hop inside the passenger seat, then he got in the driver's seat. It felt magical. And I watched everything unfold in front of me. The feeling of nervousness was now gone with Magnus beside me.

Magnus glanced at me. "It feels like it has been a long time since I last saw you."

He nodded. "Yeah, but the union ceremony took longer than I thought." Then, as if thinking of something, his lips turned into a smile. "We should have been on our honeymoon by now."

I shook my head. "Wait, Magnus, don't. I know what you're thinking. Don't even think about it."

"What? I'm just smiling innocently," he said, trying to defend himself.

"I've been waiting for this. Can't you grant my request?" He pouted,

"Please? Babe?"

I bit my lip, sighing and giving in to his request. Oh well. What can I do? Grinning at my response, he licked his lips and instantly grabbed my chin. Really, this is just him. He couldn't even wait to go to the reception!

After the official ceremony, Magnus rented this amazing hotel all for himself as his pack had complained about how we always… do it every night. Since we wolves have sharp senses, of course, they'd hear us.

At first, it embarrassed me, knowing they heard me yell Magnus's name every night. But now, it didn't even bug me.

There was only one bed and I saw that the bed was covered in rose petals, with candles and red balloons almost everywhere.

I turned to look at Magnus.

He just shrugged in answer. "What? It's our honeymoon, babe. What'd you expect? Like we're just going to play hide and seek here?"

I chuckled at him. He clearly planned it all. And he clearly had plans for me. We had just finished eating dinner and have retired to bed. Since it was only us here and some human staff of the hotel, we had the whole place for ourselves.

Magnus ordered wine and we drank for a bit. He whistled innocently, his other hand on the wine while his other hand was on my hand. "What do you want to do tonight? Tell me anything you want to do except sleeping because I won't let you waste this night."

Oh, I know damn well he had other plans other than sleeping.

"Remember, I'm pregnant, dear. Our pups will be affected if you won't take care," I reminded him and he pouted.

He then caressed my tummy and kissed it before grinning up at me.

"Oh they will understand it, right pups?"

It was not that we were sure what our pups would be, but I had a hunch that we'd have twins. And Zefren even said it himself when he inspected my pups.

Ooh, I wondered how my labor would be.

At least the room smelled nice. I might sleep very comfortably tonight.

I instantly jumped on the bed. I was only pretending I was

fine now. I was sweating bullets, nervous about what would happen tonight. Knowing Magnus, and knowing how nothing can stop us now, I was sure he would be hard to stop tonight.

"Did you enjoy tonight?" Magnus asked, lying beside me.

I nodded at him. "Yes."

What bothered me was that Magnus acted like nothing was serious now, while here I was, so nervous.

"When are we going home?" I asked nervously.

"Relax. You want to go home now when something hasn't happened yet?" he teased, a smirk playing on his lips. If it was even possible, my cheeks turned redder. I instantly stood up and hid it from Magnus. "I think I'll shower now."

I just heard Magnus's chuckles as I entered the shower. Turning on the faucet, I did my thing and washed my body. It was a good thing that the hotel had shampoo and soap there and it smelled good. Smelled like vanilla.

When I was finished, I put on the robe placed beside the door and walked out of the shower.

I almost gaped at the sight, seeing Magnus now in his robe only. I gulped, seeing his bare chest peeking out from the robe. He looked hot.

"Why are you in your robe now?" I asked, and in an instant, Magnus was in front of me.

He leaned toward me, his hot breath fanning across my face. "Isn't it obvious? I'll take a shower too. I'm feeling hot right now."

I gulped again, frozen to my spot. I felt my hands trembling now, my heart almost bursting out in excitement.

Magnus stroked my hair and said in a low voice, "We have to make the most of it. It's you and me tonight, Kamilah." And with that, I closed my eyes as he crashed his lips on mine, ravaging me with his tongue, courting my lips for a dance of passion.

He turned off the lights. His lips continued doing wonders on mine. This kiss was different from any of our last ones. He trailed kisses on my neck, down to my collarbone.

It was almost like he wanted to take a taste of everything, every inch of me. I couldn't help but moan out his name, "Ugh. Magnus."

And I covered my mouth from saying more, feeling my cheeks getting hotter in embarrassment.

Geez, did I really... just moan?

I bit my lip, looking up at him as he stared into my soul, piercing me with his emerald eyes. He gulped, almost like in agony. "Say that again.

"Call my name again, Kamilah."

I did as he told me. "Magnus."

It was like he was debating with himself, stopping himself from something until he muttered a curse,

"Damn, Kamilah. What are you doing to me?" he asked, breathing hard now.

In an instant, I let out a gasp as his hands reached to my bosom and he carried me bridal style to the bed and placed me on the soft mattress.

"I swear, you don't know how much I want you right now, Kamilah. You don't know what's going on in my mind," he mumbled. "Damn, the things I want to do to you."

I bit my lip at that "Then do it," I dared him.

He looked flabbergasted, at what I said. "What?"

"I said do it," I repeated.

He blinked at that, his face looking flushed. "I can?"

I nodded. "Yes. I'm letting you."

"But..." He trailed off.

"But what?"

As if he just won his own inner battle, he forced himself to look me in the eyes. "But I have to stop myself. I have to endure this. Please don't tempt me more, Kamilah," he said, now standing up and moving away from me.

"I can't do this. I don't want to force you. I know you are feeling shocked, that's why you're saying that," he continued.

And with that, he quickly went to the shower.

What just… happened?

I let my mind wander, calming myself down. Gosh, we almost… did it!

We were enveloped in an awkward silence when Magnus came back.

"So… what do you want to watch?" he broke the silence, acting casual now. Everything that happened earlier was just my dream.

I looked at him, seeing him sitting on the ground and I asked, "Why are you on the ground?"

He shook his head like a little kid. "No reason."

I patted the empty space beside me. "You can sit here, Magnus."

Still hardheaded, he shook his head. "But I don't trust myself. I'm afraid I can't stop myself—"

I cut his sentence off. "I trust you won't do anything to me, Magnus. Now here."

He immediately obeyed my commanding voice and went to sit beside me. Minutes later, he laid down on my lap, using it as his pillow. I stroked his hair while we watched the movie. We had ordered room service and snacks earlier since we got hungry. It was midnight after all.

And we stayed like that, chilling and watching the movie. When it ended, Magnus decided to sleep on the ground. He had called for an extra mattress earlier and his bed was set up now with only a pillow.

"Why? You should sleep here with me too, Magnus," I said, "The bed is so nice here and it would be bad of me to have it all to myself. You paid for it all after all," I tried to reason it out but he wouldn't listen.

He gazed at me. "Do you know what you're talking about, babe? Do you know what situation you are in? You want the thing that happened earlier to continue?" he asked. "That was very dangerous, Kamilah. Please don't tell that to me again."

"This is a bad decision. We should not be in the same room next time, Kamilah," he said. "It's bad for my heart."

I just chuckled at that. Really, he was overreacting. Was I really that predictable in his eyes? He was really whipped. To think I even doubted him for cheating when he was this loyal to me. I didn't know what time we slept, but Magnus just extended our stay, so we probably stayed in the hotel for a week, making the most of everything.

Epilogue

DIMITRI

I want to be alone now. I just lost my lover in the past few days. I spent all my time working my ass off, just to forget about it. My heart felt like it was going to leap out of my chest. I couldn't even hear anything, sense anything.

I felt numb.

And just when I thought I wouldn't cry, I really cried.

Just then, I felt my eyes suddenly engulfed in darkness. I felt soft hands covering my eyes, and I heard the person beside me giggling.

"Uhm… who is this? I don't have time for this, whoever you are," I snapped. People really were testing me these days. And I felt really angry at almost everyone.

Not that it was unusual. I was just stressed out while my master, Alpha Magnus, went on his honeymoon with his mate. I was left to take charge of his office, as usual. Well, I accepted this task. So I should do my best and not complain here. Work and work.

"Try to guess first and I'll loosen my grip," said the voice, still covering my eyesight.

Is he dumb? I could sense the person covering my eyesight right now. It was Gusev.

I breathed deeply. "Gusev, don't test me right now or I'll kill you."

The person huffed before losing his grip on me. I blinked at the sudden brightness and turned to look at him.

"Tsk, loosen up."

I glared at him. "Try losing your lover and maybe I'll try to."

Gusev seemed taken aback and stopped. "I did. I did lose her…"

He then sat at the chair in front of me. "Anyways, I am here to introduce you to someone."

"What? Can't you sense I'm working?" I pointed at the pile of paperwork in front of me.

He raised his eyebrows at me. "Working yourself to death? Yes. You need to unwind. I have someone for you to meet."

It was the tri-blood, Erszebet.

She smiled at me. "Hi, Dimitri." She then sent a flower to me. "Uhm… I'll give you this."

"Thanks," I glanced at Gusev who was smirking and he whispered, "You're welcome, now I got to go. I have other missions to finish."

"See ya, Erszebet!" Gusev waved at her. Erszebet smiled and then looked at me as we were left alone now. "I'm really sorry—"

"If you're here to talk about her death, then please stop," I snapped, tired of hearing that.

"Oh, my mistake," she said with her meek voice. "But I

just want to say something… I've been admiring you." Her cheeks blushed.

I blinked, but what about Almiro? I thought she wanted him? The two have been always together.

"And Almiro? You're his mate, right?" I asked. Goodness, I just lost my own and now, another man's woman was approaching me. I was not wanting to be involved in infidelity.

"What? No!" she denied. "He just likes being around me. We're just friends."

I nodded, wanting to drop it and work quietly. She'd get tired if she kept on talking to me like a wall.

"Do you want to be one too?" she asked, looking at me innocently. I couldn't help but laugh at this. Do I look like I have time to make friends with anyone right now? I swear I will kill Gusev!

"To be what?"

"My friend. I'm asking if you want to be one."

I wanted to tell her off and to scram, but I didn't have the heart to tell it to her. Not now, when she was looking at me purely, with curiousness and wonder.

"You're laughing, did I say anything funny?" she asked with a frown. "I am not a funny one, I've always been isolated so I am not good at dealing with others."

I sighed. The wind breezed, letting the paper fall from my table and I leaned down to grab it but Erszebet was quick to get it to me.

"Here." She mumbled, and I grabbed it quickly, only for me to accidentally touch her hand. I furrowed my eyebrows when I sensed a spark of electricity.

"Can you stop doing that?" I asked, believing that it must be one of her abilities as a tri-blood.

She pouted. "Stop doing what? I was only helping you… I did not even do anything."

I quirked an eyebrow. "What? So that spark of electricity…"

I froze, instantly. No, this was a no. It was not even the night of a Blood Moon so I wouldn't know who my mate was.

"What is it?" she asked.

"Oh, this is nothing."

"You felt that too, didn't you? Are we mates?" She stood up, walking closer to me.

I cursed under my breath, wanting to keep it a secret but since she found it out too… I felt at a loss for words. I had to blame it on Gusev. I swore, I'd make sure that vampire wouldn't even get to play around next time!

Epilogue

ALPHA MAGNUS

I had stopped my urges and advanced to my forever Luna as she labored, and let her body heal first. My Luna had finally delivered our twins last week. And thank goodness with our abilities, she can instantly heal herself.

I was lying in bed with my forever Luna, Kamilah, as she slept with me. I fell deeper into her long hazel hair as I inhaled deeply, smelling her shampoo scent, the same scent I called home. I gazed at her eyes, the same eyes I fell in love with.

"It has been a while since we were left alone."

Then a thought came into me and I gave her a wicked grin.

She raised her eyebrows innocently. "So?"

I scoffed. "What do you mean, "so"? Oh honey, you're playing so hard to get now." Smirking, I leaned in and whispered in her ear, "You know exactly what I'm referring to." I trailed my hands on her shoulders slowly.

She playfully patted my hand away, giggling. "I just

delivered our pups, babe. Really, how do you get that much stamina?"

I grabbed her body near me to let her know how hard I was now. "What else? You were just pregnant, dear, but there is no way I will get tired of pleasing you."

Just then, my lips started their way to her lips and I groaned. "I just miss doing this with you. You know how I'm always busy. Seize the chance now, Kamilah Ziraili," I teased, rolling my tongue as I started working on her neck, her collarbone... down and down. I made sure to kiss every inch of her beautiful scars and her stretchmarks that were the fruit of her carrying our beautiful pups.

I pulled her in deeper, needing more. I gripped her hair as my hands moved all over her body until it reached her beautiful full breasts. Massaging one, I sucked it and I moaned. I made sure to look at her while I did it, wanting to savor every reaction at each slurp and twist I did to her nakedness.

She glanced at the nursery room. "Shhh, you'll wake up the pups," she commented.

I stopped, releasing a sound, and scoffed at her. Smirking, her hands reached for my hardened cock and touched it. My breath hitched at the motion as her eyes glued to me, watching my every move and making sure to watch every bit of my reaction. She moved her hands up and down, staring at me while doing so, and in a minute, I was breathing hard, sweat forming on my forehead.

She continued, though faster, making me pant more, begging for her. I gritted my teeth, couldn't help myself as I put my hand around hers and made the motion faster, and faster, until I could feel my full hard-on dripping with pre-cum and was about to reach heaven when my hand suddenly stopped.

I stared at her, disappointed as she looked back with a

teasing look. "That's all you get, honey."

As the realization hit me, I noticed her expression changing and she quickly stood up as her face darkened but I caught up with her and licked her ear, mumbling the words, "Oh no, baby. That was dirty. You started it. You will definitely end it."

My Luna blinked and she gulped and quickly ran to the bathroom. Before she even had the time to lock it, my hands appeared and I peeked around the door. I entered the bathroom, locking the door behind me as I grinned. "There's no way out now, babe. Now, where were we?"

"Babe…stop," she warned. "The kids are asleep and—"

"You want to stop now? Now, when you made me fully erect? Babe, we'll just do it quickly." I started to comfort her as I started kissing her forehead. "I just miss you, babe. Can we do it? Please," I added with a pout.

She rolled her eyes, but I couldn't miss the hint of a smile she had as she nodded her head.

I instantly punched my fists in the air happily and dived right in, pulling her to the shower as I turned it on.

We did our business and since I couldn't get enough of her and I kind of broke my own words saying we'd do it quickly. I didn't even know how much time had passed by, as after showering, I grabbed her as we continued embracing, still hungry for each other.

This was our own world. My beautiful Kamilah, my alpha queen. I loved how I could easily embrace her whenever I wanted. All those years, my soul yearned for her because I belong to her, just as she belonged to me. It may have taken a whole century for her to accept me in her arms, but waiting for her was worth it. Forever and for eternity.

THE END

About the Author

Hiraeth Faith is a twenty-year-old dreamer from the Philippines. She is presently a Medical Technologist student as part of her premed program. She is obsessed with books and movies like Harry Potter and has been writing since 2015, beginning with Wattpad. She began writing stories because she wanted to inspire people and share her imagination with the rest of the world. Faith then began to pursue her passion for writing through online writing platforms such as Goodnovel. Please visit Hiraeth Faith's Facebook page for more information about her new books and announcements.

For inquiries: hiraethfaith@gmail.com